BLAINE L. PARDOE

TENURE 2

SOCIAL STREET JUSTICE 101

Acknowledgements:

Writing the Tenure series is both fun and challenging at times. Fortunately, the real world provides countless potential storylines for these books. Braxton Knox is a man unlike the rest of us, but one who has been pushed too far. He has lost most of his family, his career, his reputation, and his home. That transforms him into a vigilante. The story may be his, but it's one that many readers will identify with.

At the 2024 Galaxy's Edge Fan Expo, Walt Robillard gave Blaine a good lesson in knife fighting which appears in this novel.

Thanks to Ben Henderson, who offered invaluable insight into the use of AI in espionage.

Dedications:

Mike:
To my wife, Ann, who can't read this, because it's too violent.

Blaine:
To my wife, Cyndi, who can't read this, because it's too violent.

woke. wōk. *adjective*: An arrogant, self-righteous individual who claims to be aware of and engaged in societal facts and issues they deem important. Individuals who target people for online abuse with false or exaggerated accusations, then declare themselves victims when their targets respond. A judgmental person who does not contribute to society. A political movement aimed at the cancellation of others whom participants do not agree with, sans due process.

See: Social Justice Warriors and Internet Trolls, Cancel Culture, Cancel Pigs

Prologue:

As Braxton Knox exited his RAV4 in front of his cabin, he felt his muscles protesting from the workout at Valhalla Academy. He'd been taking lessons with former Staff Sergeant and owner Burt Furlock. Burt's morning lessons had been brutal, but Knox's hand-to-hand and knife-fighting skills increased every week. The skills came at a cost, not in money, but in sweat and pain.

Ronin waited on the front porch. Braxton had watched Ronin arrive on his phone. Braxton waved. Ronin rose to shake his hand. "You look like you were rode hard and put to bed wet."

Braxton sat in one of the Adirondack chairs. "Combat training. There's a sign in the academy. *Train to be a Viking Every Day*. My instructor takes that seriously." He pulled up his shirt sleeve to show the purple bruise on his lower shoulder.

"Maybe I should start taking lessons."

"It's always a good idea to be prepared." Braxton remembered being locked in the trunk of a car and driven out into the mountains to be killed. *If I hadn't had the foresight to hide a gun and knife on me, I'd be dust right now.*

"I did the follow-up you asked," Ronin said. "I thought it best not to leave a digital trail."

"How is he?"

"Nelson Broome is doing well. He moved back with his parents in Wisconsin and is transferring to Carroll University. He's kept his mouth shut. As for the guys that tried to kill your dad, they're gone. Both have bench warrants out for them."

Loose ends.

Braxton could have killed Broome and the other two, but he wasn't a mass murderer. Why he spared Broome and the others was hard to understand, let alone explain. Maybe it was guilt over others he had terminated in the attack on his cabin three weeks earlier. Knox remembered every shot, every kill. He wasn't proud of what he had done, nor was he ashamed. There were no regrets, that much he knew for sure.

They came to slaughter us. They started this war; I simply finished it.

He may have allowed them to live because he was a father and that instinct somehow stayed his trigger finger. While he had been working out at Planet Fitness in early morning hours, he had contemplated that thought many times. Braxton doubted it, but couldn't be sure.

The two that were captured with his father were easiest to explain. Murdering them in cold blood in front of his father and his former cop friends was not something he could do. They were police...they lived their lives by the rule of law. Regardless, it didn't explain why he let Broome live.

Perhaps it was the thought that the survivors would spread the word to anyone who might come after him. Choosing who lived and died was easier than explaining his actions. He stopped thinking about it.

"They're fugitives from the law, eh?" Braxton said. "Good. The fact that they have fled tells me they are afraid. Fear is a powerful weapon. Our enemies use it, and so should we."

"You've become philosophical."

"More like reflective." Three weeks earlier, ANTIFA had come to kill him, his father, and his friends. Even now, as he looked around the cabin, the signs of the battle were fading with the coming spring. Soon all evidence would be erased, though the memories of that fight were scars that would last forever.

"You still thinking about intervening in this thing in Indianapolis?"

"Yes, I am." He continued to receive mail from people offering support. Many had their own horror stories because of the woke. Others tried to insult him. Braxton read them all. The letters gave him a sense of purpose. They came from everywhere—sickening stories of ruined lives, some far worse than others. His family and career had been the focus of his life. All that had been taken from him. The letters gave him purpose.

Suzanna would want me to help other people, especially those that can't help themselves.

The letter he'd received from Jason Higby was particularly gut wrenching. Higby had owned a custom candy business. It had been doing great, until COVID hit. Higby had taken his operation online to survive. It was costly and had taken months to get running, but he was surviving around the COVID restrictions.

Then the cancel pigs attacked.

Someone requested a box of obscene penis-shaped chocolates. Higby had refused to make them. They labeled him homophobic, transphobic, and unfit for civilization as the woke defined it. They harassed his wife and daughter online. According to the letter, it led to problems at his daughter's school. When that didn't work, the cancel pigs went after his suppliers, who buckled quickly to avoid controversy.

His business plummeted. Soon he was in debt, his business an utter failure. His wife left him, taking their daughter. Higby became a pariah in Indianapolis as local news piled on. He was left with nothing but bankruptcy and loneliness.

There had been other letters that had stirred him, but Higby's rose to the top. Some of that was undoubtedly because of his wife and daughter. Braxton's family had stuck with him when the cancel pigs had come at him. Not so with Higby. It made Braxton love his lost family even more.

The other thing that had struck him was the sense of hopelessness that Higby had expressed. *This is a man who can't fight back on his own. He doesn't have either the skills or the resources. These online bullies came at him because he was an easy target. I bet they didn't actually want those penis-candies. They were setting him up, hoping he would refuse their order. That's how these people operate.*

There was more to it than that. They went after Higby's daughter. His own little girl, Angela, had been a casualty of the cancel culture mob. The result had been her death, just as sure as if they had pulled

3

the trigger. That aspect of the letter tore at Braxton's emotions, jerking his heartstrings violently.

Ronin nodded. "I assumed you would still want to help him. I pulled up some data of the people that went after this guy. There's a lot to wade through. They were posting shit about him around the clock for weeks. To the casual observer, it looks like he pissed off around a couple dozen people when he turned down that order, making things look worse than they really were."

Braxton cracked a thin smile. "You're not the casual observer."

"That's right. It's a small group. They used sock accounts, bogus accounts to make it appear there were more of them than there was. I'm still doing some work to pin down who they are. Based on some of the IPs I've seen, they don't even live in Indianapolis."

"Of course not. The internet gives them anonymity, which they believe makes them untouchable." *To them, it's all a game, making people miserable.* Memories of Debbie Driggs surged. *She too thought her actions would never come back at her.*

"Higby isn't the only one they've gone after. These jackals find a new target to go after every few weeks. It's the same MO. Sometimes they spin up fake accounts, but analysis of their messages and posts indicate it's the same little group."

"It figures," Braxton said. "So if we deal with them, we help out more than Higby."

"Basically."

Braxton drew a deep breath. It was one thing to take vengeance on those that had personally attacked him. It was different to go out as a vigilante, striking on the benefit of total strangers who had been wronged. Closing his eyes, he asked himself a simple question, "What would Suzanne want me to do?" He already knew the answer, but the question itself was important. *She'd want me to help people who couldn't help themselves.* "We need to approach this carefully. Indianapolis isn't our home turf. Law enforcement here in Portland is a joke. I don't know if the same applies in Indiana."

Ronin nodded. "You know, you can't set this guy right. He's broke because of these people. Whatever you're planning won't bring his wife and daughter back."

Ronin was right for saying it out loud.

"I know. Sometimes you can't right a wrong. You just have to be an instrument of justice when the system fails."

"These kinds of people are a plague," Ronin said. "They don't contribute to society. They exist to cause chaos and bring others down, people who don't believe exactly what they do. I've been looking at the posts these people put up and it is wild to see how bizarre their belief systems are. It's not just about progressive values, whatever those are, it's about this bizarre flexible set of morals that are constantly in flux. There's no consistency in what they post. It's all just hate."

"Hate will only take you so far," Braxton said. "At some point, these people are going to have to face up to what they've done."

"And when they refuse to accept responsibility?"

"I was a professor once. These are children. I can teach them, though that lesson may come from the barrel of Themis."

Chapter 1
Valhalla and Beyond

Two days after meeting with Ronin, Braxton was back at Valhalla Academy. It was knife day, and Burt put him through his paces. They did hand-to-hand drills on Mondays, knife on Wednesdays, and guns and disarmament on Fridays.

The practice knives were plastic and, despite not being sharp, they left an imprint. Braxton didn't care. It was important to feel the hits and avoid them. He managed to get in a few strikes of his own. It felt like progress.

When they finished, Braxton was dripping with sweat. He had done cardio at Planet Fitness before showing up and was exhausted by the knife drills. As Braxton used a small towel to wipe sweat, Burt leaned back and crossed his arms. "Do you feel like you're getting better?"

"Yeah, but I'm not where I want to be."

"Most of my students would be happy to be doing what you are. Why are you pushing yourself so hard?"

Braxton trusted Burt, but did not want to drag him into his world. "I crossed some guys who kidnapped me. They were going to take me into the woods and kill me. I got away, but only because I was prepared and they were sloppy. I don't want to put my life in fate's hands."

Burt nodded. "They handcuff you or use zip ties?"

"Zip ties. I had a knife and a gun on me. I would have preferred to not end up in the trunk to begin with."

"It sounds like you could use a tactical belt."

"You mean like for holding gear? 'Cause I've got one of those."

"No. Come on into my office." Braxton followed the hulking man. From the credenza behind his desk, Burt pulled out a leather belt. "I'm talking this kind of belt."

Braxton hefted it and it felt like a typical heavy leather belt. "What am I missing?"

Burt reached over and moved his thumbnail along a strip of leather on the backside of the belt. A thin slit pocket was revealed. Reaching in, he pulled out a key. "This is a handcuff key," he said, handing him the key. Further down he opened another slit and pulled out a small, razor-blade-sized knife. "A carbon fiber cutting blade." Near the buckle, he pulled out what looked like a wire with two small loops. "A diamond garrote wire."

"That's incredible."

"I have a friend that makes them. You're moving in places where your safety is a concern. Something like this might come in handy."

"It's like Batman's utility belt."

"Yes, but a little more covert and stylish. You can't get it past TSA, but for everyday wear, it's practical and helpful."

"The handcuff key. So are they all the same?"

"Not exactly." Burt put the items back in their hidden compartments. "Law enforcement cuffs are. There are some exceptions. Cuffs that people buy off of Wish or Temu for kinky shit, they use different keys. Most of them you can get off by hitting the lock mechanism against a hard surface a few times. I've seen some of those cheap-ass ones actually fall apart with a few hits."

Braxton appreciated the belt more and more. *Someone who does get control of me isn't likely to remove my belt. This might help.* "Does your friend take orders for these things or sell them online?"

"Not online. These aren't the kinds of things you want the public to know about. The guy that makes them prefers to keep a low profile. I could put you in contact with him, if you want. He can get you the belt and you can fill it with whatever, or you can pay a premium and he'll outfit it for you. Be warned, the handcuff keys can be a bit pricey."

"I can afford it. If you'll get me his contact info, I'll get one."

Burt nodded, then pulled out a yellow sticky-note and wrote out an email address. "His name is Jacob Pearsons," he said, handing it over. "Make sure you tell Jacob that I referred you, or he'll just delete the message."

"Gotcha." Braxton folded the piece of paper and put it in his wallet. "I appreciate it."

"There's no such thing as being too safe."

Braxton stopped for groceries, then went back to the cabin to shower up and prepare dinner. He was still struggling to cook for one. There were a lot of prepared meals out there, but he loathed all the chemicals and preservatives. Shopping meant buying smaller amounts of everything, which wasn't easy. Making tacos for one person required changing a lifetime's worth of recipe knowledge. It was a mundane task, one that reminded him of all he had lost. In a strange way, it anchored him.

After an early dinner, he loaded several weapons in the back of his RAV4 and drove over to Rudy's. They had arranged for some night shooting drills to help refine his skills. Rudy Petcock had helped him arm himself. After the attack on his cabin, Rudy had been helpful in getting rid of some of the excess weapons that Braxton had recovered, most sold as parts or whole to Rudy's more covert clientele.

He pulled up as the sun was setting. Rudy wore light gear, a shooting vest over a long-sleeved T-shirt. "Good to see you, Brax," he said.

Braxton opened the back of the RAV, uncovering an array of weapons. "So what do you have in store for me tonight?"

"I thought we'd give your AXSR a good workout…a little shoot-and-scoot drill. I've got targets out there at various ranges. Got here a while back and set up ground markers along the hillside, numbered one through ten. Your targets are marked as well with numbers. Simply put, you run to the positions in order, get into position, and fire."

It was a challenge. Themis, his AXSR, was a heavy weapon and the hill Rudy indicated was huge. He reached for his wind gauge, but Rudy stopped him. "No other gear. Leave your ballistics computer here. This is about you learning to estimate ranges and make the adjustments on the fly. Almost anyone can learn to shoot under optimal conditions with supporting hardware. You need to be better than that. I'll time you. When you hear me shoot, that means move on to the next target."

"How much time do I have?"

"Not nearly enough." Rudy grinned.

"One reason I like you, Rudy. I appreciate the challenge."

"The key is getting dialed in and adjusting using your scope's reticle based on the changes of range. A good sniper can do the mental math on the fly, and you've told me you want to be a good sniper. This will get you there."

"Understood. Any advice?"

"Watch your breathing and heart rate. You won't be depending on your tech, so go back to everything we've trained you on in terms of taking the distance and environment into account," Rudy offered as Braxton clutched the large AXSR tight to his chest. "Alright then, Brax—haul ass!"

The first sprint was easy. When he reached the firing position, he found a rock protruding from the ground and tossed out a shooting bag to brace his weapon. His heart beat loudly in his ears as he looked through the scope. He did a quick calculation. Wind speed, spin drift. He had adjusted his sights hundreds of times before, but this time was on the fly. Satisfied, he chambered a round and squeezed the trigger to the stop point, then timed the shot between beats of his heart.

The round missed by a foot, down and to the left. *Damn!* He chambered another round, adjusting his aim rather than honing in the sights. He fired, clipping the bottom center of the target. The sound of the metallic ping came a moment after he fired, followed by Rudy firing his gun. Even though he knew Rudy was going to do it, the boom still caught him off guard.

He rose quickly and ran to spot two. The new target was farther away. He missed with both shots, cursing himself for going too fast. Rudy's shot in the air propelled him on to the next target.

The third target he hit close to center on the first shot. Each sprint drained Braxton of energy. Rudy's placement of the targets varied in distances, adding to the challenge. The last one was poised at 225 meters, or so he estimated. His guess was wrong as he missed with three rounds, the last by a matter of an inch.

As he came down the mountainside, the weight of Themis was irrelevant. Maybe it was the working out or weapons training, but the heavy sniper rifle felt oddly comfortable in his arms as he rejoined Rudy who had been gathering the targets.

"You want to know how you did?" the older man asked.

Braxton sighed. "Not great, but yes, give me the rundown."

Rudy went over the targets individually, then asked a question. "Do you feel humbled?"

"I do."

"Good. I see a lot of shooters here and in the shop. Many of them are decent, but shooting at a range is nothing compared to real-life situations. This is about being able to crunch the math in your head as you move, not being dependent on tech. Your ballistics computer adds to your skills, but it isn't the root of what makes you a good shooter. You told me you wanted to be ready for serious shit. This is a step in the right direction."

"What should I do?"

"Practice. You overcome the unpredictable by training for the unpredictable. You need to get better at estimating ranges visually. I have some ways to do that. We'll do them next time. You did a lot of your shot adjustment by eye. You need to be good at that and at doing scope adjustments. If you get too dependent on one method, you'll pay for it when the time comes."

"I appreciate the feedback."

"We'll throw in a few curves next week," Rudy said. "You're going to make mistakes. It will take a while to hit your stride, but when you do, you'll be much better at the game."

Braxton took out a wad of dollars and paid Rudy. "Let's plan on this again next week. After that, I'm thinking of going on a trip."

"Good for you. After all you've been through, going somewhere to relax and have fun might just be the thing. Where are you going?"

"Indiana."

Rudy's left eyebrow cocked up. "You and me, we have a difference of opinion on where to go for fun."

"It's really not a fun trip. Someone there needs a little help."

"An old friend?"

"No. A total stranger, in fact."

Rudy smiled. "Helping someone you don't know is sometimes the most rewarding thing a man can do."

"I can't argue with that," Braxton said as he moved to the RAV4 and made sure that Themis was empty and cleared once more.

Chapter 2
Ahead of the Competition

Faye Weldon looked forward to the weekly dinners with Braxton and Ronin. She had been through a lot since being sucked into Braxton's war. She'd almost been killed, twice. The experience was sobering. Being a journalist covering cancel culture, she'd been threatened many times. ANTIFA hated her long before her association with Braxton Knox.

Faye wasn't sure why she stuck with him. Braxton's private war of retribution was over. He had dealt with those that had ruined his life. Knox wasn't done, though, and she found herself drawn into his machinations. It went beyond journalism. There was an element of excitement. A part of her always wanted to be involved with something important. She was helping people beyond telling their stories, though no one could know her role in the killings. It was exhilarating. While Faye understood right and wrong, she saw the three of them operating in the narrow line between those two states, leaning hard to right.

Is it wrong to do bad things to bad people to help set things right? No. As Braxton says, that's what real justice is.

Braxton was an open book to her. He laid his life bare. Not so much with Ronin. There was a secretive aspect to him that intrigued her. From what he had said, she knew he had a mysterious benefactor, someone in Big Tech. Every time she tried to probe his personal life, she found him evasive. That air of mystery was curious. She wanted to dig deeper, but held off. Sometimes it was worse to know the full truth about a person, even an ally. Besides, Ronin brought a great deal to their trio, a snarky, biting sense of humor. Where Braxton could be coldly calculating, Ronin at times was bitterly pragmatic.

They met at the Portland City Grill. The restaurant provided an excellent view of the city skyline, and Braxton always arranged for a discreet booth for their conversation. She arrived at the booth to find Ronin and Braxton already there. Braxton rose from his seat until she sat down, while Ronin remained seated. *That's the difference in generations.* It was an old-fashioned gesture, and Faye liked it. *That's the dichotomy of chivalry in America. Feminists say they don't want such things, but deep down, we all respect it.*

Their small talk was short. They waited until they'd placed their orders. Braxton looked like he was putting on weight...*no, not weight, muscle.* Once the waitress left, Braxton leaned in and lowered his voice. "So, Jason Higby. I'd like to hear from the two of you about what you think."

They looked at Faye.

"I pulled the few articles about what happened to him. Wild stuff. You know, up until this happened, the Chamber of Commerce named him as the new business of the year. Everyone loved this guy and what he was doing. Then the spicy virus hit. He took his business online, which was a mistake."

"That fits the Tweets, Facebook, Reddit, and Discord posts I've seen," Ronin said.

"Discord?" Braxton asked.

"It's a horrible name for a product. Discord's an online forum system...a whiney bitch board. It basically gives people echo chambers for whatever their views are. The woke love it because it gives them a place to organize against their targets. There was a lot of venom there about Higby."

"I know the type," Braxton said. "People love to pile on. It gives them a sense of purpose."

"Truth! It's handed me tons of data to accumulate from the accounts that were targeting Mr. Higby."

"Any luck in getting their names?" Faye asked.

"I'm making some headway. If you know how to work the systems, and have friends in the right places, you can get IP addresses and email accounts. That's how I know that a number of these accusers who went after Mr. Higby were bogus sock accounts."

"I thought so. That's fairly standard. Every time I cover these social justice warriors, it's the same BS. A handful of people using the net to generate a lot of noise."

Braxton leaned back and crossed his arms. Faye was familiar with that stance. *He's thinking...strategizing.* There were several things that she admired about the former professor. One was that he was always learning. The other was that he thought things through. The way he had booby-trapped his cabin in anticipation of an attack was proof of that.

After a few moments of silence, he uncrossed his arms. "I assume it's going to take some time before you can identify who was behind all of this?"

Ronin nodded. "My contacts aren't easily prodded, but they always deliver."

Braxton seemed satisfied with the answer. "It will take me a few days to get out there. I'm driving. Faye, if you're willing, why don't you go out and interview Mr. Higby? The media covered him, but only from the angle that he was wrong. You might be able to get some useful information. Also, you can be our eyes on the ground."

"Sounds good, assuming he's willing to talk."

"He will," Braxton assured her. "The man has lost everything. The mainstream media went out of their way to enable these online pukes. If you approach him with the opportunity to tell his side of the story, he'll do it."

"How do you know?" she asked.

"That's what happened with me."

I did get him to open up after he lost his wife and daughter. She was happy that he was finally telling her why he had allowed her into his circle of trust.

"Point taken."

"Driving to Indianapolis?" Ronin said. "That's a haul. Why not just fly out?"

"I don't want to check guns. I don't want Fed attention. If I drive, my firepower is far less traceable. Also, flying is an ordeal. The

14

TSA. Do you know how many times they've felt up my crack? Israel doesn't have a TSA. And they've never had a problem on their planes. You know why? Because psychologists interview every passenger. The only reason we have this massive, intrusive federal agency ordering us around and feeling up our cracks is a big show to convince people they're doing something."

The waitress refilled their water. Her arrival killed conversation until she was out of earshot. Faye waited until she was gone. "When we find the people who ruined Higby's life, what are you going to do?"

"Justice," Braxton replied.

"I assume it's the same kind of justice you gave ANTIFA?"

"Yup."

"I had to ask."

"What about your car?"

"I'm not taking my car. I'm picking up an old police cruiser. Crown Vic. The VIN numbers have been removed and there's no record of the sale. It's untraceable."

"How'd you do that?"

Braxton winked, drew a finger along his lips and mimed tossing the key away. "None of this should be taken lightly. We're taking a stand for people who can't do it for themselves. The perpetrators have to pay for their hate."

"Why not go after all of them?" Ronin asked.

"I've been studying police investigation techniques…a boring subject, but one that is pertinent to what we're doing. You have to think about this from the police perspective. Let's say we kill everyone who went after Higby. Some investigator might connect the dots. Where does that lead them? To Higby first. So now the person who was the victim gets labeled as a 'person of interest' or worse, tossed in jail. From what I saw in his letter, he's been through enough.

"No one's going to connect what we did here with what happens in a city two thousand miles away. We don't need to beat the police; we just need to out-think them."

"How did you study police investigation techniques?"

"Their textbooks are available for purchase. One would think they'd keep that stuff secret, but they don't."

"That seems stupid," Ronin said.

"I'm not complaining," Braxton replied. "Now then, let's talk about your trip to Indianapolis, Faye…"

Chapter 3
Law Enforcement

The sheriff pulled up the winding gravel driveway to his cabin slowly. Braxton was just finishing his breakfast on the porch when he saw it. He had a good reason to be nervous. The sheriff was pulling up to a crime scene where he and his compatriots had killed several ANTIFA thugs who'd come to murder them.

As Sheriff Marty Phelps got out of the car, he saw that the sheriff was alone. The cold, calculating part of his brain kicked in. *He's not here to arrest me. If he was, he wouldn't have come up here without backup.* Phelps looked around. For what, Braxton didn't know. He gave him a wave after a few moments and slowly walked up to the porch.

Braxton had called the sheriff's office every week to ask if there was any progress on his wife's murder. It was a gesture designed to throw off law enforcement. The goons that had killed his wife were dead; he had seen to that himself. Not calling them and demanding action would have been abnormal behavior. From his studies of police procedures, you didn't give law enforcement anything that might have them focus on you.

"Howdy, Mr. Knox," Phelps called out as he approached, offering a half-hearted wave.

"Sheriff," Braxton said as Phelps reached the stairs. Monsieur, his bulldog, plopped down next to Braxton, already bored with their visitor. "What brings you out here?"

"I wanted to come out and tell you personally. We've had some progress on your wife's case."

"Really? After all of these weeks? What do you have?"

Phelps came up the front steps. Phelps was portly, breathing heavy from the stairs. "We got some analysis from some paint scratches on the Outback we recovered. The state crime lab has been behind since COVID. The scrapes matched your wife's car."

"So, whoever was driving that car was the one that ran her off the road."

"Pretty sure. We got an anonymous tip that one Lucas Cox might know something about it. He's ANTIFA."

Ramrod.

"Have you arrested him?" It was the response the sheriff would be expecting, so Braxton gave it to him. Cox wasn't going to be arrested. He was long dead.

"No. We were going to bring him in for an interrogation, but we couldn't."

"Why not?"

"The kid has gone missing. Not just him, but all the members of his little ANTIFA group. All of them."

"That's strange."

"You know, that's what my deputy thought, too. I mean, these protest groups, they go off from time to time, you know, every time there's an event. We did a wellness check on his place. Hasn't been there in weeks. Add to that, the leader of this group was shot after he stole a truck."

"Sounds shady."

"They're just kids. Their stuff is mostly peaceful."

"Didn't they have a run-in with those Koreans? That didn't sound too peaceful."

Phelps shifted his feet. "Well, that's neither here nor there. That case is still open."

"So you weren't able to talk to Cox?"

"No. We got a warrant and pinged his cell phone along with the other members of that group. What we got back was strange."

"What?"

"Cox's phone went off on March 25th in the city. It never came on again. We pinged the others and on the next night, the last time they hit a cell tower was five miles from here."

"Here? Why would they be in this area?"

"I don't know. Cell coverage out here is sparse as hell. I know it's a long shot, but did you happen to see or hear anything from them at that time?"

Memories flooded his mind. Hunting them down with Themis as "In-A-Gadda-Da-Vida" roared over their cheap Chinese communicators. Blasting them at close range, one by one.

"No, sir. I think I'd remember that."

Phelps chuckled. It was fake which reminded Braxton why he didn't like the man. "I'm sure you would. It all seemed strangely coincidental, if you catch my drift."

"I'm not a big fan of coincidences. They happen, but they can't be trusted," Braxton countered.

"There's something in those words that rings true," Phelps said, hiking up his pants, which were losing altitude. "It is weird that they just all went off line and never showed up anywhere else on the network. AT&T told me you had your own private signal booster tower up here."

"That's true."

"Any chance I can have my people take a look at your data? AT&T didn't have it, but told me your box should have it."

Braxton gestured off in the distance. "I wish I could. Damn thing caught fire. I've ordered a replacement but it's not here yet."

Phelps squinted at the charred remains of the wooden tower.

"Well, that's a damn shame."

"You're telling me," Braxton said. "A friend of mine who's an IT guy hooked me up with a satellite feed."

"I guess that's part of the price you pay for living up here."

"I didn't want to come here, but after the FBI murdered my girl, I could no longer remain in that house." He didn't try to mask his bitterness.

"That was a tragedy," Phelps said.

"It was." He drew a long breath, then attempted to lead the sheriff down a rabbit hole. "How about their cars? If they shut their phones off, their cars had to be somewhere."

"Way ahead of you, Mr. Knox. My people found one of the cars, stripped and ripped—that's what we call it when crooks remove everything for parts. We found it abandoned under an overpass in a less-than-safe part of the city."

"Seems like that might be the place to look. I would like to see Cox brought in."

"Car thefts are pretty low priority. We're operating at about forty percent compared to six years ago."

Braxton nodded. "I appreciate you coming out here."

"You don't need to call our office every week. We're doing what we can to solve your wife's case. But, as you heard, it's gotten a little complicated."

"Sheriff, don't take this the wrong way, but I will continue to hound you people. I have watched enough Discovery ID to know what happens when a case gets cold. Suzanna was a damn good driver. We both know she was run off the road and killed. I want justice."

"So do I...so do I." Phelps turned back to his cruiser. "Thank you for taking the time to let me get you up to speed."

"Thank you for not doing this over the phone," Braxton said. It was sincere. He was surprised that the sheriff had come out in person. A few moments later, as the sheriff reached his car, the realization as to why the man had come to visit him seemed clear.

He knows this has been mishandled. Now he's in a dead end. If the press confronts him about the case, he will get to tell them he personally met with me. This isn't about Suzanna or those punk-ass kids. This is about his image.

Phelps waved as he turned his car around and left. Braxton only gave him a nod in response. *This is the problem with law enforcement. They are limited, by intelligence, and in the sheriff's case, a desire to remain in office. Sure, the rank-and-file officers care. They deal with real people every day on the streets. But their higher-ups are all about holding on to their pseudo power. Men like Phelps are more concerned about public image than action.* There was little doubt in his mind that his performance had been enough to sate the sheriff's desire to look like he cared.

As the car disappeared down the road, Braxton reached over and rubbed Monsieur behind his ears. "It's a sad state of affairs when I find myself trusting my dog more than the people who are supposed to protect me."

Monsieur panted heavily and leaned into his fingers. Rising, Braxton went into the cabin to finish packing.

Chapter 4
May Day

May Day came with gray skies and morning fog. Braxton and Ronin met at the Cityscape Coffee House in Lake Oswego. They took their lattes out front into the little fenced-off area with metal tables and chairs as well-heeled hausfraus strolled up and down the street, some pushing trams, some walking Pomeranians. Boys and girls cruised by on skateboards, many of them electric.

Ronin pointed to a young man riding one of those one-wheeled skateboards with a fat tire in the middle, and the rider's feet on either side. "Been thinking of getting one of those."

"Yeah, great idea. It's definitely going to improve your sense of balance." Braxton had been focused on improving himself physically and mentally and found himself always framing things against those goals.

"What's up?"

"I need a new identity. You know, we talked last week about the situation in Indianapolis. If I'm going to help that guy, they can't connect whoever it is to what went down in Portland if I run afoul of the law. I'm going to alter my appearance. I would like you to create a false identity which checks out, should anybody try to look me up online, along with some appropriate identification."

Ronin sipped his coffee. "Hmmm. You know, I've had a little experience with that. Let's start with your ID. Real ID complicates things. That's hard to fake. However, I've learned that it's not hard to fake the materials you need to get a Real ID driver's license. Linking your false identity to a valid social security number requires a contact inside of the Social Security Administration, which I have."

"So you give me docs that I take to the Oregon DMV and they just give me a license?"

"That's the idea," Ronin said, adding some sweetener to his coffee. "In terms of a fake social media presence, the real trick is to make it credible. It's going to take some prep, establishing bona fides in dozens of places on the internet. You have a name in mind?"

"Harry Callahan."

"Why do I know that name?"

"Dirty Harry."

"Oh yeah. Right. Saw that when I was a kid. Won't people suspect it's fake?"

"No. I went online and found dozens of Harry Callahans. If you think it's a problem, make it Harold Callahan. I'll just go by Harry."

"Got it. You should alter your appearance. Facial recognition software is everywhere now. You got interviewed a lot on TV, so your image is known."

"Way ahead of you. I'm going to shave my skull and grow a more formal beard. I'll wear glasses."

"Grow a man bun. That'll really throw 'em off."

Braxton winced at that suggestion. "I won't go that low. I'm still a real man. I used AI to mock up a portrait. Want to see?"

"Oh hell, why not."

Braxton poked his phone, turned it around. The image in the picture looked nothing like him. Harry Callahan slouched in gray carpenter's pants and a Trail Blazers hoodie, wearing aviator glasses, smoking a cigarette and staring at the ground.

"Hah! All right. Let me see what I can do."

"Harry has no social media profile. If they look for this Harry on the net, they find zippo."

"That in itself is suspicious."

"I don't think so. Most normal people are not self-obsessed narcissists. They may use the net to advertise their business or keep in touch with loved ones, but most people are too busy to spend much time there. At least those who work for a living. Harry's an auto mechanic. I know just enough to fake it."

"What about fingerprints?"

23

"I'll have to be careful not to leave any."

"And CCTV?"

"Well, I have the new look and a bunch of hoodies. I'm trying to achieve an ANTIFA look. Young and self-absorbed." Braxton had been planning his trip carefully. He was proud of the fact that whatever Ronin threw at him, he had a response for it.

Ronin cradled the warmth of the coffee cup in his hands. "Faye's flying out on Monday to interview Mr. Higby."

"What's her cover?"

"She's doing an article for the Prestone Foundation. This guy, Morris Prestone, set it up last year after his son committed suicide due to online taunting. Prestone used to write for *The Nation*. He's one of those former lefties who has seen the light. Nobody fights the left like a former leftie who's had a Come to Jesus moment."

"I know who he is. I read his stuff."

"What did you learn about Higby's tormentors?"

"The usual cancel pigs. Hang on. I got this off the *Indiana Daily Student*." He poked at his laptop, then turned it around. The page showed some students marching with masked agitators—all black clothes, hoodies, facial coverings. Below the cutline, it read:

> *Members of the Bloomington community, ANTIFA, and No Space for Hate march toward the Bloomington Community Farmers' Market on Aug. 24 to protest the continued presence of vendor Schooner Creek Farm. The market has been under scrutiny as of late for including Schooner Creek Farm, which is run by people with alleged ties to white nationalism.*

"Interesting," Braxton said. "They're spreading. It makes you wonder where else they might be."

"I found three guys with a lot of sock accounts, making themselves look like a bigger group. One of them lives in Indianapolis. They've done this to several businesses."

"It's May Day, the holiest day in a socialist's life. What's going on in Indy?"

"No idea, but I can tell you that they're marching for climate, food, and entertainment justice on every campus in the county. You know the routine—demanding free food, free housing, free cars, and free access to all nightclubs."

"What's   entertainment   justice?"

"Change every traditional CIS-gendered white male in entertainment for a differently-abled lesbian of color."

"You're joking."

"If you get the Disney Channel or Netflix, you know it's happening."

"I avoid TV as much as possible."

"What do you do?"

"I read books. I study things that might help us." *I grow.*

"All right. Get all the shit together about your new identity you want me to incorporate, and I'll get started. It's going to take me a week at least to get this together. Where you live, age, address, all that shit. Make sure it's solid."

"That's fine. Faye left today. I don't want my visit to overlap with hers. She's just an honest journalist doing the job the lickspittle won't do."

"Gotcha."

Braxton sat in silence for a few moments, nursing his coffee, thinking through what he might face. His mind went to Angela and how his daughter wasn't thrilled with her college options because of the wokeness on campus.

Then Ronin said, "Y'know, there are lots of places they don't put up with this horseshit. Not every town is a college town."

"I've been studying them. They are everywhere. Being woke is like being infected with a virus."

"What about Oklahoma?"

"You would think they would be safe from this BS, but they're not.   I   looked   it   up."

"You're shitting me."

Braxton took Ronin's laptop. Minutes later, he turned it back to face Ronin.

The organizers of Friday night's **"solidarity march"** in northwest Oklahoma City were clear from the beginning about the event's purpose: to honor the lives of those affected by racial injustice…

And that's how it ended. Peacefully. But it didn't come without tension for its organizers. Prior to the event, social media channels buzzed with rumors of ANTIFA groups headed to Oklahoma City from other states. Following these rumors, a group of about twenty armed men showed up at the capital ahead of Friday night's solidarity march.

Ronin rubbed his temples. "You're giving me a headache."

"You ever look at their Wikipedia entry?"

"No. Wikipedia has no bearing in real life. It is a tower of shit built on a foundation of more shit. I avoid that site like the plague."

"It's worth checking out how they spin themselves." Braxton turned the laptop back to him. He turned it around again.

> *ANTIFA is a left-wing, anti-fascist, and anti-racist political movement… It consists of a highly denaturalized array of autonomous groups that use nonviolent direct action, incivility, or violence to achieve their aims…*

"That's enough, I may puke up my breakfast. Thanks." Ronin cracked a thin smile.

"I looked at my entry and was surprised to discover that I'm a racist."

"And your response to this lie?"

"I went in there and changed it myself. I'm not a complete troglodyte."

"Duly noted. Would you like the entry to just disappear forever?"

"Can you do that?"

"Please. It's me." There was a bit of well-earned bravado in Ronin's voice.

"Do it. And find me those guys in Indy."

"Gotta go. But before I do, I want to show you something."

"What?"

Ronin pulled up the front of his hoodie revealing the butt of a 1911 .45 jammed in his waist. "I took your advice. I'm not leaving myself open to danger."

Chapter 5
Thank You for Your Patience

Faye stood in the B boarding group with other Southwest passengers waiting to board her plane from Portland. She had been willing to pay extra to avoid the B and C groups, but she'd acted late and the middle of the B group was the best they could do. She just prayed she'd find an aisle seat near the front. That way she could get off early and not stand at the rear of the plane with other weary, sweating passengers watching families of five gather their children and paraphernalia and ooze toward the front.

She traveled light. A backpack and a small suitcase for the overhead bin. No big clumsy purse. Purses were for cat ladies. *Give me a good backpack any day.* She'd breezed through security because of the way she looked and the absence of guns, bombs, liquor, or any bottle containing more than three ounces of liquid.

Travelers trickled out the gangway tube, families with young children, single ladies with shih tzus in soft carriers, business executives pulling rolling suitcases, teenagers reporting for college. After a quick turnaround to clean up the aisles, the gate agent began pre-boarding. Military veterans, families with young children. Then the A group. Then...she activated the small monitor on a pole.

"Group B, numbers 1 through 40!" *Go! Go, go, go!*

The gate agent didn't actually say that, but that's what Faye heard. There was a pileup in the boarding tube, and when Faye finally got on the plane, she was lucky to snag an aisle seat in the fourth row next to a couple of young women, one with bright blue hair, the other with purple. Faye wondered if the TSA gave them special treatment because of all the facial piercings.

The flight was nonstop and took two hours and forty-five minutes. Faye pulled out her laptop and went to work.

Those who study history know that every successful republic eventually succumbs to its own success and begins to devour itself. There's an old saying. Hard times beget strong men. Strong men beget good times. Good times beget weak men. It happened in Greece. It happened in Rome. And now it's happening in the United States. The Founding Fathers never envisioned career politicians. They were serious men engaged in a serious enterprise, bringing forth a new country, a new idea, from whole cloth. They were young. Thomas Jefferson was thirty-three when he wrote the Declaration of Independence. He studied history. Jefferson knew about Greece. He knew about Rome. In his genius and wisdom, he helped create the Constitution of the United States, the most perfect political document ever. Its greatest innovation was declaring that our rights do not come from kings, monarchs, or unelected bureaucrats. They are our natural, God-given freedoms. This poses an existential threat to politicians. Not to statesmen. But there are no statesmen left.

Politicians are mostly sociopaths. They go into politics for three reasons. To get rich without working. To enjoy special privileges, like not having to wait in line at the airport, for example. And to hurt people they don't like.

John Adams, who contributed to the Constitution, was forty when he did so. Adams said, "Our Constitution was made only for a moral and religious people. It is wholly inadequate to the government of any other."

In order to understand the situation in which the country finds itself, it's necessary to not only understand history, but to understand the sociopathic mind...

The purple-haired girl in the middle seat said, "What are you writing?"

"I'm writing a book."

"What's it about? Is it a novel?"

"No, it's about the state of the nation."

She seemed slightly less enthusiastic with Faye's response. "Are you a writer?"

Faye bit her tongue. "Yes, I'm a journalist."

"Are you famous? Maybe I've heard of you."

Faye smiled tolerantly. "Oh, I doubt it. I write for obscure foreign policy magazines."

"My name's Hazel."

Faye took her hand. "Pleased to meet you, Hazel. I'm Faye."

"Listen. I have a great idea for a novel. I could tell you, you could write it, and then we would split the profits."

Faye laughed. "Do you know how many novels are published in the US every year?"

"No. A lot?"

"One million. Most are pretty bad. Even the good ones have trouble finding traction. J.K. Rowling was turned down by twenty-seven publishers before she sold Harry Potter."

"Oh, I adore Harry Potter!" Hazel turned to her window mate. "Sue, this woman's a writer! She's writing a book right now!"

Her seatmate didn't even raise her eyes from her Android phone. "Wonderful. I'm watching this movie."

Faye glanced over and saw Eddie Murphy at the wheel of a massive plow truck.

"Are you like on Amazon or something?"

"Yes, I have a couple books out. Just look up Faye Weldon."

"I'll do that right now!"

"You must let me get back to writing. I'm meeting my publisher in Indianapolis."

"Of course. You go, girl."

Faye read what she had written.

Today's politicians don't bother to hide the destruction they do. One need only look at California, once the most prosperous state in the union, to see the folly of their policies. It is important to note that the policies are not designed to improve anyone's life but the politicians'. Thus, it behooves the modern politician to pit one group against another. Based on race. Sexuality. Land of origin. The language they speak. Even their choice in music. If the politician can convince people they're victims, then any action they take against the evil enemy is justified.

Instead of gratitude, which fosters a positive attitude that leads to progress, politicians encourage resentment. Even hate. They promise to take the resources which one group has struggled to create by dint of labor and ingenuity, and tell other groups that those resources were unjustly stolen, and that if only Group B will vote for them, the politician will return those resources which are "rightfully theirs."

Thus, Black Lives Matter. The Palestinian Liberation Front. ANTIFA, which is the real subject of this book.

She adjusted the words, tightened her prose several times over.

"Attention, please. This is the captain speaking. We are approaching Indianapolis. We should be on the ground in ten minutes. Please bring your chair backs to an upright position and close your trays. Thank you for flying Southwest."

The plane landed on an outer runway. It rolled toward the terminal, then stopped. After fifteen minutes with no explanation, a steward announced, "Sorry, folks. Seems there's another plane at our gate and we're just waiting until it's gone before we can approach. Thank you for your patience."

Thank you for your patience. Faye thought that was the real slogan of not only the airlines, but the government. It was hot and stuffy in the plane. As the wait dragged on, a baby began to cry. One idiot got out of his seat and started messing with his bag. That elicited an announcement for everyone to remain in their seats.

31

That's part of the problem too. Rather than just confront this man, they broadcast a warning to all of us. We don't hold individuals responsible, as that might upset the guilty parties, so now everyone gets drawn into their drama.

At last, the plane lurched and rolled into the gate, and the early responders, which included Faye, popped up in the aisle, eager to get off.

The steward opened the exit hatch and people streamed out. Faye burst from the stuffy tunnel into the light and cool of the terminal and headed for *GROUND TRANSPORTATION/LUGGAGE.*

As she descended the escalator to the ground floor wearing her backpack, pulling her carry-on, an unassuming man in his mid-fifties with white hair either poorly cut or awkwardly combed, wearing wire-framed glasses, an EMS jacket, and gray dockers, stood hopefully at the bottom. She smiled when she saw him.

"Mr. Higby? I'm Faye Weldon. Please call me Faye. And you must be Jason. You didn't have to come greet me."

He stuck out his hand to shake hers. "What else have I got to do? It's the least I can do after you flew all this way to interview me."

"I have a room at the Courtyard Marriott. If you'll take me there, we can have dinner after I get settled in and get started."

"Sure," he said, reaching for her tagalong bag. "I'll take that."

Chapter 6
Crown Vic

Ukiah, Oregon, population two hundred, had one main drag. Main Street. At three-thirty in the afternoon, Thursday, Braxton turned south on Camas Street, drove over Camas Creek, and just outside of town, turned into Avery's Auto Repair, an unassuming yard surrounded by hurricane fencing with a *BEWARE OF DOG* sign at the open gate. He'd shaved his skull, let his beard sprout, and wore tinted aviator glasses and a Trail Blazers hat. Braxton drove right up to the Quonset hut that served as the garage and got out. A Rottweiler came over, grinning, tongue lolling, looking for pets.

Braxton was ruffling the dog's fur when a wiry, middle-aged man wearing stained coveralls and a Packers hat came out of the garage, wiping his hands on a rag.

"You'd be Mr. Knox?"

"Yes, sir."

They shook hands.

"Who's the dog?"

"Maurice. I ordered a French bulldog and they sent me this."

Braxton looked closely to see if he was joking. Avery held a poker face until Braxton smiled.

"I call bullshit."

"You'd be surprised how many people fall for that. Come on in. I'll show you the car."

Braxton followed Avery past a rare silver Cadillac XLR on a lift and a massive Dodge truck with its hood open to the rear of the garage, where a wall split the building into two parts. An old refrigerator stood in the corner. There were parts everywhere, and a wooden workbench parallel to the curving side wall.

Avery gestured to a clean, 2002 Ford Crown Vic Police Interceptor, white, with oversized black tires with tiny hubcaps and battering ram on the front, sitting three inches taller than the civilian version.

"Here she is. She's only got 70,000 miles on the clock, and she's in tip-top shape. People think these old cop cars are run ragged, but the truth is, they are serviced exactly on schedule and are in better condition than most private vehicles."

Braxton slid into the driver's seat and gripped the wheel. There were two gaps in front with an open space between them where they'd taken out the console.

"She weighs 4,200 pounds, has a separate oil cooler, and the chassis is bulked up on steroids. I beefed up the radiator, per your message. She's got a good push bar, spotlights, and a black honeycomb grill. This one has a bullet-proof windshield, which is a perk."

Let's hope I don't need to test it.

"You mentioned you could replace the grill with a chrome civilian model."

"Yessir. Already did it. I've moved a bunch of these ex-troopers, never had a complaint. I'm kind of curious, how'd you hear about me?"

"I have a friend who found you. He's a computer expert. He said you were reputable. What he found is that you bought a lot of ex-police cars from auctions. It's a pretty unique niche."

"Yessir. I looked you up too. The Feds did you wrong with your little girl. Sorry for your loss."

"Thank you."

"From what I saw, you've been giving these commies conniptions!" He grinned displaying yellow teeth. "I ain't gonna ask what you want the car for. Your money's good. Nobody knows I got it, and nobody'll know when it's gone."

"I can pay cash."

"I like the sound of that. I've been thinking of moving to Idaho for years, but Imma waitin' to see how this separation deal goes. Most people outside of Western Oregon are sick of incompetent commies. Big movement to split it right down the middle, and we become part of Idaho."

"I hope it happens, if that's what you want." He turned their focus back to the car. "How fast will she go?"

"She's got the four-point-six and she'll do one forty on a straight stretch. Mileage ain't that good, maybe twenty-two on the highway."

"Okay if I leave my RAV here? My friend went over it to make sure there are no tags."

"Yeah sure. May not have room in the garage, though."

"That's okay. It's spent most of its life outside."

"Well, let's go in this office. Hey, it's late afternoon. This calls for a drink."

"I'll drink to that."

Framed posters of Richard Petty, A. J. Foyt, and a Ford GT 40 hung on the wall. A framed photograph of bare-chested young men in combat fatigues in a baking landscape in front of a pre-fab building in the desert.

"Where'd you serve?" Braxton asked.

"Afghanistan. Regular Army. Seemed like a good idea at the time. You?"

"Same. Once they found out I could type seventy words a minute, I didn't see a lick of combat, except when they crept in to lob mortars and fire machine guns over the fence." He opted to leave out the story of the porta johns being shot up while he was in one. War stories were supposed to be glamorous; not his. But Braxton suspected many others had ones just like it.

Avery sat behind his gun-metal gray desk covered with papers and car magazines, a computer on the table at ninety degrees. He reached into the desk's bottom drawer and brought out a bottle of Cutty Sark and set down two red Solo cups.

"Just a couple fingers," Braxton said. "I got a lot of driving to do."

"You're welcome to crash here if you like. I got an extra bunk in back."

"I think I'll take you up on that." Braxton held up his cup. "Death to communism."

They touched cups and swallowed. Avery held up the bottle. Braxton nodded. Avery held his cup up again. "There are only two sexes!"

They bumped and drank.

"I heard what happened to your family. It just seems so unbelievable, and yet all too believable. I consider myself to be lucky to have grown up in an America that was relatively free and prosperous."

"Amen, buddy."

"I got a shooting range out back."

"I gotta tell you, I have been practicing."

"With what?"

"You wanna see?"

"Sure!"

Braxton retrieved Themis from the car. He slipped it out of the wool-lined carry case and put it together on the desk. Avery whistled.

"Ho-leee shit. What is that?"

"Accuracy International. One of the top sniper rifles in the world."

"What did you use it on?" There was a hint of suspicion in his voice.

Braxton didn't take the verbal bait. "Paper targets. What else?"

"Can I pick it up?"

"Sure. What are you shooting?"

"MK 11. Same rifle Chris Kyle used."

"He was a great American."

"Fuckin' A."

They never made it out behind the garage to shoot. It was dark by the time Braxton turned in on a cot in a back room Avery used for storage. There was a bathroom in the hall with a shower. Avery said goodnight and went out back to a trailer in which he lived.

"See you in the morning."

Remarkably, Braxton slept well, with none of the nightmares that had haunted him for months. His sleep was shattered by Maurice licking his face. He had a slight hangover. He went into the bathroom and showered, the cold water delicious against his skin. When he came out, Avery was out front doing a final run-through on the Crown Vic, which was up on the lift. Avery slid out from under, his face smudged with grease.

"Yeah, just making sure everything is tight. You're good to go."

Avery lowered the car, and Braxton transferred his belongings from the Toyota into the Ford's cavernous trunk.

"You can pick up Eighty-Four east, take that down to Salt Lake, and then head east on Eighty. I got no idea how long it's gonna take you to get to Indy."

"Three days."

"You'll be driving eight hours a day."

"I don't mind. I kind of like it. No distractions."

"Yeah, the stereo system's probably not ever been used. Cops don't listen to jams much. It doesn't have a CD player, so you're gonna hear a lot of farm reports and Holy Roller religious shows."

Braxton pulled out his wallet. "Thank you, sir. Let's get this out of the way." He counted out ten thousand dollars in twenties.

"It ain't worth that much."

"It is to me. Hope to see you on the way back. Hang on to my car for me."

"I will surely do that." He signed over the title and handed it to him.

They shook hands. Braxton got in the Ford and drove toward the open gate. Maurice was in pursuit, barking, and was finally stopped by Avery, who gave him a wave. A half hour later, he hit the Interstate and sliced his way into Montana. He turned on the radio. Protesters wearing kufiyahs and waving Palestinian flags had stormed the Capitol in Washington shouting, "Free Palestine!" and "Death to America!"

I went overseas in the service so they could come here and protest. It made no sense to him. Braxton changed the channel. Avery was right about one thing: farm reports and come to Jesus stations were all he could pick up for many long, flat miles. Finally, he found a station playing country, and he stuck with it. He was surprised he liked it so much. He'd never been a country guy. Too corny. Too heart on its sleeve. He realized that the older he got, the more he liked country. Songs about patriotism spoke to him in ways they hadn't in his youth.

Ol' Waylon came on. Braxton joined in on the chorus, surprised he knew the words.

"And I turned twenty-one in prison, doin' life without parole. No one could steer me right, but Mama tried, Mama tried..."

Chapter 7
No-Tell Motel

Braxton drove east, stopping for the night at a Motel 6 in Salt Lake City. He preferred old-style motels, the kinds of places that always had vacancies and were willing to accept cash. While the big chains all wanted credit cards for incidentals, the small mom-and-pop motels didn't have incidentals with which to incur costs.

He avoided using his credit cards for transactions such as gas. If things went south, he didn't want to make it easy for the authorities to reconstruct his trail. His father was going to log in to check his own email from time to time in the cabin, creating the illusion that Braxton was still in Oregon. While he didn't anticipate problems, he made moves as if trouble was coming.

The next day he made Sidney, Nebraska. Population: 6,400. No tall buildings. Main Street, also I-80, was lined with decades-old redbrick buildings, many of which were abandoned and boarded up with gray, faded plywood. The Pizza Hut was new. He missed the old ones with the red checkerboard plastic tablecloths and the Galaga machine. Going to dinner then was fun, an event. Braxton felt things were going backwards.

Nowadays, everyone is about UberEats and Grubhub. We've lost what it is like to be a social people, out in public, enjoying life.

Braxton pulled into the Sleep Cheap motel as the sun set. A young girl sat behind the desk, sporting an abnormal number of facial piercings and tattoos. These were the kinds of decisions that come back and bit you as you aged. She was nice to him, though, even flashing him a smile when she checked him in.

He paid in cash, signing the register as Harry Callahan. His new ID passed her scrutiny with ease. Even had it been blatantly fake, she would have accepted it, absorbed as she was in her phone. The room key had a big plastic green tag with worn lettering. Inside, he saw exactly what he expected. A floral pattern bedspread that was at least a decade old. Stale air and a stained turquoise carpet. A framed print of farmland hung over the bed.

It took three trips to move everything from the trunk into the room. There was no way that he was leaving guns and ammo in the car—not in a strange town. Once he unpacked, he drove around looking for a place to eat and settled on Mi Ranchito. He got his meal to go. Sitting alone in a restaurant was depressing. It reminded him of his wife and daughter.

He ate his burrito, chips, and salsa while watching Fox News. He found the remote difficult to use, since it was glued to the bed stand. The world was in trouble. Ukraine and Israel rose to the top of the list. America's enemies smelled her weakness. It felt like a bad movie or book where he already knew the ending.

He shut off the TV and opened his book, *The Hero with a Thousand Faces*. Campbell weaved the similarities of different mythos, extracting the commonality in storytelling. The book was academic, but as a former professor, he didn't mind that at all. He was academic at heart still.

Two hours later, he closed the book, slid between the sheets, and shut off the light. Sleep came easy. Braxton had no idea how much time had passed when he heard muffled shouting through the wall. Two male voices, and a young woman. Sounded like the young lady working the desk. "Let me go!" she yelled.

Why me?

A cry for help was something he couldn't ignore. He swung his legs out, pulled on his jeans, and went to the dresser where he had laid out his weapons. The office was small. There were three people in there. Normally he would have taken Themis, counting on the sight of the sniper rifle to intimidate. It was impractical in an enclosed space. He picked up the Karambit and his Glock. Braxton slid the pressed leather holster onto his belt. He held the Karambit as if it were a set of brass knuckles.

Sounds of a struggle on the other side of the wall. The girl's voice cut off. He left his room, shutting the door behind him, and opened the lobby door.

One man wore a wrinkled blue flannel shirt from Walmart, draped over a T-shirt for some band. Children of the Stun. The other had a poorly trimmed beard and wore a faded denim shirt with sweat marks under the arms. He was behind the counter, holding the girl's arms, reaching over the small counter.

He glanced outside, noting a ten-year-old Camaro carelessly parked across two spots, hand-painted flames extending from behind the front wheels.

"You okay, miss?" Braxton said. He moved to the left, holding the knife low. He didn't want to kill them—not yet. *I don't want to end up with local law enforcement up my ass.* What he *did* want was for them to let go of the girl and leave.

"Fuck off, baldy," Blue Flannel replied.

"I wasn't talking to you. Young lady, are you alright?"

She shook her head rapidly, unable to form words. Braxton saw the streak of tears down one cheek.

"Why don't you boys just let her go?"

"This is none of your business," the beard said, shoving her to the floor, turning, muscles flexing.

Hormones and beer.

"If you leave now, no one gets hurt."

Denim shirt dude drew a cheap tactical folding knife, the kind you bought at Harbor Freight. "The only person getting hurt is you, gramps."

Braxton changed the grip, so the blade was visible. Blue Flannel pulled out a similar curved blade, spinning it like Roy Rogers spinning his six-shooter. Braxton smiled.

Denim was behind the counter. Blue Flannel made his move, swinging the blade high, coming from the left. Knox turned slightly, blocking the blow with his left forearm, bringing his Karambit down on the fleshy underside of the youth's arm.

41

The young man wailed. Blood squirted. He dropped his knife, gripping his wound. Braxton lunged forward, one foot between his assailant's feet, shoving the attacker to the floor.

Denim rounded the end of the counter and lunged, stabbing at Braxton. Knox used his right forearm to knock the blow to the side, dragging his own blade across the top of denim's arm. Burt taught him to not watch foes' faces. Look lower and to the side—his peripheral vision was quicker.

Denim's hips shifted. Braxton blocked the blow and made another slice, cutting his forearm to the bone.

The young man stepped back. Braxton stepped forward, putting his foot on denim's foot shoved. His blade caught the assailant's hand on the way down, leaving his pinky finger dangling on a thin strip of muscle and skin.

Both men lay on the floor, looking up in terror. Blood everywhere. Denim fumbled with his nearly severed finger.

Braxton gestured toward the door. "Buh-bye."

They rose so fast, Blue Flannel nearly slipped on his own blood. They ran into the parking lot. Braxton pocketed his knife and reached for his Glock, just in case they had guns. An engine with a busted muffler coughed and roared. They peeled out.

Braxton turned to the girl, who stared at him with wide eyes. "Thank you, mister."

"You know these guys?"

She nodded nervously. "We went to high school. They come by from time to time, trying to get me to come out and party with them. They've never been like this before." He didn't quite believe her last sentence.

"You might want to consider having a gun here at night when you're alone."

"My mom says that guns kill."

"Guns don't kill. People kill. You need to protect yourself."

She nodded nervously, her own adrenaline starting to play out, making her entire body tremble. "Should I call the police?"

"Nah. They ain't coming back, not until they go to the hospital. If you think they will, call the cops. Don't wait. You know the sound of their car."

"Thank you."

Braxton went back to his room and took a hot shower to calm down. There were no sirens or knocks on his door. He cleaned his knife and threw away his bloodied T-shirt. Sleep came slowly as he thought of the young girl and Angela.

She would have had a gun and known how to use it. I would never have allowed her to work a late-night job without the means of protecting herself.

Chapter 8
Penis Candy

Faye sat in the lobby of the Courtyard Marriott in Indianapolis, waiting for Jason Higby. She had offered to come to his place, but he suggested they meet somewhere else. "I lost the house and everything else in my divorce. The little flat I'm living in isn't really conducive for visitors."

She sat facing the revolving lobby door and saw him come in. Faye recognized him from when she had dropped him off. When she had first met him, he was more of a ride. Now she eyed him with her reporter-gaze. While the events that had changed his life had only occurred six months earlier, it looked as if he'd aged a half-decade. His hair was white, worn longer, not out of style, but probably to avoid the cost of a haircut. He wore wire-frame glasses. Higby was in his 40s and he was skinnier than she'd expected. The skin on his cheeks hung limp. He wore Wrangler jeans and a plaid shirt that had been ironed by someone unfamiliar with irons. He carried a brown leather computer bag slung over his shoulder. She waved and stood as he walked over.

"Ms. Weldon," he said, shaking her hand. She felt his callouses.

"Thank you for meeting me." She gestured to the seat next to her.

"I have to admit, I am reluctant to do this. It just brings up a lot of terrible memories for me," he said as he sat down.

"I understand. There's a lot of people out there who have also been canceled. Many more claim that cancel culture is a lie. They deny the negative effects of their actions. Digital mobs ruin people's lives. I want to put a face on their activities, expose them for what they really are. The scum of the earth."

Higby nodded. "That's the only reason I agreed to meet with you. I don't want anyone else to go through what I did." His voice was both weary and nervous. Her years of reporting told her to take the pacing slow with him.

She opened her notepad. "Let's start with the basics. Who are you? Where did you go to school? Tell me about your family."

"No one special. I was born here in Indy, went to Sojourner Truth High School. I learned to make candy from an old Swiss gent, Martin Federer. Met my wife when she came in to buy chocolates."

"Tell me about your candy shop."

"Well, Mr. Federer decided to retire. He was a widower and his kids were all grown. He never mentioned selling the store, but I knew he was worried that his legacy would be lost. A lot of people loved that store. Especially little kids. I had a pretty good handle on it by then, so I went to my bank to see what they could do. Let's see, I bought the store in 2011. I wanted to own my own candy shop, and it was the perfect setup. My dad always talked about the American dream. He said it started with our freedoms, and what propelled it was that any person could carve out their own part of that dream. Running my own business seemed the best way."

Higby adjusted his glasses. His blue eyes lit up. "It was a lot of fun. We had a small shop, but the real money was in special orders— you know, for parties or events. I even got written up in *Indianapolis Today* as one of the fastest rising businesses in the city."

"I read that article," Faye said. "The photo of you and your employees was wonderful."

"My wife worked there too. We had six employees at the start of 2020. Then the damn virus hit. We went on mandatory lockdown like everyone else. We did our part to flatten the curve, then it continued on. I didn't want to take money from the government. To me, that was welfare. That's not how I was raised. Besides, other people probably needed it more than me. But I needed to keep my people employed, so I had a buddy of mine get us online. People weren't doing special events much during that period, but they wanted candy. After a few months, we were selling almost as much as we did out of the storefront."

"Then what happened?" Faye asked, flipping a page. She knew the story, but wanted to hear it first person.

"This guy placed an order for a hundred penis-shaped candy bars. These things were gross. The order specified—I hope you aren't offended—veins. They wanted white chocolate sperm coming from the tip." His face twisted in disgust.

"The guy ordering was Socialjustice118—you know, that's his ID on the internet. But you have to understand, we're Christians. That wasn't the kind of order we did. I told him that. I even returned his money. That wasn't good enough for this guy. He sent me some nasty emails claiming I was against gays. That wasn't true at all. If he had ordered vagina-shaped candy, I would have turned that down too—I told him as much."

"Then what happened?"

"He started posting stuff about my business, claiming I was homophobic. My sister is a lesbian; can you imagine what that was like to try to explain to her? Others joined in, like a screaming mob. Pretty soon we never heard from Socialjustice118. He was replaced by some idiot who went by CaramelJustice. I don't know his real name. The coward hid behind his fake ID just like the others. CaramelJustice was online twenty-four hours a day, posting negative stuff about me, my family, and my business. He had some of his cronies join in. They hounded my customers, labeling them as gay-haters too. Same with my employees. He contacted the local media, and they were relentless. No one wanted to hear my side. They accepted his lies as the truth and branded me guilty. It was hit piece after hit piece."

"Your business suffered."

He sighed. "It died. People were afraid to support me out of fear they might be targeted next. I had to lay off those employees who hadn't already quit. Even my church shunned me. My pastor said I was bringing in too much negative attention to his parish. I thought they would be in my corner, but they left me high and dry.

"I tried to run the business on my own, but there were so many horrible things said about me on the net, I just gave up." Higby paused and wiped a tear from his left eye.

Faye could feel his agony. She wanted to hug him, but she maintained her objectivity and distance. This wasn't the first time she'd heard a story like this. In fact, there were too many of them. "I'm sorry this happened to you."

He nodded, tears welling. "My wife, Penelope, she couldn't take it. CaramelJustice and his followers hounded her as well as my daughter. It spread to my daughter's school and even though they were online, the kids were as bad as the parents when it came to harassment. Penelope was always very active in the community. She said that she could feel people staring at her. We began to argue. Then these online hoodlums started to post stuff about our daughter, Jennifer, on the school's message board."

Higby was silent a long moment, a dark cloud crossing his expression. "It started with her saying they needed to get away for a week or two. They did, but they never came back. Penelope stopped taking my calls. I found out why when I got a certified letter from her lawyer asking for a divorce. I thought we could work through it. I mean, we'd been married for fifteen years. It was too much for her… for them. Being unemployed, saddled with debt, I had no hope of winning custody of Jennifer. I lost it all."

"What happened after the divorce?"

Higby's face sagged. "I ended up living in a storage unit for a while, until the owner figured out I was doing it. It turns out that's against the law, but I didn't have anywhere else to go. I got a job working at the newspaper in the print shop…a waste of my college degree, but it was all I could get. I was finally able to afford a one-room apartment. It isn't much, but I am paying off the debts as best I can."

"Why didn't you go after the people that did this to you?"

Higby shook his head. "They use these tags, hide their identities. I found a lawyer, but he said that the Big Tech companies would never reveal who these people were. It's hard to sue someone for defamation when you don't know who they really are in the first place. We had some IP addresses, but without a warrant to their service providers, it was a dead end."

"These people that hounded you…do you have the information they posted online about you?"

Reaching into his computer bag, he pulled out a thick pile of printouts, bound with a heavy black clip. "I made copies for you at work. These are the ones I saw. The few friends I still have told me there's a lot of more out there. I got tired of looking at them. Each one was a stab in the back by people I don't even know."

Faye flipped through the stack. Hate leaped off the pages.

Don't do business with Higby's Candies, they are transphobic!!!
Gay-haters! Alt-right religious fanatics, all of them.
If you order from them, you're no better than they are and we will come for you!

"This is so wrong."

"I know," Higby replied, leaning back in the chair. "There aren't laws to deal with this. Yeah, we have an online harassment law in Indiana, but getting a prosecutor to actually pursue a case, that's nearly impossible."

"If you could rebuild, would you?"

He pondered her question, then shook his head. "Maybe. My fear is they would just come after me again. How can I rebuild my family? They took everything from me, all because of a lie. There are some nights I wonder if I should have just made the damn candy bars. But no, I have my values. I should have been smarter."

"No," Faye said. "Compromising what you believe to avoid their wrath is what they want. These people are terrorists. They want you to change how you act and what you believe out of fear. They are no different than ISIS or Hamas in that respect."

Faye reflected bluntly. "This was never about penis candy; this was about them exerting control. You did the right thing, Mr. Higby."

"But at what cost?" he asked as more tears ran down his face.

Faye did not have a response she could say out loud. *I can't wait to confront this CaramelJustice!*

Chapter 9
The Ringleader

Ronin sat in his command center, surrounded by curved monitors. He kept the lights low, preferring to bask in the glow of the monitors. Until a few months ago, this was where he felt best, in a world of cyber-penetrations and hacking. His employer, the owner of a major social media company, made sure that Ronin had the best hardware and tools that money could buy.

Braxton Knox changed all that. Braxton was not a person who sat back and took what the woke did to him. He took action—bold, vicious, effective. Ronin had changed, shifting from being a guy who obtained information to enable justice, to a person who got his hands dirty rendering justice.

His benefactor supported what he did in ways that went far beyond money or tools. He gave him covert contacts in a dozen different companies and agencies, loyalists like him who were more than willing to help.

When Faye forwarded him the names of all of the parties involved with destroying Higby's life, he compared it with his own research. With the email addresses, Ronin secured their IP addresses. It almost always required a warrant to get an internet provider to tell you who was behind an IP address, but there were ways around those barriers. He had friends at Verizon and Comcast, guys who were not insiders but installers. For the right money, they'd provide the information he needed. It took a few days, but he finally had names behind the social justice warriors who had destroyed Higby's life.

He called Braxton. "Where are you at?"

"Davenport, Iowa," Braxton replied unenthusiastically. "I can make it to Indianapolis tomorrow, the next day at the latest."

"Faye passed me some names she got from Higby. I've run them down."

"Excellent. What do you have?"

"The ringleader goes by CaramelJustice. His real name is Percy Kornbluth. He lives just south of Indy in a place called Whiteland."

"Percy? I bet he caught a lot of shit in school."

"He's a real piece of work, Brax. He's thirty-nine years old. He works part-time at the Indianapolis University bookstore. I posed as a hiring manager trying to verify his education on his resume. He attended class there for two years, but flunked out. Apparently he didn't bother to tell the bookstore that he wasn't a student."

"A part-time job, that's it?"

"Yeah. He lives with his mother."

"Big shock."

"His older brother was in the Army. He's a hothead in a different way. Our little troll had some run-ins with the law over the years, all violence-based. He's managed to stay out of jail, but it points to a lack of a strong male role model in the house. The older brother lives in Georgia now, with no apparent connections to Percy or his mother."

"Great family. What happened to the dad?"

"Former security guard. He bailed on the mom. I found a domestic violence police report to their house, but no charges got filed. His old man divorced her four months later and left the state. He didn't even want custody of the kids on weekends."

"So he had a bad childhood and now he takes it out against innocent people online."

"For the most part. From what I found, Percy really doesn't contribute to society. He's mostly an online presence, with six sock accounts all confirmed as tied to his IP. I pulled his high school yearbook from one of those reunion sites. He's a nobody. No hobbies, no friends other than those he rallies to his social justice cause *du jour*. Unlike his older brother, he has no real issues with the law other than he passed a few bad checks and got sued for them over the years."

"A real pimple on the ass of progress."

Ronin laughed. "Some of the IP addresses mapped to the university bookstore where he worked."

"So while he was at work, he was shitposting about his targets."

"I'm impressed, Brax. I never thought I'd hear you use the word, shitposting."

"Like I told you, I'm constantly learning. Back to Percy. He sounds like the kind of guy that the FBI says is a loner."

"Yeah. He posted about three years ago that he purchased a gun, even put up pictures of it on Twitter. Percy claimed he got it to protect himself from 'alt-righters that were threatening him.'"

"What kind of gun?"

Ronin looked at his screens. "KelTec PF9."

Braxton laughed. "A piece of crap. Was he being threatened?"

"Not really. He and his merry band of idiots were harassing a restaurant owner in Indianapolis before they went after our guy. It was the same sort of bullshit they did with our Mr. Higby. This guy posted, 'You are brave on the internet. Why don't you come down here and face me man-to-man?'" He read from another one of his open windows that flanked his gamer's chair. "Percy took that as a threat. He claimed his life was in danger."

"So he likes painting himself as the victim."

"He's done it with others he's harassed too. He wages an online smear campaign and if they say anything back to him, he claims he's being targeted by them." It was a pattern with the woke. They loved victimhood and never assumed responsibility for their actions. A generation of professional losers.

"Pathetic," Braxton replied.

"It's pretty much standard operating procedure for the woke."

"That doesn't make it right."

"When you are dealing with these people, right and wrong are fluid concepts...much like their genders. For example, two of Percy's false personas are females. Both lesbians. Some psychiatrist working their doctoral paper could get a wealth of material out of a failure like this guy."

"I picture him at home, in his mom's basement, with his pants down, surfing the internet until three a.m."

"I'd prefer not to. But if you want, I'll send you photos."

"Make sure Faye gets everything as well."

"Will do. I spoke with her earlier. She's interviewed Mr. Higby and was going to spend today talking to his former employees. She reached out to his ex-wife and got hung up on."

"When you talk to her, tell her to wait until I'm in town before she confronts Percy."

"Brax, you know Faye. She doesn't follow directions well."

"Percy is probably no threat. If she goes in there early, before I get in and we can work a plan, she'll be tipping him off. You don't give a slimeball the upper hand."

"You know that and I know that, but Faye...well, we both know she sometimes gets her blood up and does that whole crusading reporter thing."

"Tell her I need a day or so on the ground, that's all."

"Will do. I am sending you a link to a secured dropbox with everything we have on this guy and his followers. It's not great reading, but should give you an idea of what we are up against. I've done all I can from my bunker here. I'm going to book a flight to join you after we hang up."

"I have a favor to ask."

"Fire away."

"I need a garage. I want a place with rentable bays and tools. I need to make a few modifications to the car I picked up. The kind of place I'm looking for won't ask a lot of questions."

"That will take some digging. Those kinds of places don't exactly have websites." Ronin's fingers flew across his keyboard. "What are you thinking of doing to it?"

"Adding some armor."

Ronin cracked a grin. Good old Braxton. He'd done it with his cabin, and it had likely saved their lives.

"I'll get you some prospects."

"Thanks again, Ronin. I'll talk to you after I get into town and touch base with Faye." As Braxton hung up, Ronin went to work arranging his flights and scouring custom hot rod shops and rentable garage space in Indianapolis.

Once he booked his flights, he turned to Faye, sending her a link to all of his findings at the same time he did Braxton. He'd call her—try to convince her not to jump the gun. Hopefully, she would wait until Knox was there. A part of him suspected that she wouldn't. *It's her nature. It's almost maternal with her. She gets into protective mode, which sometimes puts her in harm's way.* It was one of the things he most admired about Faye, and one of the things that concerned him about her.

Chapter 10
Percy the Pussy

Percy Kornbluth sat at the service desk of the University of Illinois Bookstore, trying to mask his boredom. He hated his job. The only reason he still had it was it kept his mother off his back. She still harbored the illusion that he was going to get back in and finish his degree. Percy lied to her often, saying he had reapplied, just so she would believe he was still trying.

In reality, he didn't want to go back to school. The college expected results. Not a lot of results, but they wanted him to pass tests and turn in papers. That was work, far more boring and time consuming than his job at the bookstore. Classwork had eaten into his time online, which was something he was unwilling to sacrifice. Lying to his mother was easy; neglecting his online personas was intolerable.

When he was online, he was alive. He didn't have college kids asking him stupid questions. On Twitter/X, he was a god, albeit a minor deity. People respected him; he saw it with their likes. His opinion was important—as it should be. More importantly, he had power. Businesses and individuals feared and respected him. If they didn't, they would incur his wrath. For him, being online was akin to having a real life.

His mother didn't understand. She complained about his long hours at his computer. He often fed her little fibs about what he was doing—that he was applying for jobs, or reaching out to former professors for references, or taking some online class. His flippant words were enough to forestall his mother's nagging.

CaramelJustice was more of a real person than Percy Kornbluth. He used the word "caramel" to suggest that he was a person of color and often seeded his posts with references to being non-white. A part of Percy knew it was wrong, but he told himself it helped him better understand the plight of POCs. So far, no one had penetrated his ruse, but if they ever did, he had a lie cooked up and ready to serve.

There were other personas in his arsenal. Trixiehottie and Tracylonglegs were two lesbians. RufusBP was a transsexual. Dale5551212 was the only online presence that was a straight male, and for Percy, he was the most boring. Behind each of the characters, he had created a detailed backstory.

Having personalities from different oppressed groups was useful. When he was waging social justice, people resisted. When they did, he could drop defenses appropriate to the character. Anyone going after Trixiehottie or Tracylonglegs would be labeled as homophobic. A person calling him out when he was RufusBP was marked as a transphobe. Dale5551212 was well known for simply calling his opposition alt-right extremists. The labels were useful; they put his foes on the defensive. Sometimes it drove them to silence.

Being online for him was not a hobby, it was his life. When he was younger, he had played Dungeons and Dragons with a small group, until the dungeon master had deliberately killed his character. After that, D&D was dead to him. It was like when he played soccer as a kid. If he couldn't be the star, there was no point in playing. Percy no longer had hobbies; he had lives to live. Keeping their stories straight was no small task.

During the day, when there were few customers in the bookstore, he would jot down ideas for posts his personas could make. His manager, Rory, didn't want to waste time castigating him. Rory had told him he couldn't be on his phone at work. *Someday I am going to make him the target of my people. He'll never know it was me. The university will simply fire him.* The only thing that kept him from going after Rory was the thought that they might replace him with someone who was sterner. He used his breaks and bathroom time to make posts, outside the watchful eyes of his boss.

He saw a woman come into the bookstore. She was kind of hot. Older than most of the students that came in, probably in her thirties. Her hair was short and fiery crimson. She was slender, with ample breasts. Percy loved breasts, though he had only seen a few in real life. Just seeing her was enough for Percy to stand up straight.

She saw him and headed straight over. "Can I help you?" he asked.

"You're Percy Kornbluth, aren't you?"

How does she know my name? "Yes, I am."

"I'm Faye Weldon, a journalist. I'm doing a story about the online harassment of Jason Higby. It appears that you were the ringleader behind ruining his business. I have a lot of questions for you."

Higby! How did she figure out I was involved? Panic set in. "How did you—I mean, I have no idea what you are talking about." His face got hot.

"I know all about you, Percy. I know about your false IDs on the net. I know how you organized your little troop of friends to harass an innocent man, costing him his family and his business." From her purse, she pulled out a small digital recorder that was already on, putting it between them.

"I don't know what you are talking about," he stammered. Even to his ears, his words didn't seem convincing.

"Do the accounts CaramelJustice, Dale5551212, Trixiehottie, Tracylonglegs, or RufusBP have any meaning to you? Do you deny that you are these people? Would you like to see the evidence that you are the owner?"

Percy frowned angrily. "You can't just come barging in here and start leveling accusations."

"Percy, I know all about you. I know that you convinced your online posse to help you smear Mr. Higby's reputation. I'd love to hear your side of the story. Let's start with an easy question. Why did you do it? What was your motivation? Was it personal between you and Higby, or did you just decide to try to ruin his life for grins?"

"You can't come in here like this." He wanted to run, but he knew she would follow him.

"You're a big, tough personality online. In person...not so much. I'm sure that the LGBTQ+ community is going to be overjoyed hearing that you were representing them online. Not to mention persons of color. I bet those two groups will have a whole bunch of questions as to why you have pretended to be part of their culture."

"Look, lady, I don't know who told you I had anything to do with this Higby guy, but they lied to you." It was the best he could muster off the cuff.

"I have evidence. I can link your IP address to the emails and many of the online posts. For someone who spends their life online, you didn't do a good job of hiding who you really are."

Percy's panic ratcheted up a notch. The space behind the counter was closing in on him. He had endured panic attacks in the past, and it felt like one was coming on. His eyes looked around for something, anything that might give him a sense of security. He found nothing.

"Percy," came Rory's voice from behind him. "What's this about?"

The lady journalist turned. "Your employee here has been harassing people online. He's ruined people's lives, shut down businesses, forced people to get unemployment. He's a stalker, pretending to be lesbians and black people."

Percy caught a glimpse of Rory's face out of the corner of his eye. He wasn't pleased, but Percy was unsure who his ire was directed at.

"What my employees do on their own time is their business, ma'am," Rory said firmly. "Now then, you need to go. If you want to have this discussion, you'll have to do it elsewhere."

The journalist was unshaken. "I respect that. It might interest you to know that a number of these messages were sent from this location. That would mean that Percy here was doing his online harassment from your business. You know what that makes you? An accessory to his crimes. It means that the university is libel for his actions." She moved her digital recorder to be closer to Rory. "So, before I leave, perhaps you would like to make a statement about that?"

Rory was angry. His face reddened as he pivoted to face Percy directly. "Is this true?"

"I have no idea what she's talking about. She's just some nut who walked in here and started saying things about me." Percy wanted his words to be convincing, but deep down, he knew that they were flimsy at best.

"I can provide documentation," Weldon said.

Rory glared at Percy. "I want to see what you have," he said to the journalist. "In the meantime, Percy, you're suspended without pay."

"What? You can't do that to me. I haven't done anything wrong!"

"We've had this talk before about you being on social media at work. I'll review what she has. If she's wrong, you'll be back to work tomorrow. If not, you're done here."

Rory's words brought a smile to the Weldon woman's face. Percy felt as if he had been punched in the stomach.

Why is this happening to me? Why now? The Higby thing was months ago. I've moved on...why hasn't he? It isn't fair! I didn't do anything wrong. I was just exercising my first amendment right.

Looking at his manager, he knew that attempting to rebut what the woman said was pointless.

Slowly, he walked from behind the counter, pausing to shoot an icy stare at Weldon, then his manager.

You're going to pay for this—I promise you that. You had no right bringing this to where I work. Harassment? You're the one harassing people, not me.

As he exited the bookstore, he jerked his name plate off his shirt, tearing a small hole in the process. Percy didn't care. As he stormed away, riding the rage in his mind, he swore that the Weldon-bitch was going to regret that she'd ever crossed paths with him.

And he knew exactly what needed to be done...

Chapter 11
The Element of Surprise

On the way to Faye's hotel, Braxton stopped in at A-OK Garage. Ronin had put it at the top of the list for places to check out. From the moment he pulled up, he could tell it had the right vibe. At one point, A-OK had been a car dealership. Braxton could still make out the faded Plymouth emblem on the dull gray exterior. Plywood covered the curved showroom window where they used to put the new models. Those days were long gone. The pavement was stained with oil, grease, and antifreeze, some of it dating back to before he was born. Parking in front, Braxton went to the service door and entered, ringing a bell.

He inhaled the scent of oil and gasoline as if it were a testosterone-infused cologne. There were ten repair bays, four of which had vehicles in them. Workbenches from another era lined the back wall. He spotted MIG and TIG welding carts, metal bending gear, and an array of equipment that Braxton knew he would need. It reminded him of the garage in *Christine*.

An older man in brown coveralls limped towards him, a half-inch-thick sole on his right shoe. Two days' worth of unshaven facial hair had spittle marks from spitting tobacco. "Howdy, stranger," he said. "What can I do you for?"

"I'm looking for a place where I can work evenings. Welding, a little bodywork, that kind of thing."

"I think we can accommodate you. The rate is four hundred a month. That gives you a bay and access to the tools. Any metal or parts you need is on top of that. We have security cameras here, so the tools and such don't wander. Out back, I've got a pretty good scrapyard of parts, and if I don't have it, I know where to get it."

"I might need some help with some stuff."

"I can help you with some of the lighter stuff. The other fellas who have bays here are pretty friendly and willing to assist as needed. It might cost you a pizza, though."

"What kind of hours do ya'll keep?"

"You rent a bay, you get a key. If you want to work at four a.m., that's up to you. I run a clean shop. You spill stuff, you clean it up. If you leave the tools laying around or don't pick up after yourself, you're out of here." There was a sternness in his voice that hinted at prior military service.

"Is there some sort of contract or something I need to sign?"

"I just need a copy of your driver's license and car insurance. I don't feed lawyers with a lot of fancy contracts. In terms of payment, I want two months' worth in advance. If you're straight with me, I'll be straight with you."

Braxton extended his hand. "Sounds good. Harry Callahan."

"Rocco Renzetti," he said, shaking his hand hard.

"I hope cash is okay," Braxton said, pulling out his wallet.

"One more thing that I don't have to tell the IRS about."

Braxton counted out the bills and handed them to Rocco. The older man watched him count it out and shoved the bills in his pocket. "Alright, you get bay number four." He gestured. "Follow me, and I'll get you a key, then show you where everything is."

The tour of the garage was useful. Two cars were street rods. A Chrysler had its engine up on wood blocks, the carburetor on a towel on the workbench. While the garage itself was old and run-down, Rocco had a clean bathroom and an impressive array of tools. They talked for a few minutes, as Rocco wanted to know what kind of car he had. Braxton took him outside and showed him.

"Former cop car—nice," Rocco said. "This will get you where you want to go, that's for sure."

"Handles pretty good."

"Cop cars are always well maintained," Rocco said. "What kind of modifications are you thinking of doing?"

"Some additional protection."

"Like what?"

"Armor plates."

Rocco mulled it over for a few seconds. "Sounds like trouble."

"Let's just say I want to be prepared."

"Look, if you're going to use this to commit a robbery or something like that, I don't want to know what kinds of changes you're doing. I'd rather not have my days hung up in court."

Braxton grinned. "Not me, hoss."

Rocco cast him a cocked eye. "With a name like Harry Callahan, I can only imagine the kind of shenanigans you might be planning."

Braxton texted Faye and drove to the Courtyard. She was in the lobby waiting for him. "You finally made it," she said, hugging him. "Ronin's on his way."

They sat in the lobby until Ronin came in. Faye led them a half block to Alexander's Bar and Grill, taking a booth in the back.

"Let me tell you about Higby." She laid it out.

"You call yourself a journalist," Braxton said, "but you're more like a private investigator."

"Thanks. There's one more thing."

"What's that?" Ronin asked.

"I confronted Percy Kornbluth at his place of work."

Braxton leaned back, frowning. "Come on, Faye. Please tell me you're kidding."

"No kidding. I had to do it. I needed to see him squirm."

Braxton leaned forward on his elbows as the waiter took their drink orders. Once the waiter was out of earshot, he said, "What you did was reckless. You've tipped our hand. Kornbluth didn't know we were onto him. Now he does. You've weakened our position."

"He needed to be confronted," Faye countered. "He's every bit the internet weasel you said. Pudgy around the middle, haircut done at Hair Cuttery, pale, pimples…right out of central casting."

Ronin spoke up next. "Faye, I get it. We both do. But we had a plan."

"He's no threat," she tried to reassure them. "Saying he's out of shape would be paying him a compliment. A real basement dweller."

Ronin shook his head in frustration. It was a feeling that Braxton understood. He was mad, too, but he knew Faye. Like him and Ronin, she wanted justice. Confronting Kornbluth gave her that. Her spirit and quest for vengeance were characteristics he admired.

She got her anger up and took action. It's hard for me to criticize her, given the actions I've taken. I use violence, but that isn't her way. She weaves words, but words alone cannot deliver the kind of retribution we need.

"We wanted the element of surprise. We may have lost that. Faye did what she did for all the right reasons. I wish you hadn't," he said, locking his gaze with her, "but that is water under the bridge."

Faye seemed to understand that she had made a mistake. He could see it with the wrinkles that flared on her face. "Well, I saw the pain that he put Higby through. You could tell he's not used to being confronted face-to-face. And I wanted a piece of that little turd."

"We all do," Braxton assured her. "Trust me, justice will be served. I can't fault you for being in character and following your instincts. We work with what we have. In the meantime, show us what you've got on him so we can plan how I can and should engage with him."

Chapter 12
Family Ties

The VFW on Verona Road in Indianapolis was housed in a former three-story brick hotel built in the thirties. The VFW renovated the ground floor into a bar and a meeting hall, and rented out rooms on the remaining two floors to veterans down on their luck. Every afternoon you could find the same half dozen vets, ages ranging from their thirties to their seventies, hanging out in the cool, dark bar, drinking, telling stories, throwing darts, or playing pool.

Murray Landreth was a Gulf War veteran in his early fifties, and still looked like the bulldog sergeant he'd once been. The jowls, the crew cut, the burly body. He'd put on a little weight, as they all had since the service. He owned his own small home repair and construction business. It wasn't much, but he had a crew and a fairly solid reputation. Murray sat at a scarred wooden table with three old friends, two Gulf War veterans, the third who'd served in Afghanistan. They were playing Texas Hold'em, and Murray was fifty bucks ahead as he regarded his hand. Two jacks. He'd won more with less.

"Up to you, Murray," Jack Hawthorne said, lighting up another Marlboro. Jack lived off his late wife's insurance policy. She died when a semi ran a red light and broadsided her Prius.

Murray stared over his cards like Jack had spit on the table. The same stare that made privates and corporals jump to obey his commands. The boys just laughed. They were civilians now.

"What's the matter, Murray? You got indigestion?"

Murray pulled twenty bucks from his pocket and put it in the middle of the table with the other cash. "Call."

Hawthorne spread his cards on the table. Two nines. Phil Beck set down two tens. Bob McIntyre casually laid three queens on the table.

Murray threw his cards down in disgust. "Fuck." His phone rang. He pulled it out of his jeans pocket—it was a struggle—and looked. Every family had a black sheep, a loser. This call came in from his family's. It was his slacker nephew, the son of Murray's sister, Thelma. Percy only called when he needed a favor. But what could Murray do? Family was family.

"Yeah?"

"Uncle Murray, I need your help. Some bitch came to my place of business and cost me my job."

"Huh?" He was already regretting answering the call.

"Some fucking reporter. I don't know why she picked me. Accused me of some online stalking campaign. I don't know what her problem was. Fucking boss fired me on the spot."

"Whoa whoa. Slow down. Just a minute." Murray stood. "'Scuse me, fellas. My nephew's got his panties in a wad." That elicited a few chuckles as he stalked off to a quiet part of the bar next to a pinball machine. "Okay. Calm down. I'm listening."

"Yeah. This bitch comes into the store and starts accusing me of all kinds of wild shit. She said I was part of an online gang of hackers that cost some douchebag Christian his job. She says she has screenshots of all the shit I supposedly said and she was gonna write about it for some right-wing rag nobody reads."

"Okay, slow down. What douchebag Christian are you talking about?"

"Jason Higby. You may have read about him."

"Never heard of him."

"Yeah. Well, he had an online candy business, and some people ordered a bunch of chocolate candy shaped like penises. It's just business, right? I mean, even the Olympic teams are allowing in trans-people. The world—it's changing. Apparently, he has a problem with people that don't measure up to his Nazi standards. Anyway, he refused. It was blatant anti-LGBTQ discrimination. A lot of people objected—it wasn't just me. They reached out to his regular customers and pointed out that the dude was a bigot, and probably a Nazi, and his platform kicked him off. Somebody found his private email, and his wife's, and started hammering home the message that in this day and age, it is no longer acceptable to discriminate against LGBTQ types."

Murray didn't care about LGBTQ-alphabet-soup anything. He wasn't sure what two of those letters stood for, and had no desire to find out. As far as he was concerned, it wasn't his fight. "Is that right? What do you want me to do about it?"

"Look. Her name is Faye Weldon. She's a dish, for a white supremacist. Maybe you can, you know, talk some sense into her."

"I'm not a sense-talking kind of guy. What do you really want?"

"I want you to get her to back off. She's already cost me my job."

Murray chuckled. "And you were so well qualified. What are you gonna do now?"

"I'm exploring my options."

"My friend Bill needs workers for his lawn care business. Can you mow a lawn?"

"This isn't about me getting a new job! It's about this bitch sticking her nose in where it doesn't belong!"

"Does your mom know?"

"I haven't told her yet. She's at work. I'll tell her when she gets off."

"Yeah, that's gonna go over real good. Look, Percy, you need to knock off all that online bullshit. Get out in the real world for a change."

"How can I do that? She cost me my job!"

"I feel for ya, pal, but I don't see where this is any of my business."

"She's a real dish."

"So? I'm supposed to ask her out?"

"No. I mean, she's a pro, polished. She's hot, but bad news for guys like you. She's anti-second amendment. She also hates the US military and thinks you should all be under the control of the United Nations."

"You're shitting me." Almost instantly he hated this Weldon chick.

"She's crazy. She called the Army a den of faggots and said you couldn't fight your way out of a paper bag. Let me send you a picture of her."

"Where'd you get a picture?"

"I hacked her driver's license. I also copped a still off the security feed. Hang on."

Murray waited. His phone vibrated. Text. He hated texts. He didn't understand why anybody would use them. Murray slid it open. The woman could have been anywhere between thirty-five and forty-five, but she was good-looking. He wouldn't mind banging her.

"Run through that again. She said what now?"

"She called you a faggot."

"Me, personally?"

"No. That's her attitude toward the armed forces."

"And you know this how?"

"Come on, Murray. If there's one thing I know how to do, it's go online and dig up shit on people. Like that DUI you got last year in Salt Lake."

"You know about that?"

"Hell yes. And a bunch of other stuff."

"What the fuck are you doing digging up dirt on me?"

"You're my uncle. I want to protect you. It's part of my plan to have all that information removed from the internet so it won't cause you any embarrassment."

"You don't say a word about this to my sister."

"Of course not. I don't want to upset my mom."

"That's right. Thelma's straight as an arrow."

"Bill left her because she wouldn't put up with his drinking and pot smoking."

Murray knew otherwise. "More like she kicked his ass out of the house."

"Whatever," Percy exclaimed. "This Weldon chick needs to be taught a lesson."

"Maybe, maybe not." Murray wasn't above a little intimidation, if the cause was right. "You need to stop wasting your time online, Percy. You poking around this guy over penis candy is what got you into this."

Percy ignored him. "You're going to need help with her. Did you know your buddy Jack Hawthorne was arrested for menacing and intimidation?"

Murray hated it when Percy changed subjects violently like that. *Guess I got a little too close to home with him. What's he doing checking on my buddies?*

"What are you talking about?"

"Yeah. Two years ago. Some kid parked his car in front of Jack's house and was blasting rap all over the neighborhood. I'm not saying that was right, but Jack's first reaction was to come out of his house with a baseball bat and start taking off mirrors. Kid called the cops and Jack spent the night in the hoosegow. He got a lawyer and agreed to pay restitution. He prob'ly didn't mention that to the gang down at the VFW."

"Fuck me runnin'."

"He's also got two DUIs. One of which still has an outstanding warrant."

"Is this what you do with your time? Dig up dirt on my pals?"

"No, man! I'm trying to help. I find something that might cause some blowback, I want you to know about it. I'm in the fight for social justice, Murray. You know that. I'm trying to make the world a better place!"

Murray knew blackmail when he heard it. "And if I don't lean on this bitch, you're gonna spread our dirty laundry all over the internet."

"No way! I'm just trying to tell you I got skills. I was wasting my time at that bookstore. I'm going to check out a job with a big investigations firm. They could use somebody like me."

"What investigations firm?"

"I don't know. Pinkerton maybe."

Murray barked. "Yeah, you let me know if you need a reference."

"Come on, you gotta help me. We're family."

"Look, man, Thelma ain't gonna like it if I pop up in the news as some kind of harasser/stalker. She's got enough to deal with as is."

"I know that." Murray's sister had an arrhythmic heart and couldn't afford health insurance. She'd gone to the ER twice in the past two years. They told her to quit working, but it was the only way she could hang on to the miserable old house in which she lived. Her church chipped in, which was more than he could say about his nephew.

"I'll talk to this Weldon chick. I'll convince her to lay off of you, you know, with some knuckle."

"Thank you."

"Where do I find her?"

"She's staying at the Courtyard by Marriott at 601 West Washington Street."

"I do this for you, and all this shit you dug up stays buried, right?"

"Absolutely. Thanks, Murray. I won't forget this."

"I'm just gonna talk to her, capisce?"

"Of course. She'll listen to you."

Murray returned to the poker game.

Jack looked up. "Everything irie?"

"Everything is copacetic. Jack, you free tonight? I could use your help."

Jack looked at his hand. He threw it down. "I'm out."

Chapter 13
Hold'em

Murray and Jack drove to the Courtyard and parked on a ramp across the street.

"So this bitch is hassling your nephew?"

"Yeah. Percy's always been politically active. I remember having dinner at his house and him stickin' up for the poor, persecuted fags, that kind of stuff."

"I don't give a shit about fags. They can do what they want as long as they don't get in my face."

"I hear ya. I figure it's because the poor kid's got nothing going on in his life. He was working at the university bookstore, but the bitch confronted him right there in the store and he got shit-canned. God knows what he's going to do now. My sister has enough problems without her man-child son losing his job."

"Well, what can he do? What's he good at?"

Damn little. His nephew had always been a little *special*. Murray had tried to man him up, convince him to go into the service, but Percy wasn't that kind of kid. It was easy to blame it on him being fatherless, or having ADHD, or so his sister claimed. To Murray, Percy was just one of those kids that slid through every crack that presented itself in life.

"Stirring up shit on the internet."

"That's pretty worthless."

"Yeah. I know. Still, he doesn't deserve to lose his job. Let's you and me go sit in the lobby. I got a pretty good description. We don't want to talk to her in the hotel. They might not like it."

"What makes you think she'll come down?"

"It's five o'clock. She's gotta eat. She says she's a journalist. I know the type. They like to be around people. They like to eavesdrop. If she doesn't appear in a half hour, we'll call her room and tell her we got info on Percy. That will get us in the door."

Murray remembered one female reporter who had been embedded with his unit in the war. She posted all sorts of articles about the troops violating human rights.

People like her enjoy making people like me look bad.

"How do we even know about Percy? I mean, she's bound to ask."

Murray leaned back in the car seat, considering a response. "We were in the bookstore. She didn't see us because we kept our heads down."

"Where is this bookstore?"

"Just off University Boulevard. Down by Tenth Street and the river."

That seemed to be enough for Jack—just enough detail to craft a good lie. He changed subjects, as was his habit. "You know, I enlisted right after I got out of high school."

"Me too. Learn new skills. See the world. I learned how to keep my head down, my mouth shut, and how to change engine oil."

"You always were a motorhead."

Jack grinned broadly. "Yeah, I love me some hot cars. I got assigned to the motor pool and learned a lot. Now I'm chief mechanic at Albertson Ford." There was pride in Jack's voice, though Murray knew from previous conversations that he was having issues with his boss.

"Yeah, and you still can't get me a deal on that new Maverick."

"I told you to buy three years ago. Now we're operating on a real thin profit margin. Everybody wants more. The parts makers want more. The mechanics want more. The salesmen want more. I told you this was gonna happen."

"Yeah, never mind. I'll never buy another new car."

They crossed the street and entered the lobby—marble-topped check-in counter, bistro off to the side, white furniture.

Murray elbowed Jack and headed for the bar, where a slim young woman the color of café au lait greeted them with a warm smile. "What can I get for you, gentlemen?"

Murray sat at the bar. "I'll take a shot of Jack and a beer chaser. Whatever's on tap. Something local."

"Excellent. And for you, sir?"

"I'll have the same."

Murray watched the lobby via the mirror behind the bar. Business was slow on a Thursday night. People came and went. An elderly couple checked in, insisting on pulling their wheeled luggage into the elevator. Jack pulled out his phone. Murray kibbitzed.

"What, are you playing video games?"

"It's Texas hold'em. I'm trying to improve."

"Are you fifteen years old now?"

Jack put the phone away. "Don't tell me you don't look at your phone when you've got nothing else to do."

"I check my mail. I check the headlines. Then I put it away."

A cluster of guests stood in the elevator hall, waiting. The elevator dinged. They backed away to let other guests exit. Jack nudged Murray.

"That her?"

Murray brought up the pictures Percy had sent. "Sure is. Wait until she leaves the lobby before we get up."

The woman wore a smart sundress that fell to her knees, pale blue with white chrysanthemums, and held a backpack at her side. She went out the revolving door. Murray and Jack waited a beat before following. They emerged to see her walking down the street. She planned to eat local, just as he hoped. It was six o'clock. They followed at a discreet distance. Weldon walked two blocks before turning into Tom's Bistro, a self-effacing high-class joint. Through the glass door, they saw her speaking to the maître d' and several other people waiting to be seated.

The host picked up a menu and led her toward the back of the bar. Jack and Murray entered and another hostess appeared. "Two for dinner?"

"No, we're just visiting the bar."

The young woman flashed a smile. "Have fun."

Jack and Murray walked to the mahogany bar running from halfway back to the rear on the left side of the restaurant and took two stools and the end, from which they could view the whole restaurant. Their quarry was seated at a small table on the left beneath a framed Van Gogh sunflower.

Weldon ordered a drink and took out her laptop, oblivious. Murray and Jack were feeling pretty good by the time she ordered.

Jack turned to the bartender. "Can we get something to eat here?"

"Sure. You can eat at the bar." He handed them two menus. They both ordered cheeseburgers.

While they were waiting, Murray stood. "Imma gonna check out the restrooms." He walked away.

Jack checked his phone. His estranged daughter never spoke to him, but he followed her on Twitter. Minutes later, Murray returned.

"That hall at the back opens in an alley. There's no one outside in the alley. That might be a good place to talk to her."

The waitress brought Weldon's meal. She paid more attention to her laptop, barely picking at the pasta dish. The bartender brought the boys' hamburgers. Gone in five minutes. The boys tried to space their drinks, but they were on their third a half hour after entering. Weldon signaled for the check. Murray poked Jack in the ribs and nodded.

"I'll go first. You follow a few minutes later."

"Are you sticking me with the bill?"

Murray reached into his wallet and pulled out a fifty. "If there's more, you take care of it."

"Gee thanks."

Murray stood outside the men's room, hands in pockets, until Weldon came out of the women's room. He glanced around to make sure they were alone. The restaurant was at capacity. Everyone was either eating, drinking, or service. One quick glance toward the bar. He threw an arm around her neck, too tight for her to squawk, and dragged her out the back door into the alley. It was dark out and oil in the puddles reflected dim lights from the street. As she flailed her body to get free, she tried to kick him in the nuts. Murray dragged her around the dumpster, out of sight of the bar, and jammed her hard up against the brick wall. One hand on her throat. Jack followed, making sure they weren't pursued.

"Just shut up and listen. I don't want to hurt you, but you're playing with fire and you need to stop. Just nod if you understand."

She tried to knee him once more, but he turned his thigh toward her. It hurt anyway, adding to the rush he was feeling. "I have a pretty good idea why you're here, but the young man you've targeted has friends. Friends like me. Friends that don't like him losing his job because of a snot-nosed reporter making accusations. I want you to go directly to the hotel, check out, and get the hell out of town. Don't bother trying to report this to the police. They won't believe it and they have better things to do. If you don't do what I'm telling you to do, it will be worse next time."

She reached up, grabbed his pinky finger, and bent it harshly back until it cracked.

"Ow! Goddamn it!" He let go and backhanded her viciously across the face. She went to throw her own punch, which he blocked with a move perfected by the US Army when he had served. His response was pure instinct. He threw a haymaker at her, slamming into her jaw. Weldon hit the wall behind her, then stumbled and fell. Jack sidestepped and kicked her savagely in the ribs. Jack joined in, landing a kick to her thigh.

"Get the message?"

Jack took Murray's arm as he pulled it back for another blow. "Yeah. She got the message. Let's get out of here."

They hustled toward the street a half block away, leaving the woman withering in pain on the wet, odorous ground.

Chapter 14
The Short Arm of the Law

Wincing, Faye leaned against the wall and got to her feet. She could taste the copper from blood in her mouth and licked her lips, only to taste more. With one hand on her aching ribcage, she staggered back into the restaurant. When she appeared at the entry to the back rooms, nobody noticed. Then a woman sitting nearby gasped and stepped up to help her, putting her hand on her shoulder to support Faye.

"Are you all right?" she asked.

"Call the police. I was just assaulted."

The manager appeared. He looked like the Penguin in his suit, but the concern on his face was appreciated. He offered his arm. "Let's go into my office so you can sit down. Joan, you come along."

A young waitress inked and pierced followed, concern creasing her forehead.

She leaned on the manager, moving hesitantly back into the corridor, to a closed door on the right. The man opened it, leading her into a windowless room with a hardwood floor, wooden desk, calendar on the wall, worn and cracked leather sofa. She gently eased down.

"What happened?"

"Two men followed me when I went to the bathroom. They were waiting when I came out. They forced me into the back alley and threatened me if I didn't leave town. I'm an investigative journalist."

"Where's your phone?"

"It's back on my table."

"Joan, would you get her phone?"

"Right away, Stan."

Joan left the room, shutting the door behind her.

"Do you know who they were?"

"No. I never saw them before. I think they were sitting at the bar."

"Well, we have security cameras. The police will want to see those."

"Would you please call the police? I don't think I can talk right now." She licked her swelling lip and still tasted blood.

"Certainly."

Stan pulled out his phone and dialed nine-one-one. "Yes. This is Stan Gruber, I'm the manager at Tom's Bistro. We just had a lady assaulted in the alley behind the restaurant. Two guys. She's pretty shook up."

He listened. "Uh huh. Uh huh. Thank you."

He set the phone on the desk. "They'll be here in ten minutes."

"Thank you."

Joan knocked and entered. She handed Faye her phone.

"Thank you."

"Joan, keep an eye out for the police, and when they get here, usher them straight back here."

Joan left.

"Indianapolis used to be a real nice city," Stan said. "Ever since that George Floyd business, everything's gone to hell. A big chunk of the police force quit and the other half tiptoes, terrified to get involved for fear of being called Nazis or something."

"You should see Portland."

"Is that where you're from?"

"Yes. I'm thinking of leaving. Nobody goes downtown anymore. Half the businesses are boarded up. The last in-city Walmart shut its doors last month. Compared to Portland, Indianapolis is a thriving metropolis."

"What brings you here, Miss Weldon?"

"I'm working on a story. A cancel culture piece." Talking about her assignment was easier than dealing with the pain of the attack. It gave her focus.

"I've heard of it, but I don't have time to surf the internet."

"Did you hear about the candy maker who was forced out of business because he refused to make penis-shaped chocolates?"

Stan gaped. "No."

"Jason Higby. He lost his business, his wife divorced him, took his house and daughter. He's living at a boarding house."

"What a shame. Why can't people just leave other people alone?"

"Most of these people, we call them cancel pigs, have howling voids instead of souls. But rather than recognize that their misery comes from within, they blame everyone and everything around them."

"I never thought of it that way."

Joan knocked and opened the door. Two uniformed police officers entered, an older male, bald with a trim mustache, and a younger Latino woman, her black hair cut short. Stan stood and gestured to the chairs.

"I'll leave you to it." He left, shutting the door behind him. The two cops remained standing. Her trained eyes spotted their identification badges and she instantly memorized their names.

"May we see some identification, please?" Officer Hernandez said.

Stifling a pinch of outrage, Faye opened her purse and handed Hernandez her driver's license. She looked at it and passed it to her partner.

"What brings you to Indianapolis, ma'am?"

"I'm an investigative journalist. I'm doing a story."

"Are you injured? Do you require medical attention?" Hernandez said.

"I think I have a busted rib. There were two of them. Older white men. They came in after me and were drinking at the bar."

"Is their race important to you?" Hernandez said.

The response bothered her instantly. "I'm just giving you a description. There should be some footage from the security camera in the bar."

"Yes, we'll take a look at that, but I have to tell you, the department is down thirty percent compared to five years ago. Were you robbed?"

"No. They threatened me. They said I should stop work on the story and get out of town or there would be consequences."

The other cop's name tag said Wilson. His shoulder mic squawked. He stepped into the hall, closing the door behind him. Hernandez sat. She took out a notepad.

"Tell me everything that happened."

Faye relayed events as best she could while Hernandez wrote.

"I think I broke the one guy's little finger."

"Did you threaten to expose this Percy Kornbluth?"

"I'm a journalist, officer. I'm trying to get the story."

"You live in Portland. Why come all the way to Indianapolis for a story that frankly sounds inconsequential?"

The question irritated her. *It's none of her business, nor does it help them arrest the guys that did this.* "Do you know how many small businesses have had their lives ruined by online doxing? This is a much bigger story about our society and culture." Her voice was crisp and to the point.

Wilson returned and stood by the door, hands on his belt.

"I wasn't the one doing the doxing. It sounds like you were."

"I didn't dox anyone. I simply approached this Percy for a comment."

It was clear to her that the officers were going through the motions, and that grated on her nerves. Hernandez tried to tie a ribbon on their interview. "All right. I can't tell you how to do your job. We take assault seriously. Why don't you come down to the station tomorrow and give us a statement? In the meantime, is there anything about your assailants that stands out?"

Faye paused, forcing herself to remember the attack. Her honed reporter's skills, her attention to detail might help.

There was something...

"The guy's watch."

"What about his watch?"

"The man who grabbed me around the throat wore a watch with a Kelly-green wristband. It looked like a military watch. Maybe you'll see it in the video."

"Rita, we have to go. There's a carjacking two blocks from here."

Hernandez stood. "All right. Sorry to cut this short. Why don't you come down to the station tomorrow and give a complete statement? Here's my card."

She left the room. Wilson remained. "He could be a veteran. We have four VFWs in town."

"Kornbluth is a hard-core leftist. It's hard to imagine he hangs out with veterans."

"I'm just saying. Sorry for your trouble. We've really made a lot of progress cleaning up downtown Indianapolis in the past five years." He handed Faye his card and left.

Faye sat there for a minute trying to decide if she had to go to the ER. The pain was bad, but it wasn't that bad, and there wasn't much doctors could do for her other than wrap her in bandages.

She took out her phone and called Braxton.

"The number you have reached is not in service at this time. Please try again later."

She tapped in a short text.

Chapter 15
What's on TV?

Five minutes later, Braxton returned her call. "How's it going?"

"I was just attacked."

"What?"

"Two men. Middle-aged, but in shape. Military types, I'm pretty sure. They dragged me out of the restaurant into the alley, warned me to lay off Percy."

"Shit! Are you all right?"

"I'll survive. They may have broken a rib or two, though. But now I'm afraid to walk back to my hotel, which is two blocks away."

"Ronin and I will come get you. What's the address?"

Faye waited inside until she saw what she thought was a police car pull up in front, but then Ronin got out, walked to the door, and escorted her around to the passenger side. He got in the back seat.

"Please tell me you didn't steal a cop car," she quipped. Somehow cracking a joke made her feel a little better.

"I bought it," Braxton said. "We need to get you to a hospital."

Faye hesitated. It was probably the smart move, but she didn't want to go there. "I want to go back to the hotel."

Ronin spoke up. "Are you sure?"

She nodded in response.

Braxton angled the car around a corner slowly. "Faye, tell us what happened."

Faye recounted everything that had happened since leaving the hotel. Braxton parked outside on a side street, not wishing to appear on the garage cameras. They took the elevator to Faye's floor and went into her room. It was a nice hotel split into two sections, a sitting room first, with a sink, counter, and coffee maker, and the bedroom, which had its own door.

"You boys want something to drink? Help yourselves."

Braxton waved a hand. "We're good." She went into the bathroom and washed the cut on her lip. She inspected her sun dress which had a fresh hole in it as well. Finding the hole only made her face angrier.

Ronin had his laptop on his lap. He was never without it. "We warned you something like this might happen."

I don't need to hear this right now. "I don't care. Somebody has to confront these people before they do more damage. I recorded our entire conversation, and there's likely video from the bookstore. Ronin, see if you can get in there and grab it before it's replaced. Not to mention the bar's security footage."

"I can do that. In fact, I'll do it right now." He left the room. It was nine o'clock.

"The restaurant is still open," Braxton offered.

She shook her head. "I'm fine." She rubbed her chest and winced.

"Yeah, you look it," he quipped.

"Ronin will get the footage. That guy has connections." As much as she wanted to probe into Ronin's background, she knew now wasn't the time.

"What if he doesn't get the videos? Can you describe your assailants to me?"

"I told you. It was dark and I didn't really get a good look."

"Do the best you can. Height. Weight. Condition. Color. Hair or no hair."

"They looked ex-military. Overdue brush cuts, florid cheeks, both putting on a little weight. The one guy wore a military watch. It had all those markings for latitude and longitude, you know."

"Would it be possible to work up a visual using AI?"

"I don't know. I've never used AI."

"Me neither. Ronin can do it. You say these men were sitting at the bar?"

"Yes. I noticed them but didn't get a good look. Their backs were to me. One wore a light blue shirt. The other wore suspenders. They were watching me in the mirror."

"Maybe the bartender can remember. I'll ask him."

"Won't the police have already done that?"

"Hopefully. But we can't take anything for granted."

She appreciated Braxton's thoroughness. It was one of his redeeming qualities. "Have you eaten? Want me to order something?"

"Nah. We drove through an A&W."

"How was it? I used to love their hamburgers."

"Shit. I ordered a bacon cheeseburger. We had to pull ahead because so many people were using the drive-through. Parked in the lot. Opened the cheeseburger. No bacon. Ronin ordered a double cheeseburger. No cheese. I thought about going inside to complain but what's the point? Serves me right for using a fast-food franchise. They've all been shit since the lockdowns."

Faye winced.

"Are you sure you don't want to go to the ER?"

"Really, there's nothing they can do except wrap me with bandages and prescribe a painkiller and bill me six hundred dollars."

"I'll pick up the bill, Faye," Braxton insisted.

"Would you go down to the lobby and get me some ibuprofen?"

"Sure. But if you aren't feeling better in the morning, I'm taking you to the ER." There was a fatherly tone to his voice that she appreciated.

Braxton went to the lobby and found a bottle of Aleve for nine ninety-five. As he was paying the desk clerk, Ronin returned, gave the thumbs-up, and went to the elevators. Braxton caught up with him there.

"You get in?"

"Well, I accessed their network. Now I have to see if I can access the security feed, but I gotta warn you, chances are it's a closed system. It goes from the camera to the office and that's it. And they'll purge it on the weekend."

"Do you have what you need to get in?"

Ronin gave him an assuring nod. They rode up in the elevator. Faye let them in. The television was on. Braxton tossed Faye the Aleve. She snatched it out of the air. She tried to peel the protective plastic covering off the lid. Braxton sat next to her and saw her wince in pain.

"Let me have it."

She handed him the bottle. He took his CIVIVI tactical knife from his belt hook and used the menacing blade to cut the plastic and the foil seal, and plucked out the cotton.

"Every package is an intelligence test these days."

Faye took the bottle, got a glass of water from the tiny kitchenette, and swallowed three pills. "It's ridiculous. I have to use a tin snips on everything I buy. And of course in Portland, the few stores that remain put everything behind locked glass."

"You ought to get out."

"I'd like to, but I can't afford to move right now. Housing everywhere is through the roof."

"You're a good writer. Write a best seller."

Those words coming from Braxton, a well-read former professor, were just what she needed. "Working on it. I'm in touch with a publisher who specializes in conservative books."

"Whatcha gonna call it?"

"*Whatever Lie Serves the Vicious Child at That Moment.*"

"I like it, but it's a little long."

"*The Vicious Child*?"

"That'll work."

"I've got it," Ronin said.

Braxton and Faye turned toward him.

"What?"

Ronin held up his laptop. They watched the grainy video of two burly men sitting at the bar. "Are these your guys?"

Faye got up and walked over. She peered for a second. "That's them."

Braxton rubbed his hands together. "Now we're cookin'. How are we going to find them?"

"Assuming these are veterans, I will turn my focus there. Only one of these guys gives us a good enough image to check, I'm sad to say. Thanks to a former co-worker, I can access a national facial recognition program used by law enforcement. That will help me clean up the images so I can run it against the Army's data."

Faye gave him a stare. "At times it frightens me what you are able to do."

"I have many friends in low places," Ronin replied with a wry grin.

"Can you do it from here?" Braxton asked.

"I think so. Give me a few minutes."

Faye turned on the TV. A popular late night host entertaining a famous actor. The actor said, "How 'bout those Republicans? Are they Nazis or what?"

The audience exploded with laughter. The host clapped enthusiastically. She changed the channel. A PBS dramatization of the life of Oliver Cromwell. A black woman in a wheelchair was cast as Cromwell. A differently-abled lesbian of color played Charles the First. She changed the channel. A popular game show called *What's Your Snoblem?* in which guests vied with each other for sympathy as they complained about their lives.

A purple-haired woman with a nose ring had the floor. "I woke up one morning and my life partner was gone. She'd cleaned out our savings account and taken all my jewelry, including my wedding ring from when I was married to a man."

The host, an aging game show veteran past his retirement age, pointed at her opponent. "Max, can you top that?"

"I was suspended from social media for something I posted nine years ago. They said it went against their community standards, but they wouldn't tell me what it was. I've searched and searched for the community standards, but I never find anything."

"You think you have it rough?" the purple-haired woman barked.

Braxton looked at Faye. "Don't you think this would make a good country song?"

"I'm in," Ronin said.

It was the perfect excuse for Faye to turn off the television.

"I got the image of one of the guys cleaned up. I've accessed the Army's personnel database. They have pictures of every soldier going back three decades. Now all I have to do is feed these pictures into the system. We just sit back and wait."

Five minutes later, Ronin leaned forward. "Winner winner, chicken dinner!" He turned the screen to face the others. It showed the man who had initially attacked Faye.

Faye pointed. "That's him."

"Jack Hawthorne, Indianapolis," Ronin read. "I don't have access to his full address file. I checked tax records, but this guy moves around a lot. Cross-referencing his known addresses, and I still can't locate where this dude lives."

"Does he have any connections to Percy?" Faye asked.

"None that I can see. His social media is almost nonexistent. Wait," he said glaring at the screen. "It's not much, but his photo shows up on another Facebook post. It looks like he hangs out at The VFW Lodge #21116, 815 Verona Road."

Chapter 16
Bruises and Bangs

Braxton was up for several hours after making sure that Faye was safe and asleep. Ronin slept on the couch in her room, which had to help. Faye never said she was afraid. Braxton wasn't surprised. There was a toughness about her, a grittiness. Still, she had been assaulted, and deep down, he knew that hurt her beyond the physical pain.

The fact that two men had beaten up a woman was something he could not let pass. Faye was not just a friend; she was someone's daughter. Braxton had had a daughter. If two men had beaten her, had kicked in her ribs, they would be dead. He felt the need to provide that same cloak of protection over Faye.

She's in this because of me; that makes her my responsibility.

Things had escalated with Kornbluth, from a simple confrontation to physical violence. Braxton had visited VFWs before. He was a veteran. There would be regulars. He needed information about Jack Hawthorne and his connection to Percy, if any. *How does a soyboy like Kornbluth have friends that would go to war for him?* A puzzle.

Braxton would go to the VFW and try to find where this Jack Hawthorne lived. He would arrange a confrontation. Nothing violent. He wanted to understand the connection between Hawthorne and Kornbluth.

Eventually he fell into a shallow sleep. When he rose, he showered, dressed, and grabbed his Glock 19. While he had expertise with each weapon, there was something about the Glock. He hoped he wouldn't have to use it. He wanted to talk to Jack Hawthorne, not shoot him. But Hawthorne was a bully who beat up women. He had to play it safe.

Braxton arrived at the Courtyard Marriott and went to Faye's room. Ronin opened the door.

"How is she?"

Ronin shook his head as Braxton entered. "You know Faye. I dug a little more on this Hawthorne character. Not exactly a poster child for mental stability. He attacked some kids for blasting music in front of his house with a baseball bat."

"That sounds like an overreaction."

"From the incident report I found online, he went ballistic as his first option."

Braxton crossed his arms. *A hothead. That can be useful and makes him dangerous.* "Anything else?"

"Two DUIs. He pled down on one but not the other. He spent time in jail. His license is still suspended and, given the time that has passed, he's just not bothered to get the matter cleared up."

"Still no connections to our boy Percy?"

"Nope. As shocking as it sounds, there are some limits as to what I'm able to find out."

Braxton cracked a smile. "You're doing just fine. I appreciate the air support." He gently rapped on Faye's door. "Are you decent in there?"

"Yeah. Come on in."

Walking to the bedroom, he saw her gingerly trying to put on a shirt. The bruises on her side and the sides of her left breast were dark purple. Faye winced in pain as she buttoned the shirt. Braxton winced while watching. "You doing any better?"

"You saw the bruises, what do you think?"

Looking at her red-tinged eyes, he saw that she hadn't gotten much sleep.

"You need to get to the ER."

"That's what I told her," Ronin said.

"Fine," she sighed. "I'm doing this under protest."

"Ronin, you go with her. I don't want her alone unless we don't have a choice. I'll drive you there. It's going to take a while to get X-rays and all that crap they run you through."

"Where are you going?"

"The VFW."

Faye turned quickly, wincing in pain. "You're going in there alone? Two of them beat the shit out of me."

"I'm just a vet from out of town. I'll go in, see what I can see, ask a few questions."

Faye cocked her head. "These are not the kind of guys that like people coming around asking questions. Trust me, I know. Midwest hospitality isn't on the menu with these men."

"I promise to be the model of discretion."

Two hours later, he pulled up to the VFW. Braxton remembered the last time he had been in one. In Portland. A fellow veteran of the Global War on Terror, Art Kohl, convinced him to go for drinks. Braxton found it depressing. The vets were cordial, but it was a place for them to go and hide from their problems. The few men that Art had introduced him to were friendly, but all seemed to have issues. One was struggling through his second divorce. Another had lost his son to Child Protective Services. Drinking in a dimly lit bar didn't seem much like a solution. It was their default mode.

He got out of the car and checked his watch. Bottling his tension, Braxton went in.

It was exactly what he expected. Dark, gloomy, the stink of cigarette smoke mixed with stale beer. Despite the place just opening, there was already someone sitting at the far end of the bar with a fresh glass of beer. The bartender gave him a sideways glance. Braxton sat at the bar.

"I haven't seen you here before," the older man said.

"Visiting family. Thought I might look up some old buddies." The key to a good lie was to make sure there weren't a lot of details.

"What can I get for you?"

"Whaddaya got on tap that's local?"

"How 'bout a Sun King Lager?"

"Sounds good."

87

The bartender filled a glass, going slow to reduce the head. Braxton nodded and sipped. He checked in the mirror, making sure there were no newcomers. Probably too early for the regulars.

No rush. It was wise not to dig for info too quickly. He enjoyed the drink. Eventually, the burly man behind the bar came over. "Want another one?"

"Nah," he replied. Pulling out his wallet, he took a twenty-dollar bill and put it on the bar between them. "Hey, tell me something."

The bartender stuffed the twenty in a cash drawer and grabbed change. "Shoot."

"I knew a guy from Indy way back. Hawthorne, Jack Hawthorne. You know him?"

The bartender put the change on the bar. "Doesn't ring a bell. The regulars are here at night. You might want to drop by then."

Braxton wasn't sure, but the bartender's answer didn't feel right. *He didn't ask what he looks like, or any details other than his name. I wonder if he's hiding the truth.*

"Sounds good."

"I'll ask around. What's your name?"

"Callahan, Harold Callahan."

"What's your number?"

Braxton gave him the number to one of his burner phones.

"Where are you staying?"

"Red Roof Inn on the west side."

"That place isn't too bad. They did an overhaul," the bartender said, jotting notes on a napkin. "Does this Hawthorne guy owe you money or something?"

The question struck Braxton as odd. "No, nothing like that. We served overseas, that's all."

"I'll keep my eyes peeled, Mr. Callahan," the bartender said.

"Thanks," Braxton said, leaving the bar.

* * *

Jack Hawthorne's phone chirped. He picked it up. "Hello."

"Jack, this is Rex at the VFW."

"What's up, Rex?"

"There was a guy in here asking for you. Claims he served with you overseas. I told him I'd never heard of you."

"I was never posted overseas."

"Exactly," the bartender replied. "Guy's name is Harold Callahan. He's staying at the west side Red Roof Inn. Said he wanted to connect with you."

Jack's mind raced. He owed alimony, but his wife couldn't afford to track him down.

Who would be looking for me? Shit. That reporter. She's probably got connections.

"Thanks, Rex." He hung up.

The smart move was to not react at all. But that wasn't Jack's style. When trouble reared its ugly head, he went in swinging.

Murray got me into this mess, he needs to come along.

He called Murray. "Yo, Murray. I just got a call about someone at the VFW asking about me, claiming to be an old war buddy."

"You were never in a war."

"I know. I think this is about that chick we roughed up last night."

"Fuck me. So how do you want to handle this?"

"We confront this piece of shit—with brute-fucking force."

"Look, Jack, I'm not sure that's the right approach."

"Hey, you got me into this. You need to help me fix it. You had no problem beating up a reporter. Don't pussy-out on me about beating up her boyfriend."

"This guy have a name?"

"Harold Callahan."

Murray sighed. "Fine. He doesn't know where you live, if he did, he'd be there. He's just fishing around. Chances are he'll get bored and give up."

"And if he doesn't?"

"Then we make him wish he had."

Chapter 17
Lies on Top of Lies

Officer Rita Hernandez pulled up in front of Percy Kornbluth's house and drank in the details. Unkempt yard. Fading white paint covered the old two-story Victorian. The paint was chipped and peeling. The handrail on the stairs was galvanized pipe.

Dead potted plants dotted the front porch. Hernandez hit the doorbell.

Hernandez had come alone. Her partner had to spend time in court and she wanted to follow up from the night before. She had pulled up some of Faye Weldon's articles and been impressed. They didn't share the same politics, but there was something intriguing about Weldon. She took risks and wrote with a mix of grit and poetry.

As a young girl, Hernandez had read the old Nancy Drew series of books. Her mother got a box of them for her at a garage sale and she devoured them. *The Message in the Hollow Oak* and *The Double Jinx Mystery* were her favorites. Reading those books had inspired her to get into law enforcement. When she had dug into Faye Weldon's past after her shift, she saw a bit of Nancy Drew in the reporter.

Weldon had her detractors—a lot of them. There were online petitions to have her fired, all of which seemed to have failed. Her haters online were many, making Hernandez wonder if one of them might be responsible for the attack. Logic took over, though. One of her assailants had referenced Kornbluth being fired.

Which had led her to 1517 Jacobite Street.

Inside the house, she saw an older woman come to the door and pull the thin curtain aside to see who had rung her bell. She cracked the door. "Is there a problem?"

"Ms. Kornbluth?"

"Yes."

"I'm Officer Hernandez. I was hoping to talk to Percy."

The woman turned. "Percy!" Her grandmotherly tone disappeared. Her voice resonated angrily. She opened the door. "He's probably in his room on that damned computer," she grumbled, leading Hernandez in.

The house smelled of cats. She followed Percy's mother into the kitchen. An old table with a faux marble linoleum top from another era with four chairs. The kitchen was surprisingly clean. "Percy, get down here!" she yelled.

Footsteps on the stairs. "What is it, Ma?"

Percy was tall, just under six feet. His dark hair was receding on top, long on the sides. Rita guessed he hadn't showered in a few days. Acne dotted his pale face, a fresh pimple emerging on his chin. Pudgy around his midsection. Percy's T-shirt was from some video game. *Wing Commander III*, straining to hold his girth in place. Seeing Rita, he tried to look serious.

"This cop wants to talk to you," his mother said, pouring herself a cup of coffee from an old Mr. Coffee.

Percy shuffled in, pulled out a chair, and sat at the small table. Rita did the same. "What's this about?"

"Before we begin, can I get your name, birth date, phone number?"

Percy provided them, fumbling as to where to put his hands. He shoved them in his sweatpants pockets, then pulled them out to his side, then crossed his arms as he gave her his identification data. "What do you want?"

"I'm investigating an assault that happened downtown last night."

"I was here all night. You can ask my ma."

"I didn't say you did it."

"Well, I was here."

"He was," his mother replied, taking the seat across from Rita.

91

"Faye Weldon was the victim. Does that name mean anything to you?"

Percy shook his head slightly, eyes darting everywhere but at her. "I don't think so."

"Ms. Weldon claimed one of the men who attacked her said it was about you being fired from the bookstore."

Percy was flustered. Before he could respond, his mother interceded. "You got fired? You didn't tell me that!"

"Oh, I know who you're talking about. I didn't remember her name."

"You lost your job?" his mother pressed angrily. "Again?"

"I'm suspended." He turned to Hernandez. "This chick came into my work, made a big scene. She was ranting and raving about me having something to do with some Nazi that owned a candy store. She claimed I was harassing him on the internet…that I had ruined his business—bullshit like that. My boss had to suspend me, she made such a big-ass scene."

"Where do you work?"

"The University Bookstore. The one on Tenth Street."

She made notes without breaking eye contact. "And your manager's name?"

"Rory. Rory Robertson." His voice slowed and was softer. She had seen it many times before.

He's worried I'm going to confirm his story.

"Damn it, Percy," his mother said, slapping his arm. "It's always you on the internet, stirring up trouble."

"What do you mean, ma'am?" Hernandez asked.

Percy cut his mother off. "I'm a lot like you. You support the law and I'm all about justice. I just do my work online, exposing threats to society, making sure that the world knows what they do and don't stand for. You and I are on the same side." Pride rang in his sentences. He said the words as if he believed them.

Hernandez didn't.

"Try to look at this from my perspective," she said. "You claim a woman came in and cost you your job. Last night, she was attacked. She said it was because she had engaged with you."

Crimson rose in Percy's face. "She was acting crazy. Not only did she accuse me, she said terrible things about the military and law enforcement."

Rita continued to jot down notes as she watched his face. "That doesn't change the circumstances as I know them. Regardless of what she said, she was attacked."

"*I'm* the victim here!" he snapped. "That bitch cost me my job!" He glanced at his mother who simply bowed her head.

It's almost as if she's heard the story before.

"Percy, did you talk to anyone about this, perhaps encourage them to put some pressure on Ms. Weldon? Maybe they just took what you said and went a little too far?" She was giving him an out, hoping he would tell the truth.

"No, nobody. I swear to God."

"Percy doesn't have a lot of friends," his mother said. It was easy for Hernandez to believe that.

"Are you certain? If I were to pull your phone records, would I see something that might lead me to believe otherwise?"

"You can't do that without a warrant." Panic was starting to show. The crimson on his face faded to a pale fear.

"That's right. A judge would have to determine if there is probable cause."

His mother cut in. "If Percy says he didn't tell anyone, then he didn't. He's not a liar. He didn't even tell me."

In Hernandez's mind, it was easy to see the twisted family dynamic that was in play before her. Percy had stirred up trouble before, his mother had admitted that. *He probably spends all day on the computer, looking for things to be upset about, harassing people. When it backfires, he wraps himself in the cloak of the victim.*

She looked forward to having a discussion with his manager at the bookstore. There was always a chance that Kornbluth was telling the truth, but she doubted that was the case. There were too many nonverbal clues. His attempts to change the subject, calling himself a victim, not using the victim's name, and evoking God. She had taken several classes in how to spot liars, and these all were potential red flags.

He didn't even ask how badly she was hurt.

"So, we are clear, you didn't tell anyone about your suspension, correct?"

"Um, yeah. That's right."

"And you didn't engage with anyone to cause harm to Ms. Weldon."

"No, ma'am. I swear on the Bible, I didn't."

Hernandez started to rise and, as she got to her feet, she paused. "If I may, one more question."

"Sure, go ahead." Some of the cockiness was back in his voice. No doubt he was feeling safe that she was not arresting him.

"A total stranger shows up at your job, accuses you of something you say you didn't do, makes a scene, and costs you your job. Why didn't you call the police? Why didn't your store manager call the police? What was his reason for letting you go, Mr. Kornbluth? If you were entirely innocent, why did he suspend you?"

"I—um—she said I did some of the online stuff while I was at my job, which wasn't at all true."

"You still didn't answer my question. If she was causing such a scene, why didn't either your or your boss contact us and have her arrested?"

"She—I—she left. It all happened so fast. I mean, she came in, hollering at me, spreading her lies, then left."

"And your manager suspended you just like that?"

"Just like that."

She closed her notepad and cast a thin smile. "Thank you for your time, both of you." None of this felt right to Rita, and she was going to do her best to get to the truth—whatever that was.

Chapter 18
The Red Roof Inn Gambit

Braxton met Faye and Ronin at the Courtyard. They had wrapped her upper chest tight. The hit to her lip had stopped swelling but a dull purple bruise remained. She was on painkillers. She insisted on going to the police station to file her report.

A Latino officer came into the small room where they had ushered Faye. "Ms. Weldon," she said, taking a seat opposite of her.

"Officer Hernandez, right?"

"How are you today?"

"One cracked rib, three bruised ones, plus this—" She gestured to her face.

"Who are your friends?" she asked.

"Harold Callahan and Ronin."

Hernandez gave them a nod. "Ronin, that sounds kinda exotic."

Ronin smiled. "I have been called that from time to time. I prefer my online handle. My parents were not kind when naming me."

Hernandez turned back to Faye. "I pulled the footage from the bar. The images weren't real clear. We talked to a few of the patrons. These guys weren't regulars, at least that is what the staff told us."

That was no surprise to Braxton or Faye. "Percy Kornbluth sent them."

"I went out to his house and talked with him. He claims you showed up at his place of work to get him fired. That you told a bunch of lies about him and cost him his job. He also says he didn't send anyone after you."

"He's lying. The guy whose finger I broke told me he didn't like him losing his job because I was a snot-nosed reporter making accusations."

Hernandez nodded. "The problem is, it's your word against his. We don't know who these guys are."

Braxton stirred in his seat. "One of them is a guy named Jack Hawthorne."

Hernandez turned to him. "And you are?"

"Harold Callahan, a friend of hers."

"How do you know that one of her assailants is Jack Hawthorne?" she said, scribbling notes.

"I'd rather not say."

Hernandez gave him a look. "I'm going to need a little more than that before I go around accusing people, Mr. Callahan."

It was tempting to tell her that their world-class computer hacker had enhanced the image, gotten into some databases he wasn't supposed to, and discovered the man's name—if only to wipe the expression off Hernandez's face. "I'd rather not say." He looked at Faye.

Officer Hernandez leaned back in her seat. "I'll be blunt with you, Ms. Weldon. This Percy guy gave me the creeps. He insisted that he do the interview with his mother in the room. For a guy in his thirties, that's just plain weird. He told me that you came in, making a big scene at his job, saying things about veterans, law enforcement, things along those lines."

"I didn't do that. I was discreet."

Braxton knew it was more than that. Faye was a great investigative reporter, but her subtlety was thick with aggression.

"I know," Hernandez replied. "I called his manager at the bookstore. He said you were assertive, but not disruptive. He also told me that Mr. Kornbluth was suspended for posting on social media at work, something for which he's been written up before."

"So he lied to you."

"Yes. What I don't know is what relation these two attackers had to Percy. In order for us to arrest him and for the prosecutors to do their job, they need that connection. You got a name, that's useful, but without knowing how you obtained it, it doesn't help in making an arrest."

"Our means of getting that information are a little sketchy."

"I expected as much," the officer sighed. "But I can treat it as a tip, which allows me to do some digging. There can't be more than one Jack Hawthorne in the Indy area."

"You might want to try the VFW on Verona," Braxton said.

"Something tells me that's more than a lucky hunch."

"My attacker said to not go to the police," Faye said. "If you go there and start asking questions, it might cause problems."

"Right now, we have to shake the tree to see if anything falls out," the officer said. "Ninety percent of the time, when these kinds of guys know that law enforcement is involved, they lie low. It's especially true in cases where they don't have a personal connection to the victim and, from the sound of it, they don't."

Hernandez thanked them for their time and left. Braxton waited until she was gone. "This Hawthorne has to have some connection with Kornbluth."

"Maybe he hired them," Faye said.

"No chance," Ronin said. "Percy can't afford a car. I found a scooter registered to him and that's it. Working at a bookstore part-time, he's not rolling in enough money to hire muscle to do his dirty work."

Braxton got up. "And you can't find a connection?"

"Sorry, chief. No dice," Ronin said. "Jack Hawthorne has almost zero social media presence, usually showing up in photos on other people's Facebook and Instagram feeds. There are at least thirty-two Jack Hawthornes in Indy. I checked all of them, none have a link to Percy. Without social media, I need to get access to his phone or computer, if he even owns one."

"I'm not convinced that the bartender at the VFW was being honest with me," Braxton said. "He was cool when I brought up Hawthorne, but I have this feeling in my gut he knows everyone that ever came into that place."

"Your gut?" Ronin asked.

"Yeah, my gut. My instincts are that the bartender will get word to Hawthorne."

"Where does that leave us?" Faye asked.

Braxton counted on his fingers. "One, he could just lie low—hope that this all blows over. Two, he may loop back to Percy and/or his partner in crime. Three, depending on his personality and the risk that being exposed might cost him, he might go on the offensive."

"Offensive?"

"He knows you, and he knows that Harold Callahan is looking for him. He may seek us out, threaten us to back off."

"Great," she sighed.

"We need to get you to a different hotel," Braxton said. "Ronin and I have rooms at the Red Roof Inn. We could get you in there. You could stay in my room. No registration. I'll bunk with Ronin."

"I've stayed at worse," Faye replied.

"I'm going to swing by the VFW again, see if I can find Hawthorne. That will get his attention."

"Is that a good thing?" Faye said. "Remember, they beat the shit out of me."

Braxton understood where she was coming from. He had a tendency to lean in to trouble. Memories of his own beating at the hands of ANTIFA lingered.

Sometimes you need to kick the nest to get the bees out in the open.

"I will be the model of discretion."

"How will he get in contact with you, if that's his play?" Ronin said.

"I left my number with the bartender and mentioned where I was staying. If the bartender does know him, logically he will pass on the contact information."

"So he may come to you?"

"It's possible," Braxton said, uncrossing his arms.

"And if he does?"

"I'd like to avoid violence with this guy if we can. If we can't, then I will respond in kind."

"In that case, Faye can take my room and I'll bunk with you."

Chapter 19
The Real World

Percy was nervous. The cop showing up at his house upsetting his mother made him anxious. After the cop left, his mother yelled at him for an hour. She threatened to take away his computer, but he had convinced her that without it, he couldn't look for a new job. His mother had pummeled him about being a loser, not getting his life together. "You're just like your father, a bum!" He'd heard it all before. Her words hurt as much as if she were beating him.

Percy eventually convinced her that he was the victim, to the point where she wanted to file lawsuits against the bookstore and Faye Weldon. It was all talk, though. His mother was living on welfare. The last time he had been fired from a job, Percy had tried to convince a lawyer to take the case, but none would. They all said that there was no way to win, and if they did take the case, his culpability in matters made winning impossible. He knew better. *No one wants to protect victims of oppressors.* He knew he was doing the right thing, going after the people who thought wrong in society.

The cop revealed that his uncle had done more than just talk. He'd beaten Weldon up. That excited Percy. He pictured her being punched and kicked.

She deserved it, after what she did to me.

Now that his mother had settled down for her afternoon nap, he called his uncle to get the details and to let him know that he had covered for him with the police. It took four rings before Murray picked up. "What is it now, Percy?"

"There was a cop here. Said that Weldon got beat up. Was that you?"

"A cop? What cop?"

Percy checked his notes. He had jotted down her name and badge number to do a little social justice research on her. "Officer Rita Hernandez."

"Fuck me, Weldon got the cops involved."

"You did it then, you beat her up!"

"Percy, calm the fuck down. This is serious shit. Yeah, we roughed her up a little. We told her to not get the police involved."

"Well, she did. Don't worry, I got your back. She didn't get anything from me."

"I can't tell you how little that means to me. The Weldon chick has got somebody working for her, poking around, asking questions about where we hang out."

"Like what, a private eye?"

"I don't know. He's just asking about Jack. Nobody ever asks about him. This has to be tied to her and what we did. And now you tell me that the cops are involved. Percy, be straight with me. Is there anything else about this bullshit you dragged me into that I don't know about?"

"No. I've told you everything. Do you think this is serious?"

"Of course I do," his uncle snapped. "We beat up a reporter and she went to the cops. For all we know, she's brought in some hired muscle."

"She didn't mention your name or Hawthorne's," Percy said. "She was just looking into that reporter's attack."

"That's something. The guy had Jack's name. That means he isn't working with the cops. If he did, this cop would have mentioned him."

"What are you going to do?"

"You don't want to know."

"What was it like? Beating her up?" Percy got a stiffy just thinking about it.

"Don't make this any more fucking awkward than it already is," Murray snapped. "We just explained to her to stay away from you. That's all you need to know."

"What now? What's our next step?"

"There is no 'our,' Percy. You need to lie low, no more of your pissy-ass internet shit until this blows over. The fucking cops make this a lot more serious. You need to leave this to Jack and me."

It was hard for Kornbluth to conceal his excitement. This was more fun than taking down Jason Higby's candy business or harassing some sci-fi author. That had all been online. This was in the real world. People were getting hurt. The police were involved. And it was all because of what he had done online. The sense of power was something he couldn't shake, nor did he try.

It was like playing chess, but with people's lives. As a kid, he had always admired his uncle, especially after his father left. Murray was getting old now, though, and that meant that Percy was able to manipulate him. It was fun. Not like when he played his mother, but almost as good. Old white men have skeletons in their closet. Uncle Murray's weakness was the people he associated with. He took in a lot of his vet buddies in his home improvement company. They all had issues, which was why he couldn't grow his business. Percy's mother had tried to get Murray to hire him, but he was not meant for a life of manual labor.

"I might be able to help," he offered.

"Do you know the identity of the guy that has been floating Jack's name around?"

"Well, no."

"Do you know how the police got Jack's name?"

"No."

"So tell me, how exactly can you help?"

Percy was frustrated. Throughout his life, people had ignored him, thought he was incompetent. Going online, going after threats to democracy, made him feel good. "I have skills. You get me some information, and I can find out about this guy."

"Okay. Until then, keep a low profile. This is getting more involved than I'd thought. I don't need you stirring the pot."

"Don't you worry about me. I know what to do. Just keep me in the loop." He wanted to know what was happening because he saw himself as a part of it. Until this point, the terror that he had sowed was online. This was for real, and Percy was the mastermind.

Uncle Murray was worried about the police and this mystery man, but not Percy. *He hasn't showed up here, which means he doesn't know about me. I snowed that cop too. She thought she had me dead to rights, but in the end, she got nothing. All she managed to do was to get Ma riled up, and I was able to calm her down.*

Percy knew the time would come when he would show Murray and everyone else just how important he was. *Social justice warriors like me are vital in a society. We root out the disruptive elements. We're ushering in a new era, one with the values we know are right.* If that means damaging the lives of bad people along the way, it was a small price to pay. One day, society would recognize the gallant work he and his friends were doing.

Despite his uncle's warning, Percy decided to contact his circle of comrades, let them know what he'd accomplished. He opened a chat window and linked in Gump227 and Shatterstorm02. They were going to love hearing that he'd taken the fight to the real world. They had helped him with the Higby affair. Chances are they could offer insights as to what he and his uncle were going through.

More importantly, it was a chance to brag. *I got a girl beat up, and I didn't even have to raise a finger. I'm finally the influencer I always knew I could be.* He opened a bag of Cheetos, popped a handful in his mouth, and typed.

Chapter 20
Inquiring Minds

Murray Landreth watched the pool game at the VFW from behind the shooters. He wanted to play, but the Weldon broad had broken his pinkie finger. The cast was an annoyance. The only good news about it was they gave him a subscription for painkillers. Half of them he planned to use, the other half he'd sell.

His buddy, Jack Hawthorne, was lining up a shot which, from what Murray knew of his friend, was beyond his ability to pull off. The crack of the balls hitting surprised Murray as his friend nicked the seven ball just right, putting it in the side pocket.

"I'm on fire tonight!" Jack said.

"You were lucky," Marty Masterson, Jack's opponent, said.

"All I have left is the eight ball," Jack replied with a grin. He moved around the table, stalking the black ball from a number of angles. When he made up his mind, he bent over and pulled back the cue. "Eight Ball, corner pocket." He pointed at his objective...

He slid the cue back slowly, then jabbed it at the ball. To Murray, it looked as if the ball was going to miss, but it hit the edge of the pocket, spun slightly, then barely dropped. "Yes!" Jack called out. "Ten bucks, Marty!"

Marty reached into his leather vest pocket and extracted two wadded up fives, tossing them on the table at Jack. "You've been practicing."

"Lady Luck has spread her legs for me," Jack said, snatching up his winnings. Putting his stick in the rack, he and Murray sat. "Can you believe that game?"

"I wouldn't push it if I were you. When you push luck, it usually pushes back," Murray said, gulping his Miller. He had preferred Budweiser but after the Dylan Mulvaney fiasco, the members of VFW #21116 had dumped the brand and switched to Miller. Bud became unacceptable.

Murray saw that Jack was out of beer. "Another round?"

"Sure. Your turn."

"You just won at pool."

"Irrelevant. It's your turn. In the meantime, I need to take a piss." Hawthorne got up and made his way to the back.

Murray went to the bar, holding up two fingers. Rex was talking to some bald guy. A vet, judging by his stance. He had a small, well-trimmed beard. Muscles, but not a freak.

Rex came over and handed him two beers. "Hey, Mur, this guy is looking for a Jack Hawthorne," Rex said."

Murray discreetly concealed his broken finger.

"Someone said he was in here earlier. You know him?" the man asked.

Murray shifted his stance, blocking the newcomer's view of the restrooms. "Never heard of him."

The man turned to him. "I heard he hung out here."

"Like I said, never heard of him. Is he a friend of yours?"

"An acquaintance. We met overseas."

This is the guy that was snooping around earlier.

"I wish I could help you," Murray said, grabbing the beers. The stranger turned away and Murray went to the back of the bar and intercepted Jack as he was coming out of the men's room. Murray motioned for him to back up. They entered the bathroom.

"What the fuck, Murray. I'm not drinking beer in the pisser."

"That guy is here, the one that was looking for you."

"Callahan? Fuck."

"Yeah, tell me about it."

"This guy isn't letting up. He needs to go away."

Murray hated the idea, but he didn't have much choice. *Goddamn Percy—getting me dragged into his bullshit!* "Nobody here is going to rat you out. He's at the Red Roof Inn. We head that way, wait until he shows up, take him for a ride."

"I don't need this shit in my life, Murray."

Jack had nothing but troubles in his life. He was living in a mobile home that a mutual friend had loaned him. The guy didn't have a driver's license and the car he drove barely ran. He couldn't afford insurance. He was one bad week from living in a cardboard box under an overpass. Percy threatening to out Jack's legal problems was not helpful. Murray had been forced to sweeten the pot with a fifty-dollar bill for Jack, lest he decide it was better to beat the shit out of his nephew for blackmailing him.

Murray felt guilty getting Jack involved in this, but there weren't a lot of people he could turn to. Jack had a moral ambiguity that was useful. If they had to kill someone, he would do it, and he wasn't the kind of guy to talk to others about it.

He hoped they could just beat some sense into this Callahan character. There was a lot of risk with that approach. It would bring the police into the mix. Still, Murray hated the thought of someone lurking in the shadows, waiting to get the jump on him.

"We don't know squat about this Callahan," Murray said. "Maybe he's a PI, maybe he's hired muscle that this chick has brought in. I don't know. What I do know is that we need to seize the initiative. I don't want him to get the drop on us. We need to get to him first."

"I've already got a lot of problems. I have a bench warrant out there. I can't do more time in jail."

"You're only going to jail if we get caught, and that ain't happenin'."

Jack was not convinced. "Your nephew is a real piece of work," he said, cracking the restroom door open to look at the bar.

"He's family."

"He needs a real job—a real life. Digging up shit about people on the internet is just a fucking waste of time." He closed the door. "I didn't see anyone talking to Rex. This guy must have moved on."

Murray said nothing for a few moments, thinking through the best course of action. "We'll check with Rex. Make sure this guy didn't get any info."

"Then we go to the hotel?"

"Not in broad daylight. We need to be discreet. Night is best."

Jack nodded in agreement. They opened the door, making sure that the bald man was no longer there. They walked to the bar.

"Hey, Rex," Murray said.

"Don't 'hey Rex' me," he growled. "That guy's been here twice looking for you. And earlier, I got a visit from a cop named Hernandez. She had a booking photo of you, Jack. What kind of shit are you guys in?"

"What makes you think I'm involved?"

Rex cocked his left eyebrow and glared.

"It's all a simple misunderstanding," Murray said.

Rex's brow furrowed. "Murray, you know better than to shovel that crap at me. Look, whatever stuff you two are involved in, it's getting the VFW hall involved. I can't cover for you. Sooner or later, one of these guys is going to say you were here. We can't risk our liquor license again, so until you get your collective acts together, you need to hang out somewhere else."

Murray wanted to argue but couldn't. Rex was right. "Thanks for giving us air cover, Rex."

"Yeah, yeah," he said, frustration abating. He walked down the bar. Jack looked sorry for the trouble they were generating.

"They are really putting pressure on us."

There was no way to suppress the police, but Callahan was a different story. "We have to work the cards we've been dealt," he said in a low tone.

"I don't want to go to jail."

"You won't. I'll make sure of that."

"It probably would have been easier if we had just killed that Weldon chick." Jack scowled.

Murray had thought that as well. At the time, he hadn't been prepared to kill for Percy. His nephew wasn't worth that kind of risk.

Now things were different. It wasn't about Percy. This was about keeping them both out of jail.

"We're gonna have to lie low. So far, they're looking for you, not me. So we'll go to my place until it gets dark. Then we can go and check out this Callahan." Murray kept quiet about his anger and frustration. Jack was right, his nephew was a piece of work. His sister had really screwed up raising him. Murray had tried to help the kid, but hard work and Percy were strangers. Now he and Jack were in trouble.

Someone had to pay for this. He couldn't take it out on Percy, the kid was a lost cause. But he could on Callahan.

Chapter 21
Up Armored

Braxton had asked a few patrons in the VFW about Jack Hawthorne and got nothing. Some of their icy stares spoke volumes. Hawthorne had been there; he was sure of it. No one wanted to be a squealer, which he respected. After all, he was an outsider. Being a vet got him in the door; it didn't penetrate their local bond.

He drove to A-OK Garage and maneuvered into his bay. Removing the interior door panels, he mounted steel plates. Studying the driver and passenger seats, he decided to hang steel panels in the backs. They were heavier than carbon fiber but more effective.

Rocco showed him the scrap steel rack and gave him a five-minute orientation on the plasma cutter. Sparks rained down on Walmart steel-toed work boots he had picked up on the trip to Indianapolis. It was hot work, the kind that cleared his mind—which was why he was doing it.

There was a lot to think about. *I've been snooping around, and I'm sure Officer Hernandez has as well. Word is going to get back to this Hawthorne and whoever is working with him.* Braxton mentally went over how they might react. Cowards would go to ground. *These guys are both vets, probably not the kind of guys that hide. Hawthorne has gotten into trouble his whole life. From what Ronin has pulled on him, he is just a few steps ahead of the law already.* It spoke to the more nefarious side of his foe's character.

As he struggled to get the right angle on the hot steel, he thought through their reactions. *We've moved Faye; that might throw them off. It doesn't give them a lot of choice. Fight or flee. These are guys*

*who attacked a woman in an alley. They are fighters. It is a matter of
when and where.*

"Looks like you're getting her ready for combat," Rocco said as
Braxton used some old seat belts from wrecks in the yard to mount
the rear seat plates.

"I prepare for the worst."

"Ten-gauge isn't going to stop the heavy stuff," Rocco said as
Braxton worked.

"You're right. But for them to hit the plates, they are either
blasting through the car body or rear windshield. And I'm angling
them. Altogether that will take some of the kick out."

"You get shot at a lot?"

Braxton smiled. "More than you might think." Taking a utility
knife off a workbench, he cut the ceiling material out of the car.

"Why are you pulling that out?" Rocco asked.

"I want to weld a gun mount, kinda a holster, on the interior
roof."

Rocco looked puzzled but didn't comment, so Braxton explained.
"Look, mounting stuff on doors and such looks good in the movies. I
want my gun where someone looking in the car won't see it, on the
interior roof. Besides, if I'm forced to raise my hands, I've got a
weapon right at my fingertips."

Rocco nodded. "There's some bits of angle iron that might do the
job. No charge." He gestured to a drum that had a lot of steel poking
upward. "If you don't mind me asking, Mr. Callahan, if that's really
your name—what kind of work do you do?"

He's figured out the Harry Callahan name.

"Freelance. I help people. Try to set things right when people get
screwed over."

"Uh huh," Rocco replied. "People get screwed over a lot these
days. Not many folks go around helping them."

"I lost my family to some bad people. I want to help those that
can't help themselves."

Rocco nodded. "I've got some padding that might help with that
roof holster—and some Velcro strap material. You're welcome to it."

"Thank you. I'm happy to pay."

"Nah. Most of the guys in here are hot rodders. No offense, but I've forgotten more stuff than they'll ever know. They load up YouTube and think it will teach them how to rebuild a carburetor. What you're doing, it's different."

Braxton cut the metal, using his Glock as a pattern. Finding something to weld onto the ceiling was tricky, but the Crown Vic had a roll bar assembly built in, saving him from burning a hole in the roof. It wasn't easy, but he enjoyed it.

When he was finished, he tested it out from the driver's seat, pulling the gun out several times. Rocco inspected the end results. "Not too shabby."

"I appreciate the help."

"I appreciate the entertainment."

"I was thinking of putting on puncture-resistant tires. What do you know about them?"

Rocco looked at the tires. "You've got Goodyear Eagle RS-As on there. Good sidewalls, excellent for high-speed chases. Unless you go totally airless, and most of that stuff is still prototype, you need to go with Continentals with ContiSeal or Michelin Uptis. They're expensive, that's for sure. None are going to be bulletproof, but they will resist damage pretty well."

"Can you order me some?" He handed Rocco his credit card. Rocco took out a small pad of paper from his breast pocket and jotted down the card info, then handed it back to Braxton. "I can try. Don't you want to know the price before I order them?"

"I trust you'll do me right. Money isn't the issue it used to be." He had carefully invested the payouts he had gotten from the government and college. Despite rising inflation, his mutual funds were doing well. As his financial advisor put it, "You won't have to work another day in your life." She was right, at least about a normal person working a normal job.

"I'll probably pop by tomorrow."

"Are you going to add a turret?"

"I'll keep that in mind. I was actually thinking of ordering some police stop sticks. I'd love to rig them up under the back bumper to drop."

"You planning on being chased?"

"No one plans on that. I just like having options."

"I can weld you up some bars with spikes in them, probably a hell of a lot cheaper than ordering cop gear. The tricky part is figuring out how to engage them, but I'm sure we can resolve that."

"I appreciate it."

"It's definitely more interesting than another carburetor rebuild."

Braxton gave him a wave, then drove back to the Red Roof Inn with the window down. The smell of melted metal clung in his nostrils. His clothes were filthy. When he got to his room, he showered, struggling to keep the shower curtain from opening and spraying the floor with water. Few guests made the effort. It wasn't a scuzzy hotel, the carpeting was relatively new, as were the drapes and bedding. Far less had been spent on the bathroom, which had echoes of the 1980s. His standards had changed now that he didn't have a family. All that really mattered was that he had a place to sleep and clean up.

This isn't the kind of place I would have brought Suzanna and Angela. Now it doesn't matter.

As he got dressed, he paused and blew his nose. His snot was black. There was something strangely satisfying about it.

Most of my career, I taught...I talked for a living. It feels good to produce something.

Braxton stopped at Ronin's room two doors down. The lights were low, the only real bright spot was his laptop screen. "Any luck?"

"Yes and no," Braxton said, running his hand over his shaved skull. *Suzanna would have laughed at me for something like this.* "No one has seen this Hawthorne guy, but I got a vibe from the VFW that they know him. They're covering for him."

"Should we go stake out their parking lot?"

"No. Someone will have tipped them off by now. I'm willing to bet that they shy away from that place now that I've dropped by twice. Have you had any luck in tracking this guy down?"

Ronin sighed. "We're dealing with someone whose credit rating is so bad even the credit card companies won't do business with him. He's a cash-only guy, which makes him hard to track."

"What about the guy with the broken finger?"

"Hospitals are notoriously tight about anyone that gets treatment, courtesy of HIPPA."

"Come on, Ro, you're a world-class hacker."

Ronin grinned. "Well, these hospitals are usually part of networks of doctors and clinics. While security at a hospital is tight, not so much at a doctor's office or free clinic. My thinking is that if these two guys don't surface soon, I will get into one of these places and see if I can get to the hospital's data."

"Impressive."

"It's what I do."

"I am dying to know how these two are tied to Kornbluth. From everything you've found about this dweeb, I find it hard to believe that he would associate with a pair of hard-nosed vets."

"He's still active online. He lost his job at the bookstore, and now he's online almost full-time. Percy clocked over sixteen hours yesterday."

Imagine what he could accomplish if he was doing something productive. "What's he doing?"

"Harassing new targets. That's how it is with these people. They always have to have a target. If they don't, they cease to have any relevance. He's going after some fantasy author, claiming he's an alt-right extremist because he posted a photo of his car and he had a bumper sticker that read: *The Second Amendment, America's Original Homeland Security*. Somehow Percy made the leap from that bumper sticker to this author being a threat to democracy. He's posting a lot with his sock accounts and rallying his buddies to pile on. It's the same bullshit they did to Mr. Higby."

"Maybe one of his buddies knows Hawthorne."

Ronin grinned. "One step ahead of you. He has two friends who both have a shitload of fake accounts they run. I've narrowed that list down to the pertinent ones for simplicity's sake. Gump227 and Shatterstorm02. Gump227 is a guy named Walter Fitzsimmons;

Shatterstorm02 is Dennis Orm. Both live in the area. They connected with Percy on some left-wing message boards. I was able to run these guys down and tried to find links between them and Hawthorne. No dice. They appear to coordinate with each other. When one finds a target, the others pile on. They're as pathetic as Percy."

"These guys need to pay too," Braxton said.

This is about pulling the weeds, root and all.

"Percy's the most active. I don't want to call him a ringleader, because it implies more intelligence than he has. He spurs them on. He's clearly the head muckraker."

Braxton shook his head. "If we put an end to Percy, we're helping other people in the process."

"Why not make a move against him right now?"

It was tempting. Braxton had considered it but ruled it out. "It may come down to that. He has other people in play, though. I'd rather whittle away at his defenses, take out his muscle, make him afraid. Going for the jugular might work, but it might also deny us from getting justice for what they did to Faye. I don't want to go down that path unless I'm forced to."

"How are we going to get at his muscle? Right now, we only have one name and that guy is a rabbit."

"I think these guys will eventually surface," Braxton said. "We've generated pressure by asking about them. The police getting involved works to our advantage as well. I think they'll be compelled to show themselves at some point, to try to intimidate us further."

Chapter 22
Rumble at Rocco's

Braxton stepped out of his hotel room and surveyed the lot. He suspected that Hawthorne knew where he was. Call it paranoia or instinct, it was a tangible sensation he couldn't ignore. He put a hand on his Glock. If Hawthorne was going to ambush him, it would be at the Red Roof Inn. As he looked at the cars in the lot, he saw no signs of anyone stalking him. Every vehicle was empty.

Maybe they have gone to ground.

Braxton got breakfast from Wendy's for Ronin and Faye. Weldon looked better after some rest, but she still winced in pain. Every time she did, he felt a twinge of guilt. It was his quest to bring justice that had drawn her into the fight. Yes, she had become over-anxious, but it was his zeal that got her injured.

Faye finished her sandwich. "So what's the plan?"

"I got a text from the garage. My tires are in. I'm going over to put them on."

"That's it?" Ronin asked.

"No. I want you to do a drive-by at this Hawthorne-guy's house, see if there's any sign of him. If he's still on the lam, we'll have you or Faye take a run at the VFW hall. They don't open until the afternoon, so there's no rush."

"Faye should sit this one out," Ronin said.

"Like hell I will," she snapped. "These guys beat the shit out of me. I want a second round with them both."

"You guys aren't going there to start a fight. Just sit in the lot and see if you spot either of them."

"And if we spot them?"

"Call me. We know these guys are prone to violence. We need to be smarter than them, confront them on terms and ground of our choosing. One at a time."

"Seems less aggressive than your usual tactics," Faye said.

"I like to think I'm methodical. There's a time for force and a time to be a sneaky bastard." Braxton chomped his breakfast sandwich. It reminded him of driving to the university every day. Wendy's had been part of his routine. He wondered why he didn't long for those days. There was no nostalgia, no desire to return to his former life.

I didn't belong there. Maybe everyone knew that better than me.

He turned to Ronin. "Any luck tracking down Percy's accomplices?"

Ronin shook his head. "The guy I usually use to get IPs and addresses is on vacation. I have another contact, but he's two time zones away and I haven't heard back from him."

Braxton stepped out, his head on a swivel and checking his surroundings. Once he was sure the coast was clear, he went to his car. He checked to make sure nothing was out of place. He opened the door and got in.

* * *

Murray lay in the woods a block from the Red Roof Inn, using his rifle scope to survey the Red Roof Inn. He hated lying in the dew-soaked grass but had done it throughout his life, both in the Army and camping and hunting. His prey went to a flat black Crown Vic and checked the vehicle. "Bingo," Murray muttered.

"You got him?" Jack asked in an excited whisper.

"Oh yeah, he's out there, checking his car."

"Why's he doing that?"

Murray watched him get in the car. He got to his feet, heading for his car parked a few yards away. "This guy's a professional. He wants to make sure we didn't sabotage his car."

Jack got in the shotgun seat. "Why not just pick him off?"

"The cops are looking for you, and you can lead them to me. We just shake this guy sniper-style, and they'll be on our ass."

"I thought we were going to kill him," Jack said.

Murray started the car and followed the Crow Vic at a discreet distance.

"We are. There's a big difference between just killing someone and doing it smart. If this guy just disappears, well, that doesn't give the cops anything to work with. Nothing that can be traced to us. It will be a while before his friends even know he's gone."

"Smart."

"Yeah. Just remember, no body, no conviction."

* * *

Braxton drove to A-OK Garage as Rocco was opening. It was noon. Rocco waved and stepped aside so Braxton could pull in. He eased it into the bay. Rocco guided him in. He saw the tires he ordered stacked at the far end of the bay.

Braxton checked out the tires. "Nice wheels."

"The guy I talked to said that even if you hit a bunch of nails, these things are going to hold up." Rocco handed him the receipt.

Braxton tucked it in his pocket. "Let's hope it doesn't come to that."

"The hoist controls are on the wall," Rocco said, pointing. "Oh, I almost forgot." He turned and pulled out a steel round bar with sharp metal spikes on them. "I got your stop sticks done."

"Nice!"

"You work on the tires; I'll see how to rig them to drop." The older man sounded downright excited.

Braxton raised the car and used the air impact wrench to remove and replace the tires. Rocco helped him balance the tires. It felt good to stretch his muscles.

I need to locate the nearest Planet Fitness. I've been off my routine for too long.

Rocco worked on a hinge to hold the stop sticks behind the rear bumper. He used a pin to lock it into place, then ran the wire under the vehicle and into the driver's compartment. When finished, he tested it a few times, showing Braxton how to pull a ring at the end of the wire hard to deploy the sticks. It was cheap and easy, but might come in handy at some point.

Lowering the car to the ground, he sat in the driver's seat. There wasn't much left to do. He'd tracked down an explosive-proof gas tank based on the bladder system that WWII fighter aircraft had used.

Rocco came over with a cold beer, the bottle sweating beads. "Yo." He had another in his other hand.

Braxton took the beer. "PBR? That's still a thing?"

"I ain't buying that Bud Lite shit," Rocco said, drinking. "If they don't want me as a customer, I'm not obliged to give them my money."

"The woke are a real problem."

Rocco nodded. "Spoiled brats. I blame their parents. If they had done their jobs right, they wouldn't be on the internet all day."

"I've had a few run-ins with social justice warriors. I've never met one that was a productive member of society."

"You've crossed paths with them? I thought most of what they do is online."

"I have."

"Tell me about it."

Braxton liked Rocco. *How would he react if he knew what I did back in Portland?* Sizing up the older man, he knew he could keep his secret. "First off, I'm not Harold Callahan."

"No shit," snickered Rocco. "That credit card you gave me for the tires belongs to someone named Braxton Knox."

"That's me." He took a sip of beer, finding it strangely pleasing. "It all started when I misgendered a girl in my class…"

* * *

Murray saw Jack jogging back from the scrapyard. "It's just him and some old guy."

117

Murray surveyed the old garage. He didn't see any security cameras, but that didn't mean they weren't there. The place was pretty run-down. Even if he had cameras, chances were they weren't top of the line. He handed Hawthorne a black mask.

"What about the old man?"

"He's an old man. We grab our guy, we knock the old guy out. You have the zip ties?"

"Yeah. In my pocket."

Murray locked eyes with Hawthorne. "Don't shoot anybody unless you hear me shooting, got it?" His cohort nodded. "Take a deep breath and hold it for a second. You need to be on your A-game."

"I've got this."

"Follow my lead and we'll put this problem behind us."

* * *

Braxton was putting his tools away when he heard feet scraping on the gritty garage floor. It didn't sound like Rocco's footfalls. He turned and saw two men grappling with the garage owner. Rocco swung a wrench hitting one man in the arm. THE MAN GRUNTED IN PAIN.

Braxton rushed in. Rocco staggered back as one of the men fired a gun. The weapon cracked, preternaturally loud. The fight had changed. Braxton sprang at one of the men, hitting him in the midriff, knocking him down. Braxton struggled to regain his balance.

The other man came at him, gun in one hand, wooden club in the other. He swung the club, hitting Braxton on his right bicep. He ignored the pain when he saw the man's furious face.

Jack Hawthorne.

Braxton threw an uppercut, catching Hawthorne in the chin, rocking him back. Braxton sprinted for his Crown Vic, pulling out his Glock. He slid on some oil, twisting his ankle, and fell to the concrete floor.

There wasn't enough time to curse. Knox rolled, bringing his gun around.

Two guns pointed at him. "Drop it!" the unknown man barked.

Braxton calculated. The odds weren't in his favor. Given their range, one of them was bound to hit him.

Never fight the math.

He held his hands upward, pointing the Glock away from the men towards the ceiling.

"Toss that gun over here," the first man ordered.

Slowly Braxton put it on the floor and pushed it a few feet closer to the men. He regretted it instantly, but his mind couldn't conjure a better solution.

"Stand up," the man commanded.

As he rose, he surveyed the car and the surrounding area, looking for something to change the odds. There was nothing.

The man nodded to Hawthorne. "Tie his hands behind his back."

Hawthorne moved in next to him as Braxton drank in the details. He was wearing a T-shirt under an open flannel shirt, blue jeans, working boots. He was so close that Braxton got a good dose of his body odor, a long-fading hint of Ax Body Spray, and cigarettes. A zip tie went around his wrists, digging into his skin.

"Put the bag over his head," the man ordered. A burlap bag dropped over his face. It reeked of grain.

He heard Rocco groan. "Hey," Braxton called out through the burlap. "He's hurt!"

"It looks like a leg wound. He'll live." The assailant dragged him around to the front of his car.

"Nice Glock," Hawthorne said. It was adding insult to injury.

I'm going to get that gun back.

They forced him awkwardly through the shop, pushing and shoving him. Braxton worried about Rocco. He bumped into something. It wasn't the pain; it was the unexpected that made it feel sharper than it was.

His captors forced him out the back, through the scrapyard. They brought him to a car, slamming him into it, then popping the trunk. They bent him into the trunk. He lay on jumper cables, jabbing into his side and back. The trunk slammed shut.

119

He tested the strength of the zip ties. The fingers in his left hand were already going numb. The darkness didn't help his predicament. His arms ached as he strained to simply pull his hands free. Panic chewed at his brain, but he managed to smother the feeling.

I need to focus. Pay attention! Learn how long they drove, perhaps how fast. Every clue was something he might be able to use.

Braxton strained to hear their muffled voices through the trunk wall and rear seat.

"Damn it, Jack, I told you not to shoot. Why'd you shoot the old man?"

"I just reacted. I mean—the old bastard hit me. I'm sorry, Murray. I didn't shoot to kill him, just to stop him."

"He might bleed out. If he does, we're facing a murder charge. You're going to have to ditch that gun. There can't be anything that links us to the bullet you put in him."

"I got Callahan's Glock, so that's fine by me."

The two men shut up. Braxton knew more than he did before. He now had a name for the other man. Murray. That might be something Ronin could work with.

It's only useful if I survive this.

Chapter 23
The Defiance of the Condemned

Braxton catalogued his pockets. His keys were there. Not a great saw for cutting a zip tie, but it was possible. One of his burner phones was there, but that was of little help—there was no way to tell Ronin where they were taking him, even if he could reach it.

As he felt around the trunk, a thought came to him. *My belt!* He was wearing the tactical belt Burt got him. *I have a knife and a saw there.* Reaching along the leather of the belt, he found the hidden flaps. He smiled.

The car was moving fast—at least fifty miles per hour. *If I get my hands free and pop the trunk, jumping out might kill me. They could have shot me there in the garage. Why not?* They must want something from him. Information. *They don't know who I am, or why I'm asking about Hawthorne. Once they get that information, they'll kill me.*

Carefully, he removed the knife and cut the zip ties, then replaced it. His left hand tingled. On the verge of being painful, but he ignored it. *There's no reason for them to check the zip ties when they get me out of here. If I hold my hands behind me, they might just believe the tie is still there.* To complete the illusion, he took the severed tie and held it in place with his fingers behind his back. Cutting it and faking it gave him options.

They drove for about twenty-five minutes. The last bit was gravel. Far from prying eyes. Braxton kept the knife palmed. He knew they would be rough with him. If he had to go at them with the small knife, he would. It wasn't much of a weapon, but it was the best he had. He felt around for a tire iron. Nada.

The car lurched to a stop, backed up. They turned the engine off. The trunk opened but with the hood over his face, he couldn't see much other than a lack of light. The air was cool as they jerked him out of the trunk. He held onto the knife and the zip tie. They forced him around the side of the vehicle, then pushed his back against the car.

Someone grabbed his wallet. The man that he identified as Murray spoke. "No credit cards, but it says your name is Harold Callahan. So tell me, Harold, what is your connection to this Weldon broad?"

"I don't know what you're talking about."

Braxton braced for the punch, flexing his stomach muscles. With the hood on, it was all he could do. They hit him in the left cheek, hard. His head snapped to one side and he felt a moment of dizziness. He tasted blood.

"Wanna try again? Why were you asking about Jack?" Murray said.

"I thought he was the Jack Hawthorne I knew from when I was in the Army."

This time to the stomach. He exhaled sharply.

"Bullshit. This has to do with the Weldon chick." Another blow to his body, higher, to the diaphragm. He violently exhaled, struggling for breath. He bent over and coughed.

"If you tell us the truth, this can all come to an end."

Braxton knew that was a lie. They had no intention of letting him walk away from this. Instinct tore at him to rip the hood off and go at them, but the guns gave them a massive advantage.

Wait until the time is right.

Slowly he pulled his body upright. "I don't know what you're talking about."

They kicked him in the groin. The pain felt like sharp needles, stabbing his thighs and gut. For a moment, he saw stars in his closed eyes. He doubled over, eyes watering.

"This is going to go on until you talk," Murray said.

"I must have had the wrong Jack Hawthorne," he gasped.

"Bullshit," Jack said. "You were telling Rex we knew each other from overseas. I never went overseas, and I sure as hell never met you." The punch landed on his right ear.

"My mistake," Braxton grunted, pushing himself to standing upright against the vehicle. The temptation to pull the knife was growing.

"Who are you?" Murray said. "Some sort of private eye?"

Braxton was tempted to tell them that was the case, just to see where it went.

Once they get what they want, the beating will stop and the killing will start.

"Do I look like a PI?"

"You look like a penis with that shaved head," Jack said, landing a kick on his leg just above the knee.

"This is all a big misunderstanding," Braxton spat, as the pain in his crotch slowly started to wane. "I must have had the wrong Jack Hawthorne."

There was a momentary pause, for which he was thankful. "What if he's telling the truth?" Jack asked.

"Don't be a dipshit, Jack. He's working for the Weldon chick."

Braxton's phone rang. He had changed the ringtone. "Highway to Hell" by AC/DC. He cringed. Thus far, his bumbling assailants hadn't checked for a phone. An instant later, he felt hands patting his pants. One hand found his burner phone and pulled it out. "Check this out," Jack said.

After a second or so, Murray spoke up. "It looks like someone named Ro is trying to find you. What's the code for unlocking this phone?"

Braxton wasn't about to expose Faye and Ronin any further than he already had. "FAFO," he said, allowing himself a grin under the hood.

"Very funny, smart-ass," Murray replied.

"My father likes to say it's better to be a smart-ass than a dumbass." In his mind he knew his dad would be proud that he was being quoted under such circumstances.

I hope I live to tell him.

"You're not helping yourself at all…you know that?"

Braxton felt the pain from the hits he had taken and rose above them. "I don't have any reason to help you."

"How about you get to live?" Hawthorne asked.

He knew better. "I seriously doubt you are going to let me live. Which begs the question, why should I help you?"

That brought another punch, this time to his chest. It wasn't enough to knock the wind out of his lungs, but it hurt. "We don't have to kill you," Murray replied. "We can just make you wish you were dead."

A flurry of punches hit him, he assumed from Murray. Braxton twisted several times, trying to anticipate them and let his arms shield his body. A few times it worked, others less so. The pain from the jabs were numerous, and he knew he'd have to simply weather them. There was no other option other than try to fight back. *Now isn't the time.* He felt they wouldn't just shoot him. The shot in the garage had bothered Murray. *Maybe they'll just beat me to death. I'll attack long before that happens.*

"Jack. Jack! Ease up. I want him to talk."

The punches slowed, then stopped. No doubt his attacker was starting to get exhausted. His puncher was breathing hard, he could hear it between hits. One hit to his face was trickling blood; he could taste it on his lips. He wanted to curl up, but he refused to give his assailants the satisfaction. Braxton clung to the knife so tightly he was afraid he might cut himself. After several long seconds, Braxton rose back to a fully standing position. Defiance was all he had left.

"Had enough?" the winded Murray asked.

"Have you?"

Hawthorne's voice cut in. "He's not going to talk, Murray."

"You might be right."

"So what are we going to do?"

"We got his phone. My nephew got us into this; maybe he can do something productive for once in his life and figure out a way to break into it."

Nephew? That's the connection. I wonder if that is Percy? Braxton held his words in check, hoping his attackers would reveal more. All he did was cough, which made everything hurt with a new twinge of agony.

"Get that rope out of the back seat," Murray said.

Braxton heard the car door next to him open. "Let's drag him out on the dock. I'll get the cement blocks."

Dock, rope, blocks...*they're going to drown me.* Through the pain, he wondered how deep the water was, and if they were going to shoot him before tossing him in. After a minute or so, they grabbed Braxton and forced him to walk out onto the dock. Each footfall on the wooden deck echoed into the night.

He felt the rope being tied around his legs. It felt thick, which made him wonder if he would be able to cut it off once he hit the water. Fear nibbled at his brain as the rope got tighter. "Not so talkative now, eh, Callahan?" Murray said.

I want them to toss me in. "I'm afraid of drowning."

"It doesn't have to be this way. You tell me what I want, and I promise you a bullet to the head. That has to be a lot better than slowly sucking pond water in your lungs. Quick and easy, or slow and frightening—it's your call."

"I can't betray the people that count on me."

"Pigheaded asshole," Murray spat. "Last chance."

He shook his hooded head. *Go ahead, push me in.*

"What a dumbfuck," Murray said. He felt his foe's beefy hand on his sternum, then came the shove. Falling backwards, he hit the water, sucking in a deep breath as he splashed. He bobbed down and slowly rose, barely breaking the surface. It was just enough for him to hear another splash next to him.

There was a violent tug as the tight rope around his ankles jerked him down. Braxton was pulled down into the depths of the pond.

Chapter 24
The Depths of Despair

Ronin sat at the desk in Faye's hotel room and glared at his phone. "It's not like him to not pick up."

"You're worried about him," Faye said. "That's so cute."

"Seriously. He went to put on some tires and it's already getting dark."

"You want to go and check on him?"

Ronin nodded. "Fine," Faye said, wincing as she pulled on a shirt over her top.

"You don't need to come with me."

"Bullshit," she snapped back. "I already got the shit kicked out of me. The way I see it, these guys have some payback coming."

Ronin pulled up the address of A-OK garage. "Great, let's roll."

* * *

Don't panic. Braxton told himself that until the downward descent into the water stopped. He dropped the ruse of having his hands behind his back and pulled the hood off his head. It was dark; he couldn't see the rope around his feet. The water was much colder than when he had been thrown in, an indication that he was fairly deep. His body protested each move, firing off every place he had been punched and kicked. He ignored the pain.

Bending over he found the rope with his free hand, pulling himself closer to it. Nylon from the feeling, half-inch thick. With his belt knife, he sawed into the fibers. His lungs ached from the pressure of holding his breath, and he slowly let a trickle of air out as he worked the rope.

It wasn't easy, in the dark. He felt a pain in his foot, and realized that he had cut himself. *Stay calm. If you panic, you'll die here.* His right ear popped as he worked. He managed to cut the rope, but it wasn't letting him free. *What the hell?* Braxton started on another wrap of the nylon. His ears were gurgling and he inadvertently let out a larger burst of air. While he sawed, he inadvertently sucked in some water through his nose, and sputtered.

Sawing faster, he felt a strange vertigo wash over him. Death was close, he could feel its shadow.

Come on, damn it!

* * *

Murray saw a bubble of air break the surface on the water where they had pushed Braxton in. "He's toast by now."

"You sure?" Jack asked.

"You tied the block to his legs. He ain't coming up." Murray took another look at the fading ripples in the water and turned to the end of the dock.

"Johnny isn't going to like it if a dead body comes floating up in his favorite fishing hole," Hawthorne said.

"You know, sometimes you piss me off, Jack," Murray said as they reached the end of the dock. "First of all, that body is staying at the bottom of the pond. Second, even if it does pop up, there's nothing that ties us to it. Johnny is out of town for another two weeks. Anybody could have put a body in the pond."

As they reached Murray's car, they got inside. "What do we do now?"

"I'm going to call Percy. There might be some heat if this Weldon chick reports Callahan missing. He needs to move out, lay low at somebody's house. Second, we need to get him this phone. If he can crack it, it might tell us more about everyone involved."

Murray started the car and pulled away from the dock.

"If Weldon is smart, she'll leave town. The police will move on to fresh crimes. It happens all the time. If they don't solve it in forty-eight hours, it doesn't get solved. We need to keep a low profile for a week or two until this just goes away."

"I'm lucky to have you as a friend. Thanks, Murray."

"Trust me. We'll be fine."

* * *

Braxton cut through the second rope and flexed his aching legs. He paddled towards the surface. Looking up he saw the shimmer of the top of the water and reached it, barely. He burst out of the water under something, gasping desperately for air. The weight of his boots made his legs feel slow.

For a moment, he bobbed back down, but renewed life helped him kick and paddle with his arms back to the surface. He was under the dock. Angling for the shore, he reached up and got a grip on one of the poles that held the dock in place. Clinging to it, Knox slowed his breathing. For all he knew, they could be standing right above him.

It was twilight. Gray clouds hid the setting sun. He still held the knife in his right hand while his left wrapped around the piling. Listening carefully, he heard only crickets. He waited, regaining his composure and breath.

If they are still up there or on the shore, they probably don't know I'm alive.

Waiting in the water, his body quivered from chill and adrenaline. Moving under the dock, he looked up through the slats and saw no sign of his attackers. *They still could be on the shore, just waiting to see if I pop up.* He moved slowly to avoid any noise. He waited as his body reminded him of each hit he had taken. His breathing slowed as his grip grew weaker.

Sliding out from under the dock, he grabbed dead grass and weeds along the bank to pull himself out. He pulled his head up over the bank. He was in a pond, surrounded by trees. It was twilight. Above him, the sky was cloudy, blocking most of the stars. The moon shone around the lip of one cloud. The gravel road was deserted. It was always possible that they were hidden in the trees, waiting to see if he had emerged, but Braxton doubted it.

If they had wanted to shoot me, they had ample opportunity.

He tried to stand. The pain made him pause. He lowered his body back onto the grassy shore. His ear popped as the water drained. He tried to ignore the aches that seemed to be everywhere. His last sensation before he passed out was the smell of the pond water and how strangely familiar it was.

* * *

Faye watched Ronin check the door to the A-OK Garage. With one hand on the door, he pulled his gun. She pulled hers and chambered a round.

As she moved to the other side of the door, tightly wrapped chest pounding. The painkillers helped. She knew she could have asked for something stronger but didn't. Pain was good. Her grandfather had told her, "Our pains in life are what defines us." As a twelve-year-old, those words didn't mean much. Now it was one of her mantras.

Ronin slowly opened the door and shifted through the gap. Faye followed, heart pounding. As they moved into the garage, the smells were what she expected. Decades of petroleum products pooled into every surface. Her eyes widened.

Then came the words from Ronin, "Oh shit!"

He darted ahead of her to an old man on the floor. A pool of dark blood came from his leg as Ronin moved to him. "He's still alive. Call nine-one-one!"

Faye didn't release the grip on her weapon. For all she knew, the attackers were still there. She dialed the emergency dispatch center and got angry when they insisted on an address. "I don't fucking know. It's the A-OK Garage. Send an ambulance and the police, now!"

Faye dropped the phone in her purse as Ronin pulled a shop rag off one of the workbenches and started to wrap the wound on the old man. He groaned, which she took as a good sign.

It hurts, but you're alive.

"Help's on the way," Ronin said.

Where was Braxton? She walked around his car, expecting to find his body. She moved to the other bays, gun in hand. Nothing.

Where the hell is he?

* * *

It was a hot summer day. The sun shimmered on the lake. They had run out of sunscreen before getting into the canoe, so Braxton had gone without so that Suzanna and Angela would have it. The canoe was a rental. Suzanna took the bow, Angela between them. Braxton was in the stern. It had been a perfect day. He could still smell the lake.

He hated that dream. Most of his memories of his life before were pleasant, welcoming, seductive. Not this one. It was a nightmare wrapped in guilt.

He heard the motor for the boat but ignored it. There were a lot of boats on the water that day. It was a regret that was impossible for him to shake. Even as the memory played out, he wanted to warn his past self to turn, to see the approaching boat. It was impossible.

The boat had three, no, four kids in it. In his memories, he didn't see their faces, he only somehow knew they were kids. The wake of the boat hit the canoe broadside, rolling it over. He gulped in lake water as panic and water washed over him.

He had kicked away from the canoe. Breaking the surface, he saw his wife, stunned and angry at the same time, but alive, framed by the capsized canoe. He'd insisted on life preservers. There was no sign of Angela. "Angela!" Suzanna called as he coughed out the water he had swallowed.

Angela's life preserver bobbed up in the water, empty.

His heart sank, and he followed. Braxton dove into the water blindly, reaching for his daughter. The terror of losing his child gripped him. He kicked and paddled hard, groping in the water. He saw a leg. Grabbing it, he pulled madly, getting a better grip. Somehow he got her in front of him and the two of them broke the surface. She coughed, which made him cry, a sign that she was okay. She cried, frightened by what had happened, but very much alive. He kicked alongside the canoe as another boat maneuvered close, reaching down to help.

As they were pulled aboard, he made sure Angela was alright. She had been scared, but she was only nine years old. Braxton surveyed the lake in the dream. "I swear I'm going to knock some sense into those kids," he said out loud, mostly for himself.

"Let it go, honey," Suzanna said.

"They could have killed us!"

"Find them, then find their parents," the memory echoed in Braxton's brain. "Let them punish them."

The memory of her face froze, as if a pause button had been pressed. He savored the image. He wanted to stay in that state for the rest of his life, seeing his lost wife. Reality jerked him out of the dream. His whole body tensed. It was dark.

How long was I out?

It was impossible to tell. He was still soaked, still in pain, but alive. Already, the memories of the canoe incident were melting away. His beating took their place. He still held the knife that had saved his life.

He slowly stood, shivering from the cold spring air in his soaked clothes. Coughing only made his many bruises and aches react. That was the least of his problems.

I have no idea where I am, I've got no phone, no wallet, and I'm wet and beaten half to death.

Slowly, methodically, he walked along the gravel road. It didn't matter where it led, as long as it led away from the pond.

Chapter 25
Keyboard "Warriors"

Percy sat at his keyboard, nibbling on his Hot Pocket, basking in the dim glow from his monitors, overjoyed with how things were going. His uncle was dealing with the Weldon woman and her accomplices. He wished he had been there to see her beaten. It was the ultimate form of social justice. He felt deprived of witnessing it.

I should have asked him to record it.

The best part was the attack on her couldn't be tied to him. If the police could have done that, he'd already be in jail. *They don't have shit.* His little exaggeration to his uncle had played out far better than he had hoped. The best part of his little deception was that if there was any physical retribution, it would be against his uncle and his friend Jack.

They were both in the military. They're more than able to handle anything that comes at them.

Percy had called the bookstore to see if he could get his job back. No. He didn't want the job, really. The only reason he called was that his mother had insisted. She had gone so far as to threaten to make the call herself, which was the last thing he wanted.

Her generation is stupid. They think that having a job and being successful is what's important. What I do here, in this chair, that's what is going to change the world for the better.

He was watching two targets online, waiting for one of them to post something—anything. One was a fantasy author, Burton Walsh, who had attracted his attention when he posted that he was not in favor of using personal pronouns. Immediately, Percy and his sidekicks, Walter/Gump227 and Dennis/Shatterstorm02 had decided that Walsh was a target. Dennis was a genius at crafting memes or creating fake Tweets and Facebook posts. There were a half dozen websites that aided in creating fake social media entries that looked real. He loved the one Dennis did for Walsh, making it look like it came from his Twitter account:

> *The people that use pronouns are threats to our country. They are traitors and Nazis, each and every one of them.*

It was inflammatory by design. Using his accessory accounts, he and his friends spread the fake Tweet. To Percy, it really wasn't false. *He's the kind of guy that probably thinks that. All we did was let others know what kind of person he really is.* If things went well, it wouldn't be long before Walsh's publisher dropped him. Social justice at its finest.

The other target was a police officer named Jackson McClean whom Walter said had harassed him, pulling him over and citing him for not having a driver's license. Walter worked with Dennis to edit the audio on his body cam footage of his encounter. AI was a big help in duplicating the officer's voice. They made it sound like the police officer was the worst kind of racist. That video even made it to the evening news. Despite the police putting up the actual footage, Percy and his comrades manage to spread the word that it was a cover-up, a police conspiracy. There were cries on the editorial page of the *Indianapolis Star* calling for an investigation. He had been put on administrative leave, and now the media was spreading the lie.

Ruining careers was all part and parcel for control of the nation's culture. The people they went after deserved it. Especially that. Police were a huge part of America's problem—George Floyd showed that. And the author, Walsh, people like him could not have a voice in the society that Percy and his friends were creating.

History is going to remember our contributions. Everyone will see us for what we are, heroes—heroes for calling out the secret Nazis.

For Percy and his circle of friends, using their computers to call out fascists was what justice was all about. It was more than fun for

Percy. It was what he imagined the founding fathers would have wanted. *My great-grandfather was in World War Two, storming the beaches of southern France. He was part of the original generation of ANTIFA.*

Thinking of ANTIFA was frustrating. He'd found a local cell and contacted them about joining. They invited him to a private sit-down. It was everything he'd imagined, right down to their hoods and masks. They asked him a lot of questions. He had thought he'd done well. "Don't call us, we'll call you," they told him.

They all think they're better than me because they are in shape. They're fat-shaming, that's what they are doing.

He made a point, every Friday, to send them a little report he prepared about the targets he and his friends were going after and what they had done.

Sooner or later, they will see me for the asset that I am.

His phone chirped. His sweaty fingers stabbed the button. "Uncle Murray!"

"Yeah. Listen. There was a guy that was somehow attached to this Weldon-woman. Name of Harold Callahan. He's been snooping around our hangout, along with a cop. We dealt with him."

"You mean you—"

"Don't say anything. He won't bother you anymore."

Percy loved what his uncle couldn't say out loud. *They killed a guy—for me. This is awesome. Why haven't I used my uncle for this earlier?* "Wow," was all he could muster.

"Yeah. Here's the deal. We got this guy's phone. It's a burner, you know, one of those cheap-ass ones you get from 7-Eleven. Our guy wasn't too talkative about the code to open it. I'd like to see who he was texting and what he was telling him—confirm if he was really working with Weldon or someone else."

"What can I do?"

"Two things. One, I need you to break into this phone and get me the data. Second, you need to move out for a while. If this guy is some PI with ties to the cops, it might bring in some heat and you don't want that."

"Move out? Where do I go?"

"I don't care. You're not going to drag my sister into your shit."

"Can I stay with you?"

"Fuck no. If the cops find one of us, they find the other. Find some other place to crash."

"I don't know where to go."

"You have a friend? Ask if you can sleep on their sofa for a week or two, just until the heat dies down."

Percy cringed. He had friends, like Walter and Dennis. But they were internet friends. He had never met either of them face-to-face. Asking them would be awkward. His circle of associates was not likely to take in someone.

Where should I go?

Panic washed over him.

"Percy, can you crack this phone?"

"I—I've never done that before."

"You're always bragging that you're some sort of cyber-genius. You have to know someone that can do it."

"Most of the people I know are more social media experts."

"Jesus, Percy. You got me sucked into your damn games on the net, now I've got some heat on me. This can die down, but the time has come for you to grab one of your balls and man-up!" He heard the disgust in his uncle's voice. It reminded him of his mother's tone and he instantly resented it.

He's talking down to me, like I'm some sort of loser.

"I didn't ask you to kill a guy, Uncle Murray."

"You did. You just didn't know it. That's how these things get out of hand. If you're smart, you'll do exactly what I tell you. If you don't, you're going to be spending time in jail for being an accessory to a crime. Do you fuckin' understand?"

"I—I understand."

"Good boy. Pack your shit and get out of there. Tell your mom something, tell her you're going to a friend's to play video games, whatever works. I'll call you in an hour or so, and I'll get you this phone. I don't care what you have to do to get into it, just handle it."

"Don't worry," Percy said, stuffing his laptop in his backpack. "I won't let you down."

"Yeah, yeah. Just follow orders and this will eventually go away." Before he could speak his uncle hung up.

Percy looked around his room. He started to gather clothing, stuffing things in his backpack. *This is serious shit. I need to show Uncle Murray that I'm a man. That I can handle this.* As he grabbed some socks and jammed them in, he wondered where he was going to go. *Dennis and Walter might have some ideas.* He didn't have a lot of money, but he had access to his mom's retirement savings. He had pulled out some cash in the past without her knowing. *I should transfer some funds over, just in case. She never noticed before. She can't even log in to check the balance. That's how I got her ID and password in the first place.*

For the first time in his life, the real world was intruding on his happiness, and it filled him with anxiety and terror.

Chapter 26
The Loaf & Jug

Braxton didn't know how far he walked. Miles. Eventually, he saw a crossroads in the distance with a Loaf & Jug. Onward. One guy was filling up at a pump. He didn't look up as Braxton trudged across the concrete and pushed open the door. The clerk was olive-skinned and wore a turban. He looked up and his mouth opened.

"I look like shit, don't I?" Braxton said, glancing down at his mud-encrusted wet clothing.

"Indeed, sir. You look like shit."

"I fell asleep at the wheel and drove into a pond. I've been walking for hours."

"Which way did you come from?"

Braxton turned toward the front and pointed back down the road.

"Ah. That is Gibson's Pond. People fish there."

"Now my car's at the bottom of the pond, along with my phone and my wallet."

"You have no phone and no wallet."

"That is correct, sir."

"And how is it you drove there? There is nothing else there."

"I had a fight with my girlfriend. She threw me out. I was going to camp. I have a tent and sleeping bag in the trunk. Had."

"This all sounds very dubious. You have many bruises and cuts on your face, not exactly like a man that accidentally drove into a pond."

He's seeing through my ruse. Time to change things up.

"I know. Are you a Sikh?"

"Indeed, sir. Are you a Sikh?"

"No. I'm a Christian. But I know a little about Sikhism. If I remember correctly, your faith is known for its commitment to equality."

"That is true. We believe that all people, regardless of who they are or where they come from, are equal in the eyes of God."

Braxton nodded. "I remember reading that Guru Nanak Dev Ji strongly rejected the caste system and spread the message of 'Langar'—a community kitchen where free meals are served to all, rich or poor, to promote social equality and humility."

The clerk stared, slack-jawed. "That is correct. How do you know that?"

"I was a history professor."

"Are you no longer a history professor?"

That was a prior life. "No. I'm retired. I'm a veteran. I have a pension."

"How can I help?"

"May I use your phone?"

"Of course."

"What's the address?"

"One-four-four-two Highway Thirty-One, Pendleton." The clerk reached under the counter and placed an old-fashioned black telephone with buttons instead of a dial down.

"Haven't seen one of those in a while."

"It was here long before me. The owner uses it, and I use it when I need to speak to the owner."

"Thank you. I'll make this short." Braxton dialed Faye. Her number was embossed in his brain. She answered on the first ring.

"Braxton?"

"How did you know?"

"Thank God. We've been worried sick. Who else is going to call at ten-thirty? What happened?"

"Long story. I'll tell you when I see you. Right now, I need Ronin to come get me. Got a pen?"

"Yes."

He gave her the address. "Put Ronin on."

"Are you all right?"

"I'll live. It was a close one. I'll tell you when you pick me up."

"Where at? I'll leave right now."

Braxton gave him the address. The clerk put the phone back under the counter. He wore a name tag that said, *Ram*.

"Ram, I owe you a debt of gratitude."

Ram shrugged. "Really, it was no problem. I must admit, when you first came in I thought, oh no, what kind of crazy man is out walking around at this time of night?"

Braxton laughed. "Don't blame you."

"Where were you a professor?"

"Eastern State University in Portland."

"What kind of history?"

"Mostly ancient Greece and Rome. I don't know if that professorship is still open. They seem to be moving away from traditional topics toward frivolous subjects like interpretive dance and gender ideology."

"I could not agree with you more. I myself am taking night classes from the University of Phoenix. I hope to earn my Master's Degree in computer science this spring."

"I'm sure you will."

I owe him. He could have very well called the police and my story would have fallen apart.

"Hey, it'll be a while before my ride gets here. Give me a trash bag and I'll pick up the litter in your lot."

Ram went in the back room and returned with a thirty-gallon bag. Braxton went outside and picked up the trash. Discarded plastic cups and straws, cigarette butts, fast-food wrappers. He used a fast-food wrapper to snag a used condom. There was a lot of trash. Just as he was finishing up, Ronin pulled in, driving a piece-of-shit beige Hyundai with a ten-speed riding the rear bumper. It had the old company logo, dating the car.

Ronin got out. "You look like something the dog dragged in. What happened?"

"I'll tell you on the way back."

Ronin dug out an old towel from the back seat and gave it to Braxton, supposedly to protect his upholstery. They got in the car and Braxton felt every hit he had been given. Ronin circled the pumps and headed back to town. Joe Walsh sang about his life as Braxton turned the radio down.

"They must have followed me from the Red Roof. I should have been smarter. They nailed me at the garage. Shot the owner. Beat the crap out of me and forced me into the trunk. We ended up at some pond down the road. When I wouldn't tell them what I wanted, they tied my legs to a cinder block and threw me off the end of the pier. I'd palmed my knife—it's a little knife, they never noticed. But I still had a helluva time getting loose. I almost drowned. Came up under the pier after they'd left. They must've gotten tired of waiting and taken off."

"You should write a book. Riding around in car trunks."

"Very funny. Ha fucking ha. Both of them wore masks, but were talkers. One of them was our Jack."

"Hawthorne."

"Yeah. The other was someone called Murray."

Ronin's eyes narrowed. "Murray, eh? That might be something I can use."

"I think they are related. Murray may be his uncle."

"How do you convince a relative to commit murder?"

Braxton grimaced, "Some people will do anything for their family. Is Faye still up?"

"Pretty sure she is."

They took the elevator to the third floor. It was ten-thirty by the Hyundai's clock. Braxton knocked lightly on Faye's door. The peep hole darkened for a moment, then she opened the door.

"Oh, thank God!" she said, wrapping her arms around him. They went inside and she shut the door.

"You need a shower."

"No shit."

"What happened?"

"They grabbed me at the garage."

"We know. When we got there, the owner was passed out from loss of blood. He'd been shot. We think the ambulance got there in time. They said his chances were fifty-fifty. Would you like something to drink? I have beer and ginger ale."

In all of the excitement, he had forgotten about Rocco.

That is one more thing they are going to have to answer for.

"Better make it a ginger ale."

"Me too," Ronin said.

Faye opened up the cube fridge and pulled out three cans of soda. Braxton popped his, tipped back, and glugged half the can.

"You must be starving."

"I'll live."

"I could call room service," she joked, with an obvious reference to them being at an old Red Roof Inn.

"No, I'd rather hit the sack."

"What happened?" she demanded.

"Well shit. They must have followed me from here. They sandbagged me in the garage. Beat the crap out of me, then tossed me in a pond with a cement block tied to my feet. Let's just say it wasn't the kind of night I expected in Indianapolis."

"Are we in danger?" Faye asked.

"I doubt it. They think I'm dead. I can use that to our advantage. They're not gonna come after you here. They don't know about Ronin."

"You know," Ronin said, "that's twice thugs have tossed you in their trunks and taken you off to be killed. You're setting some kind of world record."

"I'd just as soon not. Now, if it's okay, I want a shower and then I need to hit the sack. Faye, we'll see you in the morning."

Chapter 27
Rocco

On Friday, Ronin drove Braxton to the garage to pick up his car. There wasn't any police tape. The police were so overburdened and understaffed they couldn't spare the men. Braxton's car was where he'd left it. His attackers apparently had not checked out the vehicle, which was fine by him. Braxton got in the car.

"We passed a T.J. Maxx on the way. I'm going to stop there, pick up some new duds, and a wallet."

"Got anything to put in it?"

"No."

"Then it's a good thing I made you this duplicate driver's license." Ronin whipped out an Indiana driver's license belonging to Harold H. Callahan, 451 Buttonwood Street, Portland. He handed Braxton a burner. "Take this phone. I loaded it with my and Faye's phone numbers and installed the Uber app in case you get stranded again."

"You're kidding."

"Yes, I'm kidding."

"Ronin, you're a fucking genius."

"I know! I'll see you back at the Inn."

Braxton drove to the hospital where Rocco was being treated and parked in the visitors' lot. The hospital was bound to have cameras, but no one was looking for Harry Callahan. He doubted that he would have any police protection.

Braxton got out. He wore fresh blue jeans and a blue work shirt, with a Colts cap pulled low on his forehead. He had picked up three different caps. His research into police procedures said that oftentimes hats distracted people's eyes, making it difficult for them to identify others. There was a metal detector past the reception desk, staffed by a hospital security person that was almost twice Braxton's weight. The receptionist, a middle-aged woman with smooth caramel skin, looked up. "How can I help you?"

"Rocco Renzetti?"

"May I see some ID?"

Braxton pulled out his fresh driver's license. He had to admit, Ronin was pretty smart to have ordered a duplicate license for just such a contingency. The receptionist gave it a cursory glance and handed it back to him with a smile.

She consulted the computer. "He's on the third floor, room 312. Are you family?"

"Just a friend."

Braxton walked through the metal detector. A rent-a-cop with a paunch sat on a stool reading a Michael Connelly novel. Braxton took the elevator to the third floor. The smell was always the same. Antiseptics with a hint of Febreze. Three-twelve was closed. He knocked.

"Yeah?"

Braxton went inside. Rocco lay in bed with his right leg elevated in a cast. A broad grin spread on his face.

"Didn't expect to see you again!"

"Me neither. How you doin', Rocco?"

"I been hurt worse. Bullet missed the bone and the artery. Gotta hobble around on crutches for a few weeks. Gonna be a drag at the garage."

"You got anybody to help?"

"Yeah, I got a few buddies I can call. My brother said he would help out in his spare time. Got a friend whose boy wants to be a mechanic. He's been hanging out. I'll call him. So tell me. What the fuck did those guys want?"

Braxton shrugged. "Beats me."

"Riiiiiight. What happened to them?"

Braxton shrugged and frowned unconvincingly.

"How'd you get away?"

Shrug, frown.

"Well, you're just a font of information, aren't you?"

"It's a mystery. When this is all over, I'll fill you in. I just stopped by to see if you were still kicking."

Rocco lifted his left leg. "Next time you come, bring me some bourbon. Not the cheap shit."

"I'll see what I can do."

Braxton drove to the Red Roof Inn. Ronin sat at the desk in his room with his laptop open, a broad grin on his face. "You were right. Our Murray is Kornbluth's uncle. Murray Landreth is fifty-seven, drives his wife's '06 Cadillac. Lives at 836 Rinehart Boulevard, works at Ross Refrigeration. Jack Hawthorne is another Gulf War veteran, lives at 5552 Waunakee, apartment number 406, drives an '06 Toyota Land Cruiser. I have their license numbers if you want 'em."

"Beautiful. What about their online activity?"

"Not much lately. I did notice that Percy's IP address has changed twice."

"So he's not at home."

"That's right. He's on the move."

"His uncle probably tipped him off." It made sense. Percy was more of a liability than an asset.

"You're probably right, based on what we know about him. Both he and Murray are lying low. The one email I was able to intercept between them indicated that he was pretty fed up with his nephew right now. Percy, however, is greatly encouraged and has been more active than ever, urging his minions to strike out at Nazis, Jews, white supremacists, all the oppressor classes. He's lashing out from whatever secret bunker he's hiding out in."

"Landreth's wife around?"

"She died of cancer two years ago. He's living off her life insurance and a home repair business that is barely treading water."

His mind churned. *One mystery is solved. They think I'm dead, which is a huge plus. The question still remains: How do we take advantage of this?*

"We should track this bastard, if we can."

Ronin reached into his backpack, rummaged around, and came up with an AirTag. "Let me put it in my system." He entered it on his laptop and tossed it to Braxton, who snapped it out of the air. "You gonna plant it? Or you want me to do it?"

"Would you mind?"

"What else I got to do? Imma taking my bike. It's not too far."

"Don't get caught."

They drove a half block to a Burger King on Shadeland. Braxton and Faye were still hurting from their assaults. They sat at a booth looking out on the street. It was early evening and traffic was light. Workers returning home, buses and Ubers passing, kids joyriding. Young men on skateboards. Young women on electric scooters. They watched as a heavyset woman rolled into the Burger King parking lot, got off, and let the scooter fall on the sidewalk.

Ronin picked up their order, burgers all around. Faye's was a single.

"Y'know, Ro, you could always rent one of those scooters."

"I could, but they all have tracking devices so the city can pick them up. That, and Indy only has them in the immediate downtown area, not out here in the 'burbs."

Faye laughed. "I see the same scooter lying in a vacant lot every day."

He looked it up. "It's probably stolen or dead. Forget it. I'll take my bike."

After dinner, they returned to the hotel. Ronin wore dark blue jeans and a black hoodie.

"Don't get run over."

"Bike has a light. I'll turn it off when I get to Murray's neighborhood."

"Text me when you're on the way home."

Ronin held up a thumb. Braxton walked outside with him, watched him unlock his bike from the rack, feel the tires, get on and pedal away. Braxton went to his room and turned on the television. Venezuelan street gangs had taken over Aurora, Colorado, and Chicago. In Chicago, the Gangster Disciples, Black P Stones, Vice Lords, Latin Kings, and Satan Disciples vowed to take on Tren de

Aragua. "The city's going up in flames," exclaimed a former gangbanger-turned-social-worker.

Braxton changed the channel. Stephen Colbert. "Hey," Colbert joked. "Trump supporters…do they all wear white sheets?" The audience laughed and cheered. Braxton changed the channel. Jason Statham working his way down the concourse of a cruise ship, breaking every arm in sight. Braxton changed the channel. The bisexual *Lord of the Rings* series was doing a crossover with the new James Bond, a differently abled lesbian of color. Braxton changed the channel. Soccer. He gave up. As he prepared to take a shower, he surveyed his bruises and cuts. They were all still in the deep purple stage. Just lifting his arms fired off throbs of pain.

These guys both have a lot to answer for.

He took a shower, letting the almost scalding water do its work on his muscles and aches. When done, he tossed back a couple Aleve and slid into bed.

Chapter 28
Crash

Ronin's return woke Braxton. He looked at the clock. It was nine-thirty. He'd been asleep for two hours. It felt like eight.

Ronin sat on his bed and opened his laptop. "He's on the move." He turned it around. Braxton saw a red dot moving down Rinehart Boulevard toward Massachusetts Ave. He handed the laptop to Braxton, who sat up and put it on the bed.

"Where's he going?"

"He might be going to another VFW. There are eight. Gimme."

Braxton handed the laptop back. Ronin did a search. "Looks like he's headed toward Post 907 on Carruthers Street. Wait a minute." They waited in silence.

"Yup. Just pulled in. The address is 415 Carruthers Street."

Braxton got up. He'd slept in his clothes. He went to the bathroom, splashed water in his face, took the Glock out of his satchel, grabbed a Trail Blazers cap and a leather jacket, and opened the door.

"You want me to come?"

Braxton thought about it. "I don't want you with me if things go sideways."

"I can handle myself. You know that."

Braxton paused. "All right. Come on."

Ronin stuffed his laptop in his backpack and followed Braxton out the door. The Crown Vic burbled to life. Ronin dialed in the address on his laptop which guided them down the street. Forty-five minutes later, they turned into the empty parking lot of a failed furniture store across Carruthers Street from the VFW. They parked in a shadow next to the building. They had a clear view of the VFW and its parking lot.

"That's Hawthorne's Land Cruiser," Ronin said softly, although there was no one around to hear it.

"And there's Murray's wife's Cadillac."

They watched in silence. Braxton swept his field of vision. Ronin opened his laptop. When Braxton looked over, Ronin was watching a video of two Asians wearing frog masks shooting out rubber tongues at a game board.

The open windows admitted cool air, a hint of tar. Honky-tonk music trickled from the bar. Dolly Parton singing "Jolene." Braxton relaxed. His jaw unclenched. He breathed deeply. The next thing he knew, Ronin was elbowing him in the ribs.

He woke with a start. "What?"

Ronin nodded across the street. A man was getting into the Land Cruiser. "Is that Hawthorne?" he whispered.

"It's gotta be." The Cruiser's lights went on. It left the bar, cruising east. Braxton waited until it was a quarter mile down the road before starting the car and following, headlights off. Two miles down, Hawthorne turned south on Emerson Ave. Traffic was light, the occasional truck. Kids cruising. Twenty minutes later, Hawthorne drove past Beach Grove park and headed southeast on Shelbyville.

"Where's he going?" Ronin said.

"He may not be staying in the city." Hawthorne slowed and turned right, toward the west. Braxton took his time reaching the intersection, paused to read the sign by moonlight. Ostrich Lane. He followed. Ostrich Lane wound through forested hills, debouching onto a straight line through farmland. The moon cast an eerie glow. They were a half mile behind Hawthorne when he slammed on the brakes. An instant later, he took off like a scalded cat.

"Shit," Braxton said. "He made us."

Braxton put the pedal to the metal. The big Ford V8 responded abruptly, accelerating so fast, it pressed them into the backs of their seats.

That's what I'm talking about!

Ronin hurriedly fastened his seat belt. "Does this thing have crash balloons?"

"I don't know if they work. It's kind of old."

"Let's not find out."

They raced after Hawthorne, hitting ninety miles an hour. Braxton was surprised the old Toyota would go that fast. The Crown Vic went a lot faster. They closed until they were fifteen feet from Hawthorne's rear bumper.

"What's the plan?" Ronin said.

"Let's see what happens when I ram him."

Braxton accelerated alongside, almost swooping past. Ronin had put his hood up. Braxton wore the Trail Blazers cap and a pair of rose-tinted night glasses. They glanced over. Hawthorne was aiming a pistol at them. Braxton dropped back, then swerved to the right, ramming the Cruiser's right rear corner with his push bar. His Crown Vic had a thousand pounds on the Cruiser and had been built to perform PIT maneuvers. The results were predictable. The Cruiser veered off the road, hit the ditch, and tumbled over three times. Braxton drove ahead fifty yards and pulled over. He shut the engine off. His heart was in overdrive. He slowed his breathing and slowed his heart. Ronin twisted around in the seat. He faced front, opened the door, and got out, careful not to trip in the drainage ditch. The Cruiser's lights still shone, wheels on top like a dead insect.

Braxton got out and headed down the road. "Let's go."

Ronin ran to catch up. "What's the plan?"

"Time for him to go."

"Wait a minute. Wait a minute. Oh, shit, never mind."

"Don't get squeamish on me. This is what we do. He tried to kill me and Rocco."

"You're right. Never mind."

They stepped over the drainage ditch into a recently plowed field. Ronin crouched and dug with his fingers, coming up with moist soil. He sniffed. "Corn. It's planting season."

They reached the Cruiser. Hawthorne lay half out the window, bleeding from a gash on the bridge of his nose, his left arm bent at a funny angle. Braxton stooped next to him. He smiled.

"Hi. How are ya?"

"Call an ambulance. I'm in a bad way here."

Braxton showed his teeth. "That's a good 'un. You are one ugly son of a bitch. Ronin, hit the headlights, would ya?"

Ronin crawled in the passenger window and shut off the headlights.

"Listen. I'm a veteran. I'm sorry I got mixed up in this. I tried to talk Murray out of it."

"Cute lie. You broke Faye's ribs. You tried to kill me."

"I've got money…"

"No you don't. You're suckin' air."

"I can get fifty thou together!"

Braxton removed a five-gallon plastic garbage bag from his jacket pocket. "What's Murray up to?"

"I don't know! He got me into this!"

"He's not going after Faye?"

"How would I know?"

"Okay."

Braxton fitted the bag around Hawthorne's neck and pulled it tight. Hawthorne struggled, but his good arm was trapped in the wreck of his car. Braxton waited until he stopped breathing and waited some more. When he was convinced the man was dead, he took off the bag and stuck it back in his pocket.

Braxton reached inside and dug through Hawthorne's pockets, taking his wallet and cell phone. He took two hundred-dollar bills out of the wallet and stuck it back in the pocket. He handed the cell phone to Ronin.

"Pull the AirTag and let's boogie."

They headed back toward the Crown Vic. Ronin hadn't said a word since they'd reached the wreck.

"You okay?" Braxton said.

"I'm fine."

They got back in the car. Ronin slammed his door. The air bag exploded in his face.

"Great," Ronin muttered.

Chapter 29
Peyton Manning Rookie Card

Murray groaned and rolled over. The morning sunlight was like a laser in his eye. He rolled over and tried to ignore the morning, but it was there, nagging and tugging at him to get up.

As he planted his feet on the floor, he almost absentmindedly thought he'd see his wife, Paula. In his mind, she would be wearing baggy jeans and a loose flannel shirt. Her gardening outfit. Spring was dedicated to her tomatoes and mint growing in the little garden, harvesting what she could have bought for three bucks at a Safeway.

Instead, there was nothing there. Cancer had taken her. If it had been a drunk driver, he would have had someone to channel his rage to. Cancer didn't have a face that he could punch. The disease didn't have a crotch to kick. It simply existed. Murray missed her, and that longing gave him an anger that constantly sought an outlet. If she were alive, she would be saying, "I thought you weren't going to come home drunk anymore," in that drill instructor tone of hers. As much as he hated that tone, he wished he could hear it one more time.

"I'm going through a rough patch, or haven't you noticed?" He spoke the words as if she were really there, scolding him.

Getting up, he brushed his teeth and rubbed his beard stubble. He went into the kitchen, ignoring the stack of dirty dishes for the sixth time, loaded up the coffeemaker with ingredients, and sat down at the small table. He turned on his police scanner and sighed, waiting for the Maxwell House to finish brewing. Murray's head seemed to groan, a slow steady pain that came from the alcohol he had consumed the night before.

Then he heard it. A 10-51 and 10-67, wrecker needed and reporting a death. They described the car, and he knew who it belonged to.

I know that license plate! It's Jack's!

He listened to the location, and it was on some country road outside of the city.

They'd been drinking at a different VFW last night, to throw off anyone trying to find them, be it the police or the people tied to the Weldon chick. Nobody there knew them, but welcomed them as fellow warriors. Jack had been talking about moving away from Indianapolis. He said the town gave him the creeps. Murray felt a twinge of guilt.

Damn it! This is all Percy's fault. Worthless piece of shit. Dumbass dweeb couldn't hold a menial job. He spends all of his time on the internet and now it's coming back to haunt him—and Jack paid the price. Why the fuck did I agree to help him?

If he was going to kill someone, it should probably be Percy.

He dipped his head down, closed his eyes, put his elbows on the table, holding the back of his neck as the hangover spiked his brain. The scanner reported the ambulance being dispatched. There was no hurry. Jack was dead.

The old coffeemaker finished, and he slowly raised his head, got up, and poured himself a mug full in the same dirty mug he had been using all week. Splashing in a copious amount of sugar, he made his way back to the table and took a sip. It was scalding hot, to the point that it hurt his tongue and the roof of his mouth. That pain seemed to shove back the sting of the hangover, if only for a moment. Combined with the aching of his broken pinkie finger, it felt sadly familiar to him.

Jack's death was too much for him to cope with. His mind shifted to the last death in his life. He barely remembered Paula's funeral. Most of that period of his life was a thankful blur in his mind.

Will it be the same way with Jack? Who's going to show up for him? Yes, there will be an honor guard, the guns will crack, a flag folded...but who will be there other than me?

Paula's funeral had brought many people, many of which he didn't know. Their marriage had been on the rocks for some time. Neither of them wanted to endure the expense of divorce, so they had settled in for tolerating each other. He loved her, but at times, he wanted to strangle her. Paula had been a teacher at the local middle school. She made as much as he did, and in his mind, that was one of the things that drove them apart. Her financial independence made her stand up to him more, which led to fights. She got fed up, as did he.

Her problems were part of the problems he saw with the country. Paula taught sixth grade in a middle class neighborhood. The students were a mix of races, mostly well-off parents. Yet only five percent tested proficient in math last year, and three percent in history. The former Lewis and Clark Middle School had been renamed Tecumseh. He thought it was a wasteful change, one that cost the school district money and accomplished nothing in response. She was an idealist and said it was a positive move. He wanted her to get a job at a private school, but she loved the commute. They lived just a few doors down from the school. In their better years, they walked the playing fields in the evening hours, after the kids and their obnoxious parents had gone home. Those days were now just foggy memories. He didn't cling to them. Murray wanted them to go away.

Paula had taught history. It used to be American history. Now it was Native American history, and the history of American oppression. If she could have just hung in there one more year, she would've retired with a pension. Of course, the cancer had interrupted her dreams of retirement. That was frustrating to Murray, too. She had been one of the few surviving white teachers. Sixty percent of the staff now consisted of other races. It was a purge, plain and simple. As job insurance, Paula had been compelled to spout the latest dogma, whether it was that men could give birth, or they had only ten more years before sea levels washed away all signs of civilization.

What good did it do? The cancer got her despite everything she did to hold on to that fucking job.

153

He took another long sip of his coffee and thought he could feel the caffeine surge into his bloodstream as he did. The ambulance arrived at the scene and they confirmed the victim was Jack Hawthorne.

As he finished the coffee, he wondered what Jack had been doing on that road.

That's not near his house. He had too much to drink last night to be out cruising country roads.

The only thing that made sense was that he had been following someone...or someone had been following him.

When he finished the coffee, he set the mug on the counter, then went in the bathroom, turned on the shower, and got in. Reaching it, the water was frigid. *Too fucking cold.* He was no longer a dumb kid! Turning the heat up, he waited for it to come, then stepped into the hot shower. Time seemed to freeze for him. He had no idea how long he had been there, eyes closed, skin withering.

Murray got out, toweled off, examining the rosacea on his face and arms. He was at that age. Trouble sleeping, trouble pissing, trouble shitting. Forget about getting it up. He thought about ordering Viagra through the internet, but what was he going to do with it? Jack off alone? Hire a hooker? Women that he saw as desirable didn't see him in the same light. It was hard to blame them.

As he got dressed, one thought kept going through his mind.

What were you doing on that road, Jack?

There would be no answer. Jack was gone.

What could he do? His nephew was worse than worthless. He didn't think for one moment that Jack had lost control of his vehicle. They had killed Callahan, drowned the stubborn bastard. It wasn't Callahan, but that meant that Callahan was not working alone. There were others out there and they were looking for blood. It was a sobering thought.

Jack always had my back, but he's dead. That means they may be coming after me!

He needed help. Although Murray never saw any action, he knew a guy who did. Wesley Palmer had been Special Forces and done two tours of duty in Afghanistan. They'd crossed paths at Fort Pendleton.

After Wesley mustered out, he became a contractor for an outfit called Brownwater. They did shady shit in Africa and SE Asia. Wesley had contacted Murray several years ago asking if he'd be interested. Murray had laughed.

"Wes, I never saw a lick of action."

"Oh, I'm sorry! I'm confusing you with Murray Balter!"

Murray remembered Balter because they shared a first name. Balter was a much decorated soldier. Murray had written Wesley's phone number down in case he ran into someone at the VFW who might be interested. It took him fifteen minutes' burrowing through his den, tossing out old cable bills and unread magazines, before he found the notepad in which he'd written it.

Murray dialed the number. It rang three times.

"Hello."

"Is this Wesley Palmer?"

"Who's this?"

"Murray Landreth. We served together."

"Oh. Oh yeah. Geez, it's been a long time. What's up, Murray?"

"Are you still with Brownwater?"

"Off and on." It was the exact answer that a private military contractor would give.

"I might have a job for you."

Silence…awkward and deliberate.

"What kind of job?"

"The kind we can't discuss on the phone. I'm in Indianapolis. Where are you?"

"You're in luck. I'm in Baltimore, but I'm flying to Minneapolis Thursday and I have a one-hour layover in Indianapolis."

"Can we meet at the airport?"

"Yeah. I'll come and meet you at the main terminal. It's been a while. How will I know it's you?"

"I'll wear a Colts sweatshirt."

"Okay. Hang on."

Paper shuffling.

"I land in Indy at two-thirty. Probably take me about fifteen minutes to get down there."

"Great. See you there."

Murray hung up. At first, he was relieved. Then a sense of dread began to creep up on him.

What the fuck am I doing? How am I going to pay for this?

There was one way. His Peyton Manning Rookie Card was worth fifty thousand dollars. It had been a fluke that he had gotten it. Paula had purchased a big box of cards at an estate sale and had given it to him. After she got sick, he spent hours sorting them. It filled his time, mindless organization. When he found it, sealed and graded at the bottom of the box, he was surprised he didn't have a heart attack.

Murray had almost forgotten about the card. He downplayed its value when he first found it, a little secret his wife didn't need to know about. He had always felt a little guilty about that. When the medical bills came in after her death, he had not cashed in the card, but had used money from his business to keep the creditors at bay. Once he sold it, there was a risk the IRS would want a piece of the money, so he had held off. *Paula would have understood...* it was a lie that he told himself every time he saw the card.

Paula had her grandmother's necklace. That was worth a lot of money too, so much, she had insisted that he get a rider on their insurance policy for it. He had wanted to sell it, but her sister had been claiming that it should go to her. If he sold it, she was the kind of person that would sue him over it. For the time being, he would leave it locked away in his dead wife's jewelry box.

He hated to part with it, but he knew a collector who'd been bugging him for years when he had bragged about having it. It had been the last present he had gotten from Paula, which was why he had hung onto it. Now, though, he needed the help, and help came at a price. Murray went to the closet in his den, reached up, and pulled down the big three-ring binder in which he kept his sports cards. He also had a John Elway Rookie Card. He could throw that in to sweeten the deal.

Chapter 30
Frisbee Golf

Braxton, Faye, and Ronin went to breakfast at a Waffle House down the street from the Red Roof Inn. Ronin had picked it out. They took a corner booth. The waitress was a pert twenty-something with a pierced nose and fully tatted sleeves. Braxton never understood the need for people to tattoo themselves up. Ronin had once asked a programmer he worked with about everyone having tattoos, and she said it was an expression of individuality.

"If everyone's doing it, how are you standing out?"

His coworker didn't have an answer to that...

"Something to drink?" tattoo girl asked.

"Coffee."

"Coffee."

"Me too."

"Perfect."

Braxton waited until she'd left. Hubbub drowned out their conversation from the locals who sought solace or sobriety in the dingy Waffle House. "Well, now it's down to Murray and Percy," Braxton said.

"I'm wondering if we should just let it go," Faye said.

"It was your ribs they broke. They tried to drown me. Let's not forget the reason we are here, Mr. Higby." He saw that the last part hit Faye hard.

"If we let it go," Ronin said, "it will embolden others."

Faye pursed her lips. The waitress returned with their coffee.

"Would you like to order?"

Braxton and Ronin ordered omelets. Faye ordered a fruit salad.

"Um, this is the Waffle House. We don't have fruit salad."

"Fine—how about the chicken salad?" she growled.

Faye waited until the waitress left. "I trust you guys. If anyone deserves justice, it's these people."

"Ro, can you stick an AirTag on Murray's car?"

"He's using his dead wife's Cadillac. I can do that."

They ate. The waitress returned. "Can I offer you any dessert?"

"Not me," Braxton said.

"I'm full," Faye said.

"Just the bill," Ronin said.

The waitress set the bill on the table. "You pay at the counter up front."

"Thank you."

She walked away.

"I'll have the shit on a shingle," Ronin joked.

"Perfect," Faye said with a thin smile. "I'm working with children."

When they returned to the hotel, Ronin unpacked his bike.

"In broad daylight?" Braxton said.

"Yeah. It's early."

"That might be tricky."

"I *am* kinda tricky."

"Okay. I trust your judgment."

"As well you should," he quipped back.

* * *

With a baggy gray hoodie and backpack, Ronin was indistinguishable from most teenagers. He pedaled away, phone mounted on his handlebars. He rode past one boarded-up store after another, casualties of the 2020 riots. Walmart. Indy Scripts. Dollar General. The one Walgreens still open had armed guards at the entrance. Gangs had covered every storefront with graffiti. Huge, stylized letters, some incomprehensible, some spelling out the gangs' names. GRACKLE ST MOFOS. STUMPTOWN HUSTLERS. Ronin appreciated the aesthetic, but the style itself spoke of decay and lawlessness. Ronin didn't like it when he saw it in comic books. He didn't like it when he saw it on the street.

Ronin rode onto the bike trail that ran through Pleasant Run Parkway. Bikers going the other way wore bespoke biking duds, skin-tight, asses in the air, helmets on. A lot of electric bikes. Ronin had been looking. He'd test ridden the Co-op, and it had a lot going for it. It would go thirty miles on a full charge, but the motor only cut in when you pedaled. When you didn't pedal, it didn't draw on the battery. It had five power levels, each stronger than the last. It made going up hills a breeze. On the other hand, the seat was pure torture, and it was way under-geared. He figured the issue had to have something to do with electric bikes in general, because there were hardly any with more than seven gears, and none with dual front sprockets.

Then there were the bikes you didn't have to pedal. The trouble with those was they didn't look like bicycles. They looked like miniature gadgets with two wheels. The wheels were smaller than regular bike wheels. They looked like something urban hipsters would ride, when they got too old for electric skateboards or scooters. There were plenty of those on the bike trail. None of the riders wore helmets.

He passed electric skateboards and scooters. None of those riders wore helmets, either. A third of the scooters were those high-zoot models with one big fat wheel in the center that the rider straddled. Ronin had been thinking of getting one himself. He imagined his electric garage. Bike, scooter, skateboard. Everything but an electric car.

Several "community scooters" lay half-submerged in the creek. Tossed there by people who thought vandalism was fun, no doubt.

Indianapolis did a good job of hiding its homeless people, keeping them off the main roads. Off the beaten path, the homeless were everywhere. Many had tents. Some used blue tarps that looked like they came from Harbor Freight. Many were just campsites surrounded by garbage. Shopping carts everywhere, some jammed with personal possessions. Some had bicycles. Ronin wondered idly if they'd been stolen. A few of the bicycles were attached to baby carriages crammed with clothes and camping gear. Clothes. Stolen plastic milk crates. He rode past a junkie shooting up, back against a tree. When he was done, he tossed the needle in the river. Other homeless hobos hunkered with each other, passing bottles of five-dollar port, or malt liquor.

It was no worse than Portland. Maybe better. At least you could still visit downtown. Downtown Portland was a ghost town. Every private store had closed up shop. The lawyers and investment houses remained. They would always be there, sequestered behind armed guards in brick buildings. Powell's Books still stood, although it was dicey getting around the junkies who'd set up camp on the sidewalk.

He passed Tecumseh Middle School on Verona Road on the east side. The school was built in the seventies, one-story redbrick surrounded by hurricane fencing with an athletic field mostly for soccer. Murray's house was within eyesight of the school.

Ronin pedaled into a park across the street and locked his bike in a rack with several others. It was nine. The park had a Frisbee golf course. Ronin had checked before he had come. He reached in his backpack and pulled out a Frisbee. The goal was to land the Frisbee in chain hammocks that had been set up as "holes." There were nine hammocks. Ronin tossed at hammock #1. The Frisbee skimmed the hammock but didn't land. Ronin walked up, picked up the Frisbee and dropped it in the hammock, in case anyone was looking. As if anybody gave a shit. The fifth "hole" was closest to the Landreths' home. The house was well kept from what he could see, which surprised him. He threw his Frisbee in a broad parabola he knew would take it across the street over by the Cadillac that was in the driveway. It skidded over the fence, bounced off the Cadillac's trunk, and landed next to it.

Ronin jogged across the street, entered the parking lot through the unlocked gate, ran to the Caddy, bent to retrieve his disc, and slapped the AirTag under the trunk, held in place by a big slab of Gorilla Tape.

He returned to the park and finished out his game. It made more sense to walk away, but Ronin had a compulsion to see things all the way through.

Chapter 31
Nagging Feelings

Officer Rita Hernandez came in as usual and checked the morning reports. It was less policy as it was a force of habit, something her former sergeant had ingrained in her. The first screen was dull, no names that triggered anything. It was all the usual stuff. Some gang activity in Tuxedo Park. No big shock there.

That neighborhood is a blight on the city.

Random gunfire, no one hit, but some kids were frightened—as they should be.

Then, on page two, a car crash and fatality. Jack Hawthorne.

Hawthorne...it can't be a coincidence.

She accessed the report and photos and looked at them. He was dead. Broken bottles of booze in the vehicle and he was twice over the legal limit. The accident photos were not as horrific as they could have been. Based on the way his body was positioned, to her at least, it looked as if Hawthorne might have survived the crash, if only for a few minutes.

Faye Weldon's friend. What was his name? Callahan! Yes, he had dropped Hawthorne's name as one of her attackers. Now he was dead. If he was involved in the attack on Faye Weldon, she had nothing more to fear from him.

If I get some downtime during the shift, I should reach out to her and let her know.

Her partner took a sip of coffee. "Rita, we need to get rolling."

She hit the page down key and saw more crash scene photos. The rear bumper of Hawthorne's car had a vertical dent. She had seen that once before, when she had used the PIT (precision immobilization technique) maneuver on a fleeing suspect's car. It was favored by the police, a hit on a rear bumper at the right angle would send a car in a spin, thus ending the pursuit.

The vertical marks were unique to a police vehicle's front nudge bars. She stopped for a moment and stared at the bumper. It wasn't the best photo, but it was distinct.

Was Hawthorne involved in a chase at some point? It wasn't in his records. That can't be it.

Looking at the marks they didn't look weather-worn, so chances are he didn't buy the vehicle like that.

That left one inescapable conclusion. A police vehicle may have been involved.

"Rita, ticktock," her partner said.

She logged off, grabbed her gear, and followed him to their cruiser. As she got in and buckled up, all she could do was contemplate what she had seen.

Maybe something else caused that dent. It might not have anything to do with the wreck. Hawthorne was intoxicated at the time. It could be just what it had been ruled, a single car wreck by a drunk driver.

"I said, signal in our ten-eight," her partner said, jarring her out of her thoughts.

Rita transmitted the code as they pulled out of the lot. "What's with you today, Rita?"

"Nothing, just thinking, that's all."

"Keep your focus here," her partner cautioned. "I need your head in the game."

"You got it."

As they took off, she mulled over the images. Something didn't feel right. It would be easy to let it go, but Rita inherited her persistence from her grandmother.

I need to do some digging into this, even if I have to do it in my spare time.

* * *

Percy had asked some of his online friends if he could crash with them. Gump227 never got back to him at all. Shatterstorm02 said that his father didn't let him have friends over, especially those he only knew from the internet. Gump227 had been a disappointment. When Percy reached out to him to stalk or harass someone, he was lightning-fast with responding. Now he was asking a little favor and he was just ignored. It was almost as if his friends on the internet weren't real friends.

That can't be right. These dudes have always had my back every time we took down some overprivileged white dude. They both must have a lot going on, that's all.

He checked with one of his former coworkers at the bookstore, but they ghosted him, not responding to his three voicemails.

The people at work were probably happy I got let go. They were always jealous of what I brought to the table.

That meant he had to stay at hotels. Part of it was exciting, that he had to be on the road, hiding from alt-right crazies. Thanks to access to his mother's retirement accounts via his laptop, he was able to advance himself the necessary money to afford rooms. He had moved each day to a different place, just in case they were trying to zero in on him.

The biggest headache had come with the phone that his uncle Murray had given him to crack. There was a lot on the internet about how to do it, but so far, most of that information had proven either outdated or bogus.

He had gone on the dark web in search of someone who could do it. He found two people who claimed they could do it, but both required Bitcoin deposits. As much as he touted himself as a cyber-whiz, it was more bravado than reality. He had to Google buying Bitcoin and how to do transfers. He found the information more confusing than useful.

If I had been making the kind of money I deserved, I would have gotten into Bitcoin early on. It was these alt-righters who held me back.

That left him with the unwelcome task of telling his uncle that he couldn't break into the phone. Rather than admit he lacked the skills or tools, Percy opted for an easier path. He came up with a well-crafted lie. To him, it wasn't really bad. No one would be hurt with his lie, which made it okay. It wasn't even really a lie, just a stretching of the truth. In Percy's tiny universe, it justified what he would say to his uncle.

As he returned from McDonald's to the Motel 6, his phone chirped. He set down the bag, muttering. His food was going to get cold. When he saw his uncle's number, his heart raced.

He's probably calling about the phone! He prepared to serve up his dish of mistruths.

"Hello?" he said as he picked up.

"Percy. Listen up."

He was overanxious. "Look, if it's about the phone—"

"Percy, shut up and listen. My buddy Jack Hawthorne was killed last night."

"I—uh, wow. I mean, I'm sorry to hear that."

"Percy, pay attention. I don't think that Jack just wrecked his car. He was far from his home, where he had no reason to be. I think someone killed him."

Those words shook Percy deeply. "Killed, as in murdered?"

"Listen up, Percy. I took care of one of Weldon's thugs, but this means there may be more of them."

Panic gripped him. Percy's heart pounded. He got up and locked his door as he held the phone tight to his ear. "M-more of them? What are we going to do?"

They will be coming for me. I'm the brains behind all of this.

"You are going to stay on the lam while I work this out."

"What are you going to do?"

"That isn't your concern. I need you to stay focused. Have you gotten that phone cracked yet?"

He wanted to blurt out his lie. That it wasn't possible. That events were unraveling. "I—no, I haven't been able to."

"Look, whatever is on the phone might save both our asses. Stop fucking around and take care of it." It wasn't a request; it was an order.

"Don't worry, Uncle Murray. I'll handle it."

"You better. This is all *your* fault, Percy, and because of you, I got dragged into this shitstorm."

"What are you going to do?"

"Don't you worry about that. If this Weldon chick and her people were involved with Jack's death, I intend to make them pay."

Chapter 32
The Plan

Braxton had purchased a can of flat black spray paint and had touched up the grill push bar on the Crown Vic from where he had nudged Hawthorne off the road. There had been a small mark on it, and he wanted to make sure there was nothing that might link him to Hawthorne's accident.

As he double-checked his work, his mind was already racing ahead. There were more players involved in the Higby matter than he had expected. Percy definitely deserved the kind of justice that he delivered, as did his uncle, Murray.

What of Percy's accomplices? This Gump and Shatterstorm persons are just as guilty as Percy. They pounced on Mr. Higby at Percy's insistence. Taking out Percy will still leave them to move on to their next target. That's the problem with these keyboard warriors. They never face repercussions for their actions.

One thing that bothered him about Percy was not just his online enablers, but those that enabled him to wreck people's lives. Percy was a little man. He couldn't even hold down a job that allowed him to live on his own.

What kind of parent coddles their kid into his thirties like that? No doubt she had given him his computer, she paid his internet bill, cooks his meals, cleans his clothes...she makes it possible for him to be an online shithead.

Percy's mom needed to be reckoned with as well.

Once he was satisfied with his paint job, he capped and tossed the paint into the trash. Braxton was struggling with another concept, which was all about Higby. Administering justice wouldn't really help him. The damage was already done. *He's lost his business, his employees lost their jobs, and he lost his wife and livelihood.* Thinking about Higby's wife leaving him made him love his own departed wife even more. *Suzanne stuck with me when the shit hit the fan. Higby never got that kind of support from his wife.* No matter what, he needed to be compensated for what he lost. *We can't replace his wife, but maybe give him a chance to rebuild.*

Returning to Ronin's room, he saw both Ro and Faye working on their computers. It was good to see Faye writing again. The attack on her had shaken her.

Ronin pushed himself away from his screen, and looked over at Braxton. "We were talking while you were gone."

"About what?"

"What's your plan?"

"I'm thinking."

"And?" Faye asked. "You must have some idea. I remember how you set the stage at your cabin. You're all about plans. You think things through."

"First, we need to relocate. There's a La Quinta six miles from here. I made us reservations there. One thing we can assume is that they know that I was at the Red Roof Inn. Moving will leave them in the dark."

"That makes sense," Faye said. "I may need some help with my bag."

"No problem," Ronin assured her.

"Taking out Hawthorne will shake Murray," Braxton said. "He can either retreat, or go on the offensive. When you push people, make them afraid…they make mistakes. That's what I'm thinking."

"Go on," Ronin said.

"Percy needs to feel more pressure. He's on the run. So we prune his support system more. This Shatterstorm and Gump guys that play this little game with him, they need to be hit. We need to do it in a way that they get word to Percy—ratchet up his fear. He needs to feel real-world pressure, not that online bullshit. Are you able to pin down where these guys live?"

Ronin grinned. "Already done, chief."

"Good. I want Percy sweating, looking over his shoulder."

"My main contact that I use to pin down IP address physical locations is still out of pocket."

Braxton nodded. "Not a problem. If you can't find him, I can make him come to us."

"How?" Faye inquired.

"He's a momma's boy. He's reliant on her. Sooner or later, he's going to go home." Braxton knew the type from students he used to teach. A lifetime of participation ribbons and trophies had eroded many of their desire for independence. Their parents reinforced their weaknesses by continuing to give them money, shelter, or both.

"So, where do we start?" Ronin asked.

"What about Gump227. His name's Fitzsimmons, right?"

"Yeah. Walter Fitzsimmons." Ronin tapped his fingers furiously on the keyboard and pulled up several files. "He lives on Gatewood Drive in Greenwood, just south of the city. Nice neighborhood, a hell of a lot nicer than where Percy parks his ass. Graduated from Greenwood Community High School. Extracurricular activities were the computer club, and in his yearbook, he got a gag award for being the Most Likely to Play D&D on a Saturday Night."

"A real ladies' man," Braxton said.

"Yeah. He went to Ivy Tech Community College and got his admin degree in computer science. His parents divorced and his mother moved out of state. Daddy is a lawyer with a medium-sized firm downtown. I found a few civil lawsuits. Walter apparently had an issue with balancing his checkbook. His online accounts, almost a dozen, are all harassment accounts. He didn't do a good job of hiding them."

"So much for the community college computer science degree," Faye said.

"He's living in his dad's house. Daddy remarried—someone just four years older than Walter."

"This is like Bill's character from *Bill and Ted's Excellent Adventure*," Braxton said.

"You're not wrong about that. He's got a car, a 2000 VW Beetle."

"Does he have a job?"

"He works at Target. Night shift, stocking shelves."

"Another community college endorsement," Faye said.

Braxton crossed his arms. Confronting Fitzsimmons at home, in a nice neighborhood filled with Ring door cameras, wasn't desirable. Best to get him at work. "Can you see if the employee parking area at Target has cameras?"

"I'll drive over there and check. I'm guessing not. These big box stores only really care about the customers ripping them off. They will most likely have cameras on the inside of their loading docks to track their employees there, but the parking lot will be heavy on monitoring potential shoplifters."

"You know, sometimes it bothers me that you know this kind of stuff," Braxton said.

Ronin beamed. "I'm a walking repository of arcane knowledge."

"Like your mysterious benefactor?"

Ronin's patron was a major Big Tech player, presumably on the west coast. He never named him.

Ronin waved his finger. "Nice try. Yes, he's a big help, but he keeps himself at arm's length from this kind of stuff. He hates the woke as much, if not more, than we do."

"Is there a firearm registered to that house?"

"I don't have access to that data. Remember, a lot of gun ownership in this country isn't registered. Someone dies in your family, you take their gun, and it doesn't get registered. Even if I had access to the ATF's database, it wouldn't be an accurate source."

Ronin's right. That just means we must always presume that our targets are armed.

Braxton turned to Faye. "How far along is your article?"

"First draft is done. I need to do some polish on it. Why?"

"I don't want to make a play against this Fitzsimmons character until you've submitted it."

"Why?"

"The police might try to connect us to what happened to Hawthorne. They might think that it's somehow tied to your article. Police investigators look for connections. If the article isn't finished, they might think that was all a ruse for us coming to town and taking out these people. If your story is submitted and published, we simply look like tourists, hanging around Indy to take in some sights while you recover. We can't have you flying while your ribs are as bad as they are."

"So I have to sit this out?"

"Not entirely," Braxton replied. "I need something from you, something that you are best suited to do."

"What's that?"

"Percy's death needs a purpose, one that sends the right message. If I just kill him, it invites investigation and possible arrest. Percy's demise needs to be a thing where he decides to end his own life out of guilt. Something that shows the whole world that he was mentally unstable, and that everything he did was wrong."

"What do you need from me?"

"A manifesto. A glorious admission of guilt, implicating his friends. A confession that what he did to Mr. Higby was wrong. You're a writer, which means you're best for that task."

"I usually don't write fiction," Faye countered.

"Percy is never going to admit he was wrong. It's not part of the makeup of these social justice warrior–types. If he had a conscience, or a soul, this manifesto is what he would write. I think you're up to it. With that, the police will have no reason to come looking for us."

Faye rose, wincing slightly. "You consider all of the angles, don't you?"

"I study things. I guess that's one thing the Army taught me: the importance of continuous learning. Understanding police procedures allows us to keep them at bay. We are extracting justice, and those that see themselves as the sole proprietors of that role will do whatever it takes to hold on to that kind of power. Vigilantes pose a threat to law enforcement. If such a movement were to be known, there might be others that choose the path we have. They have always come down on vigilantes. Look at Wyatt Earp, or Bernie Goetz, the subway shooter. Not long ago, Daniel Perry, a Marine, choked a man who threatened the lives of everyone in a subway car. What did they do to him? They charged him with negligent homicide. The man was a hero, but the crazies cast him as the villain in the story. Bottom line, the media will roast us alive if we are exposed. We will be painted as extremists and far worse. The establishment will come down on us because we represent a threat to their power."

Braxton sighed, then continued. "I know our focus is on taking down the woke, but in reality, we are a destabilizing element to the powers-that-be. We are the embodiment of people who take the law in our own hands because the justice system is so hopelessly broken. Our enemy isn't just the woke, it's the legal system that enables them to ruin other people's lives."

Chapter 33
Bohemian Rhapsody

Murray waited on the main concourse just before TSA. It was three-thirty. He'd been standing around for a half hour as travelers crowded McDonald's, Cinnabon, Gifts and Panda Express. The mixture of aromas from the food court made his stomach growl. A woman carried a pet carrier with a miniature Yorkie inside that yipped as she passed. Murray wanted a cigarette. He was just about to go outside when Palmer appeared at the top of the escalator. Even with sunglasses and a hat, he was easy to recognize. The military bearing, the leather satchel over his shoulder.

He needed help. If one of Weldon's goons killed Jack, he might be next.

Or worse, what if they go after Percy and my sister gets attacked?

Things had been escalating and experience told him he needed a professional.

Murray waved. Palmer looked away and frowned. Murray waited for him at the bottom of the escalator.

"Do you have any luggage?"

"Just what I'm carrying. Let's go somewhere quiet and talk."

There was no crowd at Auntie Anne's Pretzels. Murray bought them coffee, then they sat at a table inside the rail as travelers pushed by.

"Do you have the money?"

Murray looked around, removed an envelope from his cargo pants pocket, and discreetly opened it under the table. Palmer took it and counted.

"That'll do. Tell me about the guy."

"Harold Callahan."

Palmer grinned mirthlessly. "Harold Callahan."

"You know him?"

"I know *Dirty Harry*. Are you sure that's his name?"

Murray felt like an idiot. "No. But I have his driver's license and pictures. He came to my VFW looking for me. The boys didn't give him shit. They got this off the security camera." He handed over the driver's license and the blurry photo.

Palmer turned the ID over and inspected it. "If it's fake, it's the best I've seen. All right. Give me all the details. Who all's involved?" For the next twenty minutes, Murray recited how his nephew Percy was an online cancel pig targeting anyone with whom he disagreed. He talked about the confectioner. He told how Faye Weldon had come to town to interview him, how Percy had implored Murray to put the fear of Yahweh into her, how he'd enlisted Jack. It was especially difficult to relate the circumstances of their drowning. Then there was Hawthorne's death. Murray knew that someone had chased him down and run him off the road. Palmer wrote everything down on a little lined pad he pulled from his shoulder bag.

"So you killed this Callahan? You're sure?" There was a casualness in his question that spoke to Palmer's icy professionalism.

He nodded. "There was no way he slipped those knots. He's fish food, for sure…he has to be." Murray glanced around to make sure no one was in listening distance to his confession.

"Which means he has friends. And you're positive that your buddy just didn't crash his car?"

"Jack was a drinker, but he's always been solid driving after he drinks. He had no business on that road at that hour. Someone chased him there; I'd put money on it. They must have run him off the road."

"You are. When I get to Minneapolis, I'll do a deep dive into this mess. Pretty sure I can figure out who your mystery man is. I'll return to Indianapolis on Saturday. Understand this, I won't contact you. I'll take care of the contract and leave town. I will text you how to make the rest of the payment. You will make the payment within twenty-four hours or I'll come back here."

Murray was close to panicking. "Rest of the payment?! Man, that's fifty thousand dollars! I thought you said that was your fee!"

"It *was* my fee until I found out you don't know anything about the man you want me to kill. Now I have to do homework and legwork. That will cost you another twenty-five thou."

Murray cringed at the number. There was only one other source he could dip into for that kind of cash. His wife had an expensive diamond necklace she'd inherited from her mother. She'd kept it in a jewelry box at the top of the bedroom closet along with her other jewels. After her death, he had thought about pawning it, but had held back. Murray would have to take the necklace, and perhaps one or two other keepsakes, and cash them in. He knew a pawn shop, but they only paid a quarter of what the item might be worth retail.

According to his former sister-in-law, it was a two-carat blue valued at over a hundred thousand dollars. His wife's sister had told him and asked about it. If she came around again, he'd tell her that it was stolen. He doubted she would believe it. She'd been threatening to sue him to get it, and she was the kind of person who would do that. Complication after complication. He weighed the risks. The risk of whoever had been working with Callahan coming after him next was too great. He had to do it.

"I can get you the money, but I need more time. My only assets are my wife's jewelry. They're worth a lot but I have to find a buyer and I can't exactly advertise on Craig's List. I got the fifty thou selling my Peyton Manning rookie card. Fortunately, I know a wealthy collector who was willing to pay full price. Jewelry's different. I don't know anyone who would pay what it's worth which means I have to find a pawnbroker who will give me a fair shake. It's worth a lot more than you're asking."

Murray stopped. He looked up.

"Would you like the necklace? It's a two-carat blue diamond. It's worth at least a thirty thousand dollars, probably a lot more."

Palmer made a face. He sighed. "Do I look like that bald dude on Pawn Stars? This is why I don't like dealing with amateurs. I deal with cash money, not barter."

"How will you find him?"

"He's working with this Faye Weldon, right? There are ways. I have contacts who can gain access to pretty much any database in the world. They can do it to the Pentagon and a few other three-letter agencies. I've used them before. Hiring me means you get the benefit of my resources."

"Aren't you concerned that they'll betray the United States? We both served."

Palmer laughed. "This isn't the same country we served, Landreth. I don't know who this government represents, but it's certainly not guys like you and me. Don't worry about it. They won't touch the Pentagon."

"Callahan might have been a vet. Is that going to be a problem?"

Palmer peered at him, forehead wrinkled. "You may have stumbled across some useful information. I take back what I said. Yeah, I'd like to know about his record." He glanced at his watch. "Well, that's it. Gotta go. I have your contact info. You won't hear from me until it's done. You'll probably find out about it before I have a chance to call you. Do whatever you have to do to scrape up that twenty-five. I'll be in touch."

Palmer hefted his carry-on and trooped back to security. Murray wondered if the TSA felt up his crack every time he flew, like they did to him. Murray heaved himself to his feet and walked to outdoor parking lot number three. Outside the main gate, he waded through the usual jockeying of people dropping off. It was the same on the pickup level. Airport employees in day-glow vests moved up and down the line warning people that unless they were actively dropping people off, unless they saw people getting out of the vehicles and fetching their luggage, they had to move.

A man said, "It will only be a minute! She's on her way."

"Sir," the pissant enforcer said, "this is the drop-off lane. You want the pickup lane. You have to exit the airport, take the loop, and come back."

"Can't I just phone her and tell her where I am? She's on her way."

"No, you have to leave. Leave now, or I'll issue a citation."

Cursing under his breath, the man chirped his tires.

Murray walked to outdoor lot number three, beeped open the door, started the engine, and joined the line of motorists waiting at the one checkout gate that was open. At least there was a human being at the window. She charged him five-fifty for his hour stay. He merged with the highway and headed home. He turned on the radio.

"Mama, just killed a man—put a gun against his head, pulled my trigger, now he's dead—"

He changed the station.

Chapter 34
Restitution

Ronin confirmed that the employee parking lot at the Target where Walter Fitzsimmons worked did not have cameras. Braxton parked behind the Dick's Sporting Goods next door and walked over the berm blocking the view of the rear of the store to the neighborhood behind it. The next shift came in at ten p.m. He settled in with a pair of binoculars, watching for Walter.

Walter arrived five minutes prior to work in a light blue Volkswagen Beetle. He didn't look like a keyboard terrorist. Braxton expected him to be pudgy and out of shape. Fitzsimmons was not exactly athletic, but not out of shape either. He was about five feet, two inches. He wore a red Target shirt. No acne, nothing repulsive. Braxton was disappointed. Fitzsimmons was just another face in the crowd. The only thing that hinted at geekdom was his black-rimmed eyeglasses.

Ronin joined Braxton a few minutes later, after Walter entered the rear of the store. "Did you see him?"

"Yeah. Not what I pictured."

"His high school photo made him look darkish."

"He's normal-looking."

"You sound disappointed."

"I am. I imagined Dan Levy."

"Bad guys come in all shapes and sizes."

Braxton lowered the binoculars. "We have some time before his shift is done. There's a Denny's nearby. Let's grab coffee."

"How do you intend to confront him?"

"By being friendly," Braxton replied. He pulled out his Karambit knife and grinned broadly.

* * *

At the end of Walter's shift, Braxton was in the employee parking lot. Employees trickled out. Walter went to his car, looked down, and began to curse. Braxton sauntered up. "What's wrong?"

Walter kicked the tire. "Flat tire."

"You need help with the spare?"

"Ugh. This shit always happens to me. I think I have one. I don't know. I've never changed a tire before."

"Let's take a look," Braxton said, eyes sweeping to make sure they were unobserved. He squatted. "Looks like someone slashed it."

Walter knelt. "Son of a bitch! Who would do that?"

Braxton pulled his Beretta. "I did."

Fitzsimmons's eyes popped. "Whatever you want, you're welcome to it." He started fumbling for his wallet.

"Hands where I can see them," Braxton said softly.

Fitzsimmons nodded. "I don't want any trouble. I won't resist."

"Put your hands in front of you, wrists together." The young man complied and Braxton tied them together tightly with a zip tie he had brought along. "You're going to stand slowly and we are going to walk behind Dick's to my car."

"Look," Walter sputtered. "My dad has money. He's got a stash at the house. I can show you where it is. Just don't hurt me."

Braxton turned him, then nudged him with the Beretta. He had lost his Glock to Jack and Murray. "Less talk, more walk." When they arrived at the car, Braxton did a full pat down on Walter, pulling his phone and wallet. He pushed Walter into the back seat, blindfolding him with a strip of dark cloth he had cut from a sweatshirt. Fitzsimmons trembled, providing Braxton with some satisfaction as he sat behind the wheel next to Ronin.

"Where are we going?"

"A ride in the country." He fired up the Crown Vic and pulled out. He knew this particular road a little too well. Driving past the

Loaf & Jug, turning down a dirt road, stopping at a pond. The clouds blotted out the moon and stars. The sun would come up soon, but in the last few hours before the dawn, it was pitch-black.

He parked the vehicle, got out, and pulled Fitzsimmons from the back seat. Manhandling him roughly, he forced him out on the dock, then spun him so the blindfolded man was facing him.

"My dad is a lawyer, he has money!" Walter exclaimed. "I'm worth more to you alive than dead. Let me make a phone call."

"What's the passcode on your phone?" Braxton asked.

"One, one, A, two, B."

Ronin chuckled and Braxton looked at him. Ronin shrugged. "It's part of Kirk's self-destruct code for the starship Enterprise." It was clear that Ronin actually admired that bit of geekdom. It was a reference that Braxton understood too.

"Alright. So, Wally, let me show you where you are."

He tore away the mask. Walter looked around, facial expression of sheer terror. "Where are we?"

"The middle of nowhere." Braxton turned him around so that he was looking out past the end of the dock.

"I—I'll get you whatever you want!" Walter's wobbly voice said.

"You don't seem to understand," Braxton said with a menacing tone. "This isn't something that daddy can buy your way out of."

"Wha-what do you want?"

"I want justice."

"I don't understand."

"You are Gump227, aren't you?"

"How do you know that?" He could tell by the change of the tone of Walter's voice that knowing his online identity made him nervous.

"I'll ask the questions, Wally. You and your little friends have a lot of fun at the expense of other people, don't you?"

"I don't—I mean, that was all just fun and games."

"Don't try to deflect your guilt," Braxton said. "One shove in that cold water and you'll drown." He paused. "You, Percy, and Dennis like inflicting misery on innocent people. You ruin them financially, break up families, bankrupt them and the people that worked for them—you're nothing more than an online terrorist."

Walter sniffled. Braxton's allegations were making him cry. "I didn't mean any harm."

Braxton gave him a light shove towards the end of the dock, just enough to make the younger man stiffen. "Yes, you did."

Walter sobbed. "Honest. I didn't mean to hurt anyone."

"Sure you did. Hurting them made you feel like you mattered, maybe for the first time in your life. You had power, and you inflicted it on others. It felt good to you, and you know it. You were a big man on the internet, judging other people with no risk of it ever coming back to you. Well, you're not hiding behind a fake name on the net now. This is the real world. Wally, this is what retribution looks like. Imagine your arms and legs bound, and being thrown in the water. Imagine gasping for air and sucking in cold pond water instead. That's what you deserve. It's what you've earned."

"Please! I won't do it again, I swear!"

Braxton turned him around. He'd pissed himself.

"You have no credibility with me. Your word means nothing. I let you go, and you'll run to daddy then the police. Your type always wants to be the victim."

"I won't!"

Braxton hit him in the cheek, right below his left eye. Fitzsimmons fell down, crying. In that moment, the rage Braxton felt over the loss of his wife and daughter seized him, squeezing hard, crushing his chest and his soul. Then a voice came to him, it was Angela...a memory of the two of them reading *The Fellowship of the Ring*. *"Do not be too eager to deal out death in judgment."* He remembered her reading Gandalf's words out loud. In that moment, his dead daughter spared the life of Walter Fitzsimmons.

"Your buddy Percy. Where's he hiding?" Braxton asked.

"I don't know."

Braxton kicked him in the gut, causing Fitzsimmons to curl up and wail in agony.

"Tell me what you know about Percy."

Wheezing for air, Fitzsimmons said, "Please, I don't know anything about him. He reached out to me on the internet and we tag-teamed a few alt-righters. I didn't mean for anything bad to happen."

Braxton kicked him in the back of the knee. "What you meant to happen and what did are two different things. What's Percy up to now?"

"Hiding. He asked to stay with me, but my dad doesn't allow that. He's on the run, I guess. I really don't know."

Braxton paused, looking down at him. It was tempting to push him into the water and let him drown. He wanted to, but the plan demanded something else. "Wally, you want to live, don't you?"

"Yes! Please…"

"I've come to believe that people need reminders of their past wrongs. It helps you stay on the right path. Our scars define us. Do you understand?"

Walter nodded nervously, but it was clear that he didn't. Braxton took out his tactical knife, locked the blade, and thrust it into Walter's Vans sneaker. The blade went deep into his foot. Fitzsimmons wailed, doubling over, as Braxton pulled it out. Fitzsimmons howled. Braxton wiped the blade on Fitzsimmons's shirt.

"Now you have something to remember. Proof that I'm serious. And I'm not alone. This won't kill you, but if you don't follow my instructions, the next time, you die. It's that simple."

The color drained from Fitzsimmon's face. "I don't want to die."

"Few do. There are some rules you'll have to follow. You break one, and you will never see the bullet that takes you out. Just a bang and red mist. Understood?"

"Anything!"

"Your days of online harassment are over. We're monitoring all your accounts, including the bogus ones. You decide to play social justice warrior again, you are toast."

"I won't. I'll delete them!"

"You've caused a lot of damage to a lot of innocent people. You're going to have to pay restitution to your victims. That demands redemption. You're going to reimburse them for the harm you caused."

"How—how much?"

"How much damage did you do to their lives? Think hard on that. I would think thirty-or-forty K per victim might be a good starting point."

"My dad'll never do that. It's too much."

"Think of it this way. If he actually cares for you and your life, he'll pay. If he balks, ask him how much he's willing to pay for your grave marker instead. And if he gets any ideas about hiring a PI or going to the police to come look for me or my allies, he's going to join you in the ground. Killing a lawyer is something I would savor. Understood?"

"Yes," he managed, then sobbed again.

"You tell no one about us other than Percy. If you decide to tell others, or involve the police, you'll be dead."

"I understand."

"As for Percy, there's a message I want you to pass onto him. Pay close attention, you need to get this right…"

Chapter 35
Doubling Down at the DoubleTree

Wesley Palmer stared at the driver's license for Harold Callahan and waited for a response to his inquiry. His hotel room at the DoubleTree was nice and he enjoyed the terry cloth and microfiber robe they provided. Life had never been this posh when he'd been on active duty. Being in the private sector, raking in the big bucks, made it all worthwhile.

Palmer had gotten back from a stint in Ukraine a month earlier. While the US officially didn't have boots on the ground there, the PMCs (Private Military Contractors) were covertly there, providing training and in-theater "guidance." His grandfather had been a vet from the Cold War and would approve of him killing Russians, even indirectly.

Working for a private military contractor gave him access to a number of resources that normal citizens didn't have. It was a favor-based economy, sometimes requiring a little money to grease a wheel.

Callahan was a puzzle. The ID was legitimate. The address he listed was bogus, an empty lot. While there were a few Harry Callahans in the US, none of them matched the man from Murray's ID. It was a fake identity. In his line of work, people that had such things did so for a simple reason. They wanted to protect their real lives. That meant they had things they cherished and/or people they loved. Both things were potential targets to a man like Palmer.

Callahan had two licenses. He reported one lost right after receiving it. In the post-COVID world, they issued a replacement online.

This guy is smart, a planner. He thinks through contingencies. Such people are usually dangerous.

The Red Roof Inn offered no useful information. He called and was told that no one by that name or that of Faye Weldon was a guest there. That in itself told him something. If Callahan was dead, he'd still have a room there. The folks at the Red Roof wouldn't know that he was dead or not. That meant he might very well be alive, despite the assurance that he had gotten from Murray that he was dead.

His encrypted chat came to life.

```
What can I do for you, Sandstorm?
```

His fingers were a blur:

```
I sent you an image. Can you crunch it with
some facial recognition magic?
```

```
You know I'm not supposed to do this.
```

Wesley grinned and typed his response:

```
You weren't supposed to cheat on your wife
during our last tour of duty either. Come on,
be a brother one more time.
```

```
You are such a dick. Stand by.
```

It took ten minutes, during which he refreshed his coffee. Then it came up.

```
Here you go. Don't do this ever again or I
will make sure the IRS audits your skinny ass.
```

It was a threat he respected. He thanked his buddy at the Defense Intelligence Agency with a promise of a bottle of scotch, then turned to the files. The image matched several photos of one Braxton Knox. Knox had cut the hair, but it was hard to not see the similarities in earlobes, chin, and eye-spacing. The ears always gave a man away.

A search of Braxton Knox was revealing. The target of ANTIFA and the Justice Department, Knox was a veteran who had lost his job over personal pronoun misuse.

Well, that's bullshit on a stick.

He actually found himself admiring this Knox guy for taking a stand against such idiocy. Knox lost his wife in a car accident and his daughter to a botched FBI raid of his home on civil rights violations.

The more he read, the more intrigued he became. The college that fired Knox settled a lawsuit with him, as did the Department of Justice. While the exact dollars were not published, he had to imagine that Knox was wealthy as a result of that.

Knox was no slouch. The man had a PhD and was a history professor before he'd had his job and reputation ripped away from him. He tried to find accomplices, allies that might also be in Indianapolis who would have killed Hawthorne in retribution for Knox's death, but he found nothing. As far as the internet was concerned, he disappeared weeks ago.

Palmer found a connection to Faye Weldon almost by accident. He had gotten a lot of the details about Knox from a story that she had written about his case. That solved one question as to how they were connected.

Why is he out here with her? Is it possible they are romantically involved?

Searching Weldon, he found several hard-hitting articles against the woke. Online, she had an army of haters that had come after her, even a few police incidents of violence. Wesley understood her. He had little use for the crazies on the internet too.

I wonder if Murray's nephew harassed her?

He logged it as a reminder on his notepad as something he would have to dig deeper into.

Knox had a father, Grayson. Vietnam vet. During the time his son was being harassed, there had been a shooting at the assisted living home where he lived, but no charges had been filed. Other than Braxton Knox's father, he didn't seem to have any other family.

The man had almost no social media footprint; he couldn't even pin down a phone number or email address. All of this left Palmer with more questions than answers.

Why was someone from Oregon in Indianapolis using a fake ID?

Palmer decided to look into Percy Kornbluth. It looked like the guy spent his nights harassing people. A self-proclaimed social justice warrior. That explained Weldon's interest. Percy was the kind of person whom she would expose. He lived with Murray's sister. Percy was a loser of the highest caliber from what he could see.

What kind of man mooches off his mother and harasses innocent people for fun? Murray is willing to spend a lot of money to help a worthless human being.

Percy existed only to attack others rather than doing something meaningful. For Palmer, such individuals were confusing. He had spent his entire life doing something that required action. He held people in low regard who harassed others on social media.

Using a fake ID and password, Palmer pulled up Braxton Knox's service records. Palmer was unimpressed. He had expected someone with elite skills. What he found was a fellow vet, a typical soldier in almost every regard. Only one reference to him being under fire.

Leaning back in his chair, he ran through what he'd learned. Callahan was Knox. He had gotten a bogus ID to obscure that fact. Knox was friends with the reporter, Faye Weldon. According to Landreth, Knox was dead. Someone killed Landreth's buddy, Hawthorne, presumably someone linked to Knox and Weldon. All of this began when Weldon got Landreth's nephew, Percy, fired.

Chances are slim that Weldon, a reporter, would force Hawthorne off the road. That complicates things. There are people in the mix I haven't identified yet.

Palmer enjoyed knowing who the players were before getting into a fight. Despite his digging, he didn't have what he needed.

Hacking into Weldon's phone was tricky without having the phone itself. Warrants were not easy to get as a private citizen, which, technically, he was. *Charlie Brass over at the NSA should be able to track their unencrypted messages and emails.* Brass owed him a big favor. Brass had been a point of contact for Wesley on a few missions. Palmer had gotten drunk with him one night and he admitted that he'd had an affair with the babysitter, and she had threatened to tell his wife. Palmer, being a comrade in arms, had made that problem disappear. Since then, Brass had been on his leash whenever he needed information that only the NSA could get.

Charlie would complain, tell him that this was the last time he could do this. He would then tell him how hard it was to do without getting caught. Palmer would listen patiently, knowing that, in the end, Charlie would come through.

It might take a few days, but he would soon have access to Faye Weldon's life, then he would learn who he was up against.

Chapter 36
Bravado at La Quinta

They pulled into the La Quinta Inn. "I'm surprised you let him live," Ronin said.

Braxton shrugged. "That was the pond where they tried to kill me."

"I figured."

"My daughter wouldn't have approved of me killing him. In a weird way, she saved him tonight. The way I saw it, Walter is just a bottom-feeder. He pounced on people that Percy sicced him on. Killing him would have been easy. Letting him live gives Percy reasons to be afraid." He thought back to Angela. It made his stomach tighten. "Who knows? Maybe this will be a life-changing event for the kid. Percy—he's an instigator. Walter, he just follows along. Getting a knife in the foot and having your life threatened is a great opportunity to turn your life around."

He'll have a limp for a while, that much is certain.

Braxton wanted to talk about hearing Angela's voice but was unable to form the words.

"That's one of the reasons that I stick with you," Ronin said. "If you were just some serial killer out to kill people with different ideologies, I couldn't help you. You're—thoughtful."

"Don't get all gushy on me. I apply lethal violence when it's needed, that's all. When someone comes at me and those I care about, I make sure they don't do it again."

"Like Hawthorne."

"He and Murray beat the shit out of Faye. Nobody does that—not on my watch."

"I like the idea of having him pay restitution. Do you really think his old man will go for it?"

"He may want to avoid paying, but Wally's fear will make him think otherwise. He's probably spent a big piece of his life paying for his son's failings. Yes, this is pricey, but so is losing your kid's life, or your own. The parents of these woke warriors need to be responsible for enabling their kids. This is as much a wake-up call for his old man as it is Walter."

"He's got a long walk home."

"I did it, soaking wet, beat half to death."

"You didn't have a knife wound in your foot."

"Every step is going to remind him of what happened." Braxton mentally pictured Wally hobbling into the Loaf & Jug.

That clerk is going to be wondering what is going on out at that pond.

"Next on our hit parade is the other kid, Dennis Orm."

"I'll pull up the info on him," Ronin said.

Braxton yawned loudly as he pulled the Crown Vic into the parking lot. "You do that. Right now, I need some shut-eye."

"I hear ya," Ronin replied.

Braxton pulled out his card key for his room. He plopped on the bed, not bothering to pull off his clothes or slide under the bedspread. Sleep came quick.

When he woke, he was stiff. He shaved and showered, inspecting his cuts and bruises. The smaller ones were starting to fade from purple to brown. He changed his bandages. The aches told him he was alive.

Braxton went to Faye's room and rapped on the door. She opened it and smiled. "I take it things went as planned last night."

"In a way. We are using the Fitzsimmons kid to get some money to their victims. He's also going to pass on a message to Percy."

She cocked her head. "You didn't kill him?"

"No. I didn't see the point."

"Good—I hope."

"He got a clear message if he or his dad decided to get the police or anyone else involved."

189

"That's encouraging."

"How did things go on my request?"

"The manifesto? I did a draft. It wasn't as easy as I thought. I write nonfiction. For this, I had to get in the head of some kid who sits around ruining lives because it's fun. It took a while, but I think I captured the essence of what you wanted." She handed him a printout on La Quinta Inn stationary from the tiny business center in the lobby. Braxton reviewed it, trying hard to suppress the urge to critique it as a university professor. Years of being an instructor was ingrained in him. Sentences that could be shortened. Using "that' instead of "who." He suppressed it. Faye knew what she was doing. It was good. Even used some of Percy's slang.

"There's some sloppy grammar in the second paragraph."

"That's deliberate. I went over his Tweets and posts and Reddit. He misspells and misuses words consistently. Assuming this ends up in the hands of the police at some point, I want them to think Percy wrote it."

He handed her back the sheet. "You've made him seem crazy. I like it."

"It wasn't fiction. I pored over his online activity. I portrayed him as he is. He's a textbook narcissist. You see it when he goes after people, then when they respond, he claims he's the victim—as if he had no role in their reaction. All that matters to Percy is a reaction in life, positive or negative. What I did was write a manifesto that embodied him and his thinking."

"Obviously, we need this on something other than La Quinta letterhead."

"That's all they had in the business center. I'll get you something more generic."

Ronin rapped on the door. Faye let him in. Ronin yawned and stretched, shaking off sleep. "Well, that was an interesting night."

"It was different," Braxton said.

"I ran some routines this morning. Our boy Fitzsimmons just terminated all of his social media accounts."

"So he found his way home."

"And probably the hospital."

Braxton wanted to smile but didn't. "Hopefully, he passed our message onto Percy. Did you get anything from his phone?"

"I'm monitoring his email. He sent your message to Percy about an hour ago."

"What was the message?" Faye asked.

"Something to frighten him," Braxton said. "Percy sucked his uncle and Hawthorne into his shit. They tried to kill me. Percy needs to know I'm coming for him. I'll whittle away his support, then I will take him out."

Faye cracked a sly grin. "Just what we need. Some good old-fashioned toxic masculinity."

"So, Dennis Orm?" Ronin said.

"Dennis Orm," Braxton confirmed. "What are we dealing with?"

"He's still pretty active on the internet, at least as of last night. He posted a diatribe about the author they've been harassing, Burton Walsh. They claim he's a white supremacist because his last books didn't have any persons of color in them. Oh, he's also a Nazi."

Big surprise, everyone they hate is a Nazi.

"As a historian, I hate when people misuse that word. *They're* the Nazis."

Faye jotted down the author's name. "I take it you have a profile on this guy, Ro."

"Yup. He's a homebody. Lives with his mom. He has a lot of internet security, but nothing I couldn't overcome. That makes him smarter than Percy and Walter."

"No sign of Walter tipping him off?"

"Nope. I'm sure Walter is still trying to process what happened last night."

Faye's phone rang. She picked it up. "New information? Sure…" She looked at Ronin and Braxton. "I'm at the La Quinta Inn, room two-fifteen." Faye hung up and slowly put the phone on the tiny table.

"Problem?" Braxton asked.

"Officer Hernandez. She wants to swing by. She says she has some new information."

"Hawthorne's dead. She may have some questions."

"Maybe you two should vacate the room."

"I think it's best for us to stay. I don't think it looks good for us if we aren't here. It's like we have something to hide."

"Um, we do," Ronin said.

"Hernandez doesn't know that."

* * *

Hernandez arrived twenty minutes later. If Braxton and Ronin's presence surprised her, she didn't show it. "Thanks for seeing me. I'm on my lunch break."

"Have you found the men that attacked me?" Faye said.

"That man you mentioned, Jack Hawthorne, he died two nights ago."

"How?" Ronin asked.

"Car accident. His blood alcohol level was very high. His car went off the road."

"Did you find anything that might implicate him in my attack?" Faye said.

"Not yet. In fact, other than you dropping his name, that's the only connection we have to your case."

"His name came up when we started asking around about Faye's assault," Braxton said. "We were hoping you could shed some light on him."

"I asked around where I thought he might hang out, but no one seems willing to talk. I was hoping you might be able to tell me who dropped his name to you."

Faye shrugged. "I should have written down his name."

"I would have thought a reporter would have done that."

"I just had my ribs broken. I wasn't operating at my usual level of efficiency."

"I see. Well, unfortunately, with Hawthorne dead, it limits how much digging I can do."

"Is there going to be a funeral?" Braxton asked.

"I don't know. I assume so. Why?"

"Just curious. Faye was attacked by two men. If Hawthorne was involved, then his accomplice might show up and pay his respects."

"There's only so much time my sergeant is going to allow me to poke around this case. I'm sorry, that's how it works in terms of priorities."

"I understand," Faye replied.

Hernandez started for the door, then turned. "Does that Crown Vic out there belong to one of you?"

Braxton nodded. "Yeah, it's mine."

"Former cop car," she said, with a hint of coyness in her voice.

"That's why I bought it. Big-ass engine, great suspension, and they're always well maintained."

"The older ones are more reliable," Hernandez said. "You could really run someone off the road in one of those."

"I wouldn't know. I guess that's possible."

Hernandez opened the door and left the room.

Chapter 37
Heisted Hard Drives

Dennis Orm lived with his mother in an older, post-Victorian house. The wrought iron fence was covered with vines. The small front yard had dead spots under the oak trees. It was painted a dark green with white trim, probably quaint ten years earlier when the paint was put on. Now it just looked tired and worn, like many of the other houses in the neighborhood. The chances of cameras were slim.

Braxton and Ronin had driven by before sunset and parked around the corner. They could see Orm's house and soaked in every detail. The home they parked in front of was abandoned, a heap of plastic-wrapped newspapers piled on the front stoop. Watching Orm's house, Braxton saw a few lights on.

"Any evidence he's there?"

"I'm waiting for him to make another post. He's trying to mask his IP address. Once he posts, I should be able to confirm that he's there." Ronin had determined that Dennis didn't own a registered firearm, nor did his mother. That didn't mean they were safe. Just because they weren't registered didn't mean there wasn't one in the house.

An hour later, the first-floor lights went out. One of the second-story bedroom lights went on, then went dark. The basement light was still on. Ronin monitored his laptop, washing his face in the dull light from the screen. The windows fogged up. Braxton turned on the car and ran the defroster.

"You think Hernandez suspects something?" Ronin said.

"It wouldn't surprise me. There's a certain pit bull quality to her. This was a simple assault. Normally, the police would move on with this kind of case. She's not a detective, but she's still digging."

"Persistence is a virtue."

"That depends on your perspective."

"Where's our boy Murray?"

Ronin checked. "Still at his house. I think we took away his drinking buddy."

"That little stop and stay at the airport—it's chewing on my nerves."

"In what way?"

"I'm not sure. He wasn't there for a pickup; it was too long of a time. He wasn't dropping off someone either. That's pretty fast."

"I can poke into that later," Ronin said.

Putting pressure on Murray was something he enjoyed.

Murray has got to be concerned with Hawthorne's death.

Percy must have gotten the message from Fitzsimmons and was scared shitless. Braxton felt confident.

Ronin's laptop dinged. "Our boy is posting from that house."

"Let's roll."

Walking fast, Braxton and Ronin went up the steps. Braxton carefully turned the doorknob. It wasn't locked. Slowly pushing the door open, they entered.

"Basement," Braxton whispered. To the right, the stairs went up to the second floor. Ronin moved silently under the stairs to the open basement door, lit from below.

Braxton pulled his backup Beretta out. He had already chambered a round. As his dad had taught him, a gun was pretty worthless if it wasn't ready to fire. The sound of music rose from the basement; it was 38 Special, "Caught Up in You." A tune he knew well. Memories of lip-syncing it in the kitchen with Suzanna had to be held at bay as he focused on the task at hand. The steps were wooden. When he hit the fourth step, it groaned, making him wince. The sound of the music from the basement drowned it out.

Ronin was so close, he almost put his foot next to Braxton's. As Braxton reached the bottom of the stairs, he saw a portly young man facing three large monitors. The one in the center was a curved screen. Two PCs were there, one belching out a green light.

Why would anyone light up the guts of their PC?

There was a life-sized dummy in sci-fi combat gear...*is that from Halo?* Braxton had almost been startled by the mannequin, fearful for a fleeting moment that it might be a real person.

He aimed the Beretta at the back of the chubby man and moved aside to allow Ronin to step down. The song changed to Pat Benatar's "Shadows of the Night." Orm didn't notice. He stared at one of the open windows.

Ronin accidentally nudged a cardboard box on the floor, wincing at his sloppiness.

Dennis Orm didn't turn around. "Mom, you know the rules, you're supposed to yell before coming down here."

Braxton had no doubt there was a good reason he wanted warning. Neither of them spoke.

Slowly, Dennis pivoted his heavily padded gaming chair around and froze when he saw the Beretta aimed at him. The pudgy man had no discernable chin to speak of, only a thick layer of flesh that flowed down from his cheeks and chin to his chest. He had a poorly maintained mustache and tiny beard, the only indication his face ended and his neck began. His black hair was greasy, unwashed for days, slicked back with his fingers. His dark brown eyes were wide open, locked on the Beretta. Braxton doubted he could have identified either him or Ronin, his gaze was so set.

"Who are you? What do you want?"

"Dennis Orm, Shatterstorm02?" Braxton asked.

He nodded in terror.

"Turn the music down," Ronin said.

Dennis pivoted and fumbled with the mouse, turning down Pat Benatar to a decent level. "Whatever you want, you got it. Just don't hurt me," Orm replied, turning the chair to face them.

"You're a pretty busy guy," Braxton said. "Working with Percy and Walter, harassing innocent people, ruining their lives. That must give you a lot of satisfaction."

"Who are you?" Dennis demanded nervously.

Braxton allowed a thin smile. "We're the guys that show up when people like you go too far."

It was clear that Dennis was starting to realize why they were there, and that he was trapped in his own lair. Ronin held his Beretta on him as well. "Look, I didn't mean to do any harm."

"Don't lie to me," Braxton said. "You enjoyed what you did. It was fun for you. The three of you, with your fake accounts, tormenting people because you got your rocks off doing it."

Orm's lower lip trembled. "I did," he sputtered. "I'm sorry. I didn't mean to hurt anyone."

"There you go, lying again. You don't care if you hurt people."

"It was supposed to be fun."

"But it was more than that," Braxton said. "You cost people their jobs, cost others their families. All so you could enjoy internet strangers smashing the like button. Cheering you on."

Dennis held up his sausage-like fingers, spread out as if to deflect a bullet. "I'm sorry! I never thought about it!"

"That's probably the most honest thing you've said so far. Have you been in contact with Percy?"

"CaramelJustice? Yeah, he asked if he could stay here. I didn't reply."

"Do you know where he is right now?"

"No. I don't. I swear."

"As if your word carries any weight with me. Listen up, Denny, I'm a person that administers justice against slimeballs like you. If you can't tell me where Percy is, I'm not sure how much use you are to me."

"I don't know. Percy has gone off-line. It's not like him."

"Denny," he said, stressing the nickname he had given the porky man, "people like you sicken me. You create chaos. You inflict emotional pain. Worse yet, you think it's fun. Frankly, you deserve a bullet between the eyes."

"No..." he said, his pale face going even whiter. "I promise, I won't do it anymore. I'll delete my accounts, all of them. Just don't shoot me...please!"

"I don't trust you," Braxton said. "You'd say anything to get us to leave you here alive."

"I'll do it right in front of you," Dennis replied, looking over his shoulder at the far monitor.

Braxton said nothing for a few moments, letting tension work. He looked at Ronin, "Watch him. When he's done, pull his hard drives."

"My hard drives?" Dennis asked.

"Yeah. Because they have all of your data, every nook and cranny of the internet that you've gone to."

Dennis nervously nuked his accounts. When he finished, Ronin shut down his PCs, took out his small tool pouch, and started to open the PCs. Dennis looked like he was going to throw up. "I built that system from scratch, custom cooling system, top of the line..." he moaned.

Ronin opened it, removing a few screws and jerking the case off. It took him less than two minutes to extract the hard drive. "You'll survive," he muttered as he started to work on the second PC.

Braxton stood between the two, making sure he had Dennis's full attention. "Focus, Denny, focus. You're getting a lucky break. Change your ways, and you live. Continue with the illusion you are somehow making society better with your online bullshit, and I'll kill you. Understood?"

Orm nodded so fast his chins were out of sync.

Ronin finished.

Braxton pointed at Orm's head. "Put your hands on the desktop."

Dennis complied.

"Now spread out your fingers, both hands."

Braxton cleared the chamber on his Beretta and pulled the magazine. He slammed the handle down hard in the center of Dennis's spread hand. Braxton felt the crunch of bones. The blow carried the hate Braxton had for keyboard warriors like Orm. Dennis shrieked like a girl, cradling the shattered hand.

"Keep quiet," Braxton said.

Tears ran down Orm's cheeks. Dennis held his hand upright, two of his fingers curling. A bit of bone poked through his skin, leaving a trickle of blood. Braxton surveyed what he had done and was satisfied. "Now, put the other hand down."

"No, please—"

Braxton brought the gun up and put it on his sweaty temple. "Choose wisely." Even unloaded, the gun was a threat that couldn't be ignored.

Sobbing, Orm slowly placed his hand on the desk. Braxton grabbed his wrist, pushing down hard so he couldn't withdraw, then raised the gun, raining multiple fast blows on Orm's chubby fingers. Dennis tried to jerk his hand back, but Braxton hammered, fast and furious. When he was finished, he let go.

Dennis's face was crimson. Tears poured from his eyes. His right-hand fingers were broken. "Dennis," he said in a low tone. "Calm down. The worst is done. You're not going to go to the police. If anyone asks, your PC fell over and broke your hands. Healing is going to take months. There will be more pain, but you are still alive."

Dennis tried to wipe his tears with his sleeve, but even that movement hurt. "I can't type."

"Well duh," Braxton said. "When you do recover, remember what happened here tonight. You won't harass people any longer. Because if you do, or if you decide to go to the police, you'll be dead."

"You know," Ronin said in a low tone as he packed up the hard drives, "he can still talk."

"Are you saying that I should cut out his tongue?" Braxton said, half joking.

Dennis shook his head. "No! Please! I won't say anything, I swear."

Braxton paused, just to let him perspire more about the threat. "Alright, Denny, you get to keep your tongue." There was a hint of disappointment in his voice. "But if you cross us, all bets are off."

As they headed for the stairs, Dennis's crying started in earnest.

Chapter 38
The Dark Web Debacle

Percy pulled into the parking lot for Advanced Auto as he'd been instructed. He felt like he was living in a spy thriller, rendezvousing with a mysterious person he had found on the Dark Web. He felt like a secret agent, fighting in a war against the alt-right.

"Secret agent man," he sang softly to himself. "Secret Agent man, they've given you a number and taken away your name."

Percy was unable to hack the phone. He *had* found out how to purchase Bitcoin. He transferred money out of his mother's retirement account to get the Bitcoin needed, and transferred that to a professional hacker he'd found on the dark web... Blitzerboy.

Five thousand dollars was a lot, but if it got him the data for his uncle, it was worth it. He transferred the Bitcoin and got confirmation from Blitzerboy, along with meeting instructions. Now he stood under the streetlight, waiting patiently. Blitzerboy was fifteen minutes late. Nervously, Percy looked around. He was alone. Headlights passed, but no one turned in.

He wouldn't rip me off, would he? Percy didn't know who Blitzerboy was in real life; such was the nature of people who did the kind of work he did. *Secret agent man.* As each minute passed, he began to worry that he had been ripped off. From what he had read about Blitzerboy, he was a social warrior, just like Percy.

How could he take my money and not show? We're on the same side, fighting white supremacists.

Minutes passed. Percy paced under the streetlight. His phone rang. He pulled it out. The number was not in his list of contacts. He hadn't given Blitzerboy his phone number, but this was a world-class hacker.

He probably got it on his own.

"Go for Percy," he answered.

"Percy, listen up," Walter Fitzsimmons said, clearly upset.

"Walter. This isn't your usual number."

"Yeah, I know."

"What's up?"

"Just shut up and listen," he said, breathing heavy. "I got visited by two guys. They took me at gunpoint out in the country and beat me up. They were going to kill me, I'm sure of that."

"What two guys?"

"Shut up, Percy!" Walter snapped. "They told me to pass on a message to you. The one in charge said they were coming for you and your uncle. They're going to kill you for what you've done. The leader, a bald guy, said that if you ran, you were just going to die tired."

The words hit Percy like a fist to the gut. He glanced around the parking lot. Percy was no longer looking for Blitzerboy. His eyes pierced the darkness, looking for the two men that Walter had mentioned. "Did you call the police?"

"No. They said if I did, they'd kill me. They told me I needed to pay restitution to the people we were targeting. My dad is furious. He's already confiscated my PCs and cut me off from the internet."

"You're a victim," Percy said. "You need to go to the cops. Let them round these guys up."

"I don't think you get it. If my dad brings in the cops or outside help, he'll end up dead. These guys are serious. I have nine stitches in my foot. They jammed the blade right through."

Percy's heart pounded in his ears. Standing under the parking lot light made him feel exposed.

Who are these guys? My uncle said he dealt with one of them. The Weldon bitch must have a whole bunch of Proud Boys working for her. It wasn't enough that she cost me my job; now she's going after my friends.

"Look, I need all the details about what happened. My uncle can make this go away."

"Fuck you and your uncle!" Walter snapped. "I'm out. I'm never communicating with you again. Do you get it? I've never been so afraid in my life. These guys are going to kill me if I don't do exactly what they said. They walked me out onto a dock and said they'd drown me if I didn't do what they said. You can't protect me. You can't even protect yourself."

"Look, I can make this work. My uncle—"

"Fuck off, Percy." Walter hung up.

Percy returned to his car, nervously looking around. Nothing was going the way he planned. Blitzerboy was a no-show, having already received his Bitcoin transfer. Now Gump227 was telling him there were killers on his trail. Sitting in the driver's seat, he called Uncle Murray.

"What is it, Percy?" Uncle Murray answered.

"This is getting out of control. One of my friends got visited by two guys. They beat him up, threatened to kill him." His words flew out of his mouth, slurred together.

"What are you talking about? Who got beat up?"

"Walter, Walter Fitzsimmons. He's one of my friends. They had him call me, tell me that they're coming for you and me."

His uncle said nothing for a few moments. "Fuck. Two guys, it was two guys?"

"That's what he said. One was bald."

"Fuck me! A bald guy? He said a bald guy?"

"Yeah. Why?"

"Where are you?"

"I'm in a parking lot, waiting for a guy to break the phone you gave me."

"Where are you staying?"

"The Holiday Inn Express near the airport."

"Alright. Head back there as soon as you can. Fuck! I thought we killed that guy. How the hell did he survive?"

"You know the bald guy?"

"That's whose phone you have. Jack and I drowned him."

Callahan was dead; Uncle Murray had told him that. *These guys are killers. That fucking witch reporter has hired a hit squad to go after us.* Terror gripped him. How could he post this on X? *When people find out that I have hired killers stalking me, it will make me a more important figure on the net.*

"What's our plan?"

"I've contacted a professional. He's going to take care of them. I need to let him know that the guy I thought was dead is alive. Sonofabitch, this is going to cost me a fortune. You just sit tight until I tell you otherwise. Get that phone cracked. I need to know who this guy's contacts are."

Percy flinched. He wanted to help his uncle, but didn't want to admit that he had been ripped off and was no closer to breaking into the phone's data. "I'm on it. Trust me."

"Listen, Percy, none of your bullshit on the internet either. These guys mean business."

"Don't worry. You can trust me."

"Pay attention, you fat fuck—when this is over, you are going to need to change your life. This shit has gotten way out of hand, and it's all your fault."

Percy heard what his uncle was saying, but he was more concerned with getting back to his hotel safely.

I always knew that the right-wing extremists were dangerous. I'll expose them all for what they are doing!

Starting the car, he imagined the interview that he'd be giving MSNBC after his uncle dealt with these murderers.

This is my shot at fame!

Chapter 39
Eyes on Targets

Wesley Palmer pulled his brand-new used Silverado into the parking lot of the La Quinta Inn and shut off the engine. He never rented. He paid cash and drove it from Minneapolis. Instead, he went online and found a beater and paid the owner cash. It ran and reeked of cigarette smoke. Those were its good qualities. He'd abandoned the car he'd gotten to Indianapolis with.

In the rear seat, under a blanket, was a used M&P 9 he'd purchased from a fellow contractor. He had been assured that the gun had never been used in a crime and it had been written off in a house fire by a previous owner. The Mossberg shotgun that was also in the back seat was a purchase from an estate sale. Palmer wanted to avoid a paper trail if things went south and law enforcement got involved.

When he had been in the Army, he had spent plenty of time in OPs (observation posts), staking out possible targets. While he hated the stench of Marlboros, he'd smelled worse back in the sand.

The hotel's placement was a mystery. It was along I-70 right at the beltway, I-465. It wasn't near anything. The parking lot backed up to cornfields. The corn was three feet high, the first planting of the spring. Anyone staying there had to drive a few miles to get to food or anything else they might need. His eyes surveyed the ground for cover.

The corn would be good for concealment, but there's nothing around here to provide hard cover.

His buddy at the NSA, Charlie Brass, couldn't get him access to Faye Weldon's phone. It pissed off Palmer; he had been counting on

Charlie giving him full access to Weldon's phone and thus, her life. Charlie apologized up the ass, but it still made Wesley angry.

Charlie got him a spyware app the Agency used that would allow him to determine its location. That had led him back to Indianapolis and the La Quinta Inn. It was better than nothing.

Wesley's plan was to find Weldon and observe the people with her. This was a game of sorts, and he wanted to know all the players before he acted. Sliding back in the torn driver's seat, he lowered his Army ball cap and watched the side door near where Weldon's phone pinged. He wore gloves so as to not leave fingerprints in the old truck.

Hours passed. People came and went. None of them were Weldon. He took pictures just in case. He ate a protein bar.

It was at thirteen-fifty hours when Weldon came out. She wore an unbuttoned flannel shirt over a plain black T-shirt. Wesley snapped her picture. Right behind her came a man wearing a hoodie, in his thirties, with a day's growth of stubble, and glasses. Wesley took several zoomed in photos of his face.

A third figure came out and Palmer knew him instantly.

Braxton Knox!

Murray had assured him that Harold Callahan/Braxton Knox was dead. As he snapped two photos of Knox, he knew that Murray had blown it.

How do you fuck up a drowning?

Wesley's mind danced with the new information as the trio walked to a flat black ex-police Crown Victoria. For Knox to have survived, maybe his military record was wrong—deliberately.

Is it possible that he was Special Forces? Did they doctor his service records to cover it up?

It would explain how he had the skills to survive. Palmer's own service record hid things as well. Ops he'd run and who the targets were. Unless you read between the lines, you might think he was just a Special Forces operator.

Knox drove. Wesley followed at a discreet distance. They drove to a Culver's. Wesley had eaten there before. *Home of the Butter Burger.* He parked at the Taco Bell next door and watched.

Three opposing players total. One unknown, Braxton Knox, and Faye Weldon. He would need to get a facial recognition scan on the unknown male. That, or he could just take them out. *Do I really need the intel beyond this? If Weldon had other people working for her, wouldn't they be here too?*

He ran through scenarios. Planting an IED on the Crown Vic might work, but he might not get all of them. From where he sat, he could pull one of his rifles, line up a shot, and fire. The first shot would be the best. After that, they would start diving for cover. He was fairly sure that Taco Bell had security cameras, though, and a mass shooting at a Culver's was going to draw a lot of attention. While the truck wasn't easy to trace, there was a good chance they'd ID it from footage and then there would be problems.

If he took them out, he wanted to do it from a distance. The best place might be at the La Quinta. While the parking lot had cameras, it backed up against that cornfield. Callahan's car was easy to spot. Who else would drive a used police Crown Vic? Access was a winding country road from the highway exit a mile away. There would be a lack of witnesses and zero chance of showing up on camera footage.

I could set up a sniper post in the corn, shoot at them when they're outside and exposed.

It wasn't the most desirable place, but it would be efficient.

I would have to position the truck on the access road, so I can get to it easily after I take them out.

That left the question—*do I continue to follow them, or go back and stage my ambush?* These kinds of side jobs were the ones he liked to finish as quickly as possible. The payment in cash was mildly problematic. Palmer's sister owned a string of laundromats that he had invested in, and she helped him launder cash into usable income. It would take a few months before he could enjoy the full proceeds from this job, but it would be worth it.

Wesley made his decision as he watched them eat their meal in the booth near the window.

I'll go back, set up, and take them out when they return. I'll tell Murray that I need another ten thou to cover killing Knox for good. I won't tell him in advance, only after the fact. I'll even give him the pictures to prove it. He'll bitch, but he'll pay. After all, I'm cleaning up his mess.

Three shots, three dead. Easy peasy, lemon squeezy...

Chapter 40
The Sniper

Ronin pushed his blue tray off to the side and replaced it with his laptop.

"What now?" Faye said.

"After what you said earlier, I'm now concerned about Murray's visit to the airport," Ronin said.

"The question is why," Braxton said.

The server/bus lady came over. "Can I interest you in anything else?"

"Just the check, please," Braxton said.

They waited until she walked away. Braxton put a hand to his face.

"He was meeting somebody."

"Who would he be meeting?" Faye said.

"A hired gun."

"Oh no."

"I know how this guy thinks. He's in a tight spot. He knows we're coming for him. His drinking buddy is dead. The question is, how would he even know such a person?"

"Well," Ronin said, "he was in the military."

"Where are you looking?"

"Well, he was at the airport from 2:45 until 4:15. During that time, over four thousand passengers arrived at the terminal. They get about fifteen thousand a day. A lot are there for layovers, you know, connecting flights. I accessed their flight data for the time period, eliminated foreign nationals, women, or people using regional airports, or those arriving from exotic places."

"How'd you do that?"

"Indianapolis Airport Authority. A lot easier than penetrating the TSA."

"Kind of arbitrary," Braxton said.

Ronin shrugged. "Several thousand remained. I limited my search to military veterans. Two hundred and twelve veterans passed through the airport that day. I then narrowed it to veterans who worked as contractors. Nada. Which means if Murray did meet an assassin who had military experience, he has other experience as well. Like not getting caught."

"No suspects?" Fay said.

Ronin held up a finger. "So I accessed the security cameras in the main concourse. It wasn't hard to locate Murray. He always wears that same coat. I found him at the base of the escalators leading to security in the main concourse."

Ronin poked, placed the laptop against the booth wall so that Braxton and Faye could take a look. "See him?"

"Yeah."

"Okay, watch. Minutes later, a tall man carrying a leather overnighter descended the escalator wearing a dark blue sports jacket and a Yankees cap pulled low over his face. He walked up to Murray, they spoke briefly, then headed for the exit."

"That's our guy," Braxton said. "Nice work."

"Well, wait a minute. The hat and shades made him difficult to pin down. So I looked at all flights that landed in the forty-five minutes leading up to this. There are security cameras on the concourses. I programmed the ID to look for the hat and the shades and found our man exiting Delta #2946 at 3:39. I then checked their passenger list and found a Mr. Marvin DeWalt of Hicksville, Long Island. I checked Mr. DeWalt's curriculum vitae which listed his home address as 9794 E. Blankenship Road in Nassau County." Ronin reached for the board.

"This is 9794 E. Blankenship Road." It was a 7-Eleven.

"So who is he?" Faye said.

Ronin shrugged. "Working on it."

"Could it be a fellow veteran with whom he served?" Braxton said.

"Could be, but accessing all the veterans Murray served with requires more time and data than I can handle. Here's what I can do. I can estimate height and weight. I can make it congruent with Murray's time in the service. But what if they didn't know each other back then? What if Murray acquired this asset only recently? He does know a lot of veterans."

"Well, the hat and shades are worth something," Braxton said. "You could use them to do face recog in area hotels and motels."

"There are only so many hours in the day."

"Well, we have to assume he's already dialed in. Which means we have to take precautions. He could be out there right now. I'm going to do a little reconnoiter. You guys stay inside. If you go to the rooms, stay away from the window."

"There's nothing tall enough around here to give him a good shot."

"Let's be safe, just in case."

They went to the elevator. When Faye and Ronin, and Braxton got off on the third floor. Braxton unlocked his room, pulled his binoculars from the backpack lying on the sofa and went back out. He took the elevator to the top floor. The third. He went to the stairwell. The stairs went to the roof. The heavy metal door had a lock, but it had been left open. He cautiously pushed it open and looked around. He was the only visitor. Braxton regretted there was no concealment, but a sniper targeting the hotel would hardly be looking up. He would train his rifle either on their windows, if he knew where they were, or the door.

Braxton understood the mentality of snipers. They were very patient. They could sit still for hours on end, waiting for a target to appear. He crouched before he got to the rim and slid forward on his ass, cautiously raising his head until he could see. Directly across from the hotel was the Waffle House, and behind that a ridge with a billboard. Habib Rodriguez, attorney-at-law. "I'll Get You Off, One Way Or Another."

Braxton dialed in with the binocs. The billboard was mounted in a copse of juniper, which provided some concealment, but not for someone in Braxton's position. And there he was, in his ball cap and sunglasses, lying between two bushes, wearing dark clothes, virtually invisible to anyone at street level. No rifle. He seemed to be observing. Braxton used his phone to snap a couple photos, magnifying the view as much as he could. Themis was in the trunk of his car which was parked in the lot on the other side of the hotel. Braxton was no great marksman but he could drill one through the target from his position. He was not about to draw attention to himself by doing that. He went to the back of the roof and looked around.

It was just past nine. Down the block was a strip mall, most of the stores boarded up, covered with graffiti. The only remaining business was Dave's Liquors. Several vehicles were parked in the lot, including a white Silverado. Braxton zoomed in on the back plate. Minnesota license plate. It looked familiar. When they had been at Culver's for dinner, he had seen a similar Silverado cruise through the parking lot, then park next door at the Taco Bell. At the time, it didn't stand out, simply something he noticed with his head being on a constant swivel. He wrote the license plate number down.

Braxton returned to the figure in the bushes. He could exit the hotel, go down the street a couple blocks, cross the road undetected, and come up on the sniper from behind.

And do what? Take him out? How? Braxton knew nothing about the man except for the probability that he was a professional.

Should I confront him? It was tempting, but introduced new risks. He returned to the room where Ronin sat at his laptop. Braxton handed him the license plate number.

"What's up?"

"White Silverado parked down the street. See what you can find out about it."

"What makes you think he's using this?"

"Just a hunch. I think I saw it when we were at Culver's."

"Someone tailing us?"

Braxton shrugged. "Anything is possible."

Ronin went to work. Fifteen minutes later, he turned. "License plate belongs to a 2012 Chevy Suburban."

"Bingo," Braxton said. "See if you can plant an AirTag before he takes off. I'll go back on the roof and call you if he's not there."

"Let's you and me go up there right now."

They returned to the roof. The door was still jammed open. They went to the front, hunkered down. Braxton looked through the binocs.

"Damn." He shifted position and looked up the street just in time to see the Silverado pull into traffic and drive away from the hotel. "There he goes."

He passed the binocs to Ronin, who zoomed in and followed the vehicle until it took a turn and disappeared.

"The liquor store," Ronin said.

"What about it?"

"They are bound to have a security camera."

"So what? What's to see?"

"You never know until you look."

Chapter 41
At the Gym

Ronin found Dave's Liquors' home page. It was one of those all-purpose apps designed for ease of use, featuring a cookie-cutter logo and a staged photo of the store during happier times—a couple laughing as they exited with a case of beer. The sidewalk gleamed, and the neon sign in the front window shone brightly. From there, Ronin accessed the server and introduced a glitch. The "Order Online" button became inoperable. The store opened at nine; he gave it until ten before sauntering across the street.

As he entered, the electronic bell chimed. The store was empty. Ronin glanced around, taking in the local brews, a wide selection of wines, and every other alcoholic drink imaginable except absinthe. He picked up a pint of Johnnie Walker and approached the front desk, hitting the bell.

Minutes later, Dave emerged—a flustered, middle-aged man in a Colts sweatshirt, glasses sliding down his nose. His hair had receded, revealing a sweaty, pink scalp.

"Hey, how are ya?" Dave said, ringing up the sale.

Ronin pulled out a credit card.

"Do you have cash? My system's down."

Ronin reached into his wallet and paid in cash. "What's going on with it?"

"I wish I knew. Couldn't happen at a worse time. Thirty percent of my business is online, and it's the first day of the week. God knows how long this'll take to fix."

"Do you have a tech support team?"

"I use Geek Squad when I can, but they're hit or miss. Turnover's higher than Congress!"

"I'm a computer tech. I could take a look, if you'd like."

Dave gaped. "You're kidding me."

"No, sir." He extended his hand. "Ron Kramer."

They shook.

"Seriously? If you can fix this, I'll give you a hundred bucks in credit."

Ronin rubbed his hands together. "Let's see what I can do."

Dave led him to the back, where an office and restroom flanked a warehouse. The office contained a basic setup: a computer screen displaying the same photo from the website and several app icons. Dave sat down and clicked on the online ordering app. A message appeared: *THIS FUNCTION IS NOT AVAILABLE AT THIS TIME. PLEASE TRY AGAIN LATER.*

"All yours," he said, stepping back.

"Okay." Ronin settled into the chair and began assessing the situation. He opened the app's backend and accessed the server logs, quickly identifying the glitch as a compatibility issue with their hosting provider.

As he worked, Ronin activated an AI tool he'd built for penetration testing, designed to simulate attacks on systems to identify vulnerabilities. The AI rapidly analyzed the code and network traffic, flagging weak points in Dave's security protocols. He noted how easily the online ordering system had been compromised.

The front door chimed. "I'll leave you to it," Dave said, stepping outside.

While Ronin continued his analysis, he decided to check the security cameras linked to the system. It took mere seconds to locate footage from the previous day. He spotted a Silverado parked askew outside the mall, its rear window framing a view of the cargo area. He zoomed in, noting the clutter—a fast food bag, a coffee cup, and a boarding pass. Using image enhancement algorithms, he sent the clear shot of the boarding pass to himself.

Once satisfied, he returned to the order app and reversed the glitch. The online ordering service was restored.

Minutes later, Dave reentered the office. "Whoa! You're a genius! What did you do?"

"I adjusted a few settings on the hosting site's framework. Also, I noticed some vulnerabilities in your security setup. You might want to consider an AI-based security solution to proactively monitor for threats."

"Man, you're a lifesaver! Come out and I'll give you a gift card for a hundred bucks."

Just then, a woman stood in the wine aisle holding a bottle of Chardonnay, while a man in a suit checked out with a bottle of Buffalo Trace.

"You don't owe me anything. Just take care of your customers."

"All right, but at least take the Johnnie Walker. Your money's no good here."

"Thanks, Dave!" Ronin pocketed the bottle and walked back to the hotel, where he passed Braxton and Faye having breakfast.

Braxton waved. "Hey! You gonna join us?"

"Nah, I'm too stoked. Got to get to the room and check something."

"You had some luck, I take it?"

"Let's hope."

Back in his room, Ronin magnified the image of the Silverado's cargo area, focusing on the boarding pass. It was still a bit blurry, but he used an app called Genius Scan to enhance it. There it was: Seat 14B, Delta flight #2046, Baltimore to Minneapolis with a layover in Indianapolis. Next, he hacked into Delta's flight records.

Braxton entered silently as Ronin sifted through the flight manifest.

"John Hawkins," Ronin muttered.

"Yeah? But who is he, really?"

"Let me check the purchase details."

Twenty minutes later, Ronin found that the ticket had been bought online with a Mastercard belonging to John Hawkins. Digging deeper into Hawkins's history, he uncovered a twelve-year pattern, which had now changed, indicating the card had likely been stolen. Using an NSA-developed program to trace the card's transactions, he narrowed his focus.

John Hawkins was a tire retailer in Cherry Hill, an upscale Baltimore neighborhood. Ronin punched in the number.

"Big O Tires."

"May I speak to John Hawkins?"

"Speaking."

"Sir, did you recently lose your credit card?"

"I did. Who's this?"

"My name is Ron Kropenski. I work for a consumer fraud agency. Your card was used to purchase a plane ticket from Baltimore to Minneapolis. Are you aware of any other unauthorized transactions?"

"No, just that one. I canceled the card immediately. They must have made the purchase before I did that. What do you need?

"We're trying to identify the thief. Do you know where the card might have been stolen?"

"Yeah, Genesis Gym. I go there almost every day. A week ago, I realized my card was missing after paying for my membership."

"Did anyone at the gym seem suspicious?"

"There were a couple faces I didn't recognize."

"Would you mind telling me what locker you used?"

"Yeah. I always use the same locker. Well, I used to. Locker A 22."

Ronin made a mental note. *It's possible the thief used AI to analyze security footage or even hacked the gym's system to access customer information. I'll check the gym's security protocols*

"Thanks for reaching out. If you find the culprit, will you notify Mastercard?"

"Yes, I will."

"Great! Thank you."

Getting access to Genesis Gym's security cameras was pathetically easy. An eight-character password—12345678.

It's almost like these guys ignored every warning about security ever offered!

Video from the Genesis Gym locker room showed a man in sweats and tennis shoes sitting on the bench staring at his phone while an older man finished changing clothes, shut the door, and spun the combination lock. He left. Ronin enhanced the image. Locker A 22. He changed focus to the newcomer. As soon as Hawkins left, the man sprang up, went to the locker, and spun the lock. He knew the number. He may have used AI to zero in on John Hawkins for that purpose, which meant that he had visited the gym before.

As he stayed on the line, drinking in the dead air, Ronin realized that understanding the interplay between AI and security was crucial in both defending against and executing breaches. He needed to dig deeper into the tech landscape to connect the dots.

Ronin used face recognition software and fed it into the National Security Database. Within seconds, it had a match.

Wesley Palmer.

Chapter 42
Community Bicycle

Palmer was on the clock. He was due in Tampa in five days to assist a client who wanted his wife dead, and it had to look like an accident. It was another side gig, something his superiors didn't need to know about. To get to that job, he needed to finish this one up.

The more he thought about it, the more he wanted the current contract to look like an accident. A rifle attracted too much attention. His client hadn't mentioned Knox's two companions. He couldn't take them all out with the rifle. That meant sidelining his sniper plan from the cornfield.

If they got into one car, that would be better. Automobiles were compact spaces and accidents often covered up hints of foul play. Palmer knew how to follow a target without being noticed. He had done it often overseas.

These guys aren't that caliber of target. They do not know who I am or what my mission is.

Hawthorne's death threw a monkey wrench into the plan. Someone might notice the similarity. On the other hand, no one really knew what happened to Hawthorne. He might have been startled by a deer. Then again, it could be his accident was caused by Knox. Palmer didn't like the looks of Knox's Crown Vic. It was heavy and had been modified. His truck was probably about the same weight, but it would be better to use something bigger, with more mass; like a garbage truck. The trick was to steal the vehicle without attracting attention. He didn't know how long it would take before he got the opportunity. He didn't want witnesses. That meant waiting for them to drive somewhere remote. Preferably at night.

Palmer recalled passing a sanitation company headquarters in Brownsburg on his way into town. He drove Route 135 rather than the Interstate. The company had its own fenced-in lot a quarter mile off the road, a lot filled with dozens of enormous sanitation trucks. They were sure to have security and cameras, but he knew how to get around that. Sanitation trucks stopped for lunch and toilet breaks. There were long moments when the truck was parked unattended.

Who in their right mind would burglarize, or try to steal one?

There were often extra uniforms hanging inside for those days when the ones they wore got soaked in shit. Or chicken fat. It was a simple matter for Palmer to access the website and look at their routes. Looking at their name, he chuckled. Troll Sanitation. Their mascot was a troll in a Tyrolean hat holding a garbage bag.

Troll was particularly active in southwest Indianapolis where their headquarters were located, as well as the airport. Palmer had seen the Troll trucks when he'd landed. Getting the truck was easy. First, he had to get the uniform. Then the truck. Getting Knox and his buddies was more difficult. He needed to observe them for a couple of days to establish patterns. No patterns would make it more difficult. But Palmer knew there were patterns. Obviously, Murray was their next target. He could always ride with Murray. Make him an easy target and then, when they attacked, fight back. The cops would never buy Murray as some kind of avenger. He was too inept.

Palmer thought about slapping a tracking device on the Crown Vic, but Knox struck him as a little too wise not to look. No, the best way to track it was to follow. Palmer sat in the Waffle House down the street from the La Quinta Inn. It was two in the afternoon. The people eating there only ate waffles in the morning. As he gazed out the window, he noticed people riding electric bikes down the street. They were ubiquitous.

Palmer went online. "Pacers Bikeshare has 325 white e-bikes available at 50 stations across the city. The bikes are available 24 hours a day, 365 days a year. The Pacers Bikeshare program is funded by a combination of public and private partnerships, including a $1.2 million federal grant from the U.S. Department of

Transportation. You can access the bikes using the BCycle mobile app or by walking up to a station."

Fat City. He'd seen people riding, seen e-bikes discarded like trash in the gutters. The nearest station was four blocks away. He could leave his Silverado in long-term parking and walk it. Put on a hoodie and a backpack and he was indistinguishable from the latte-slurping students and aging intellectuals who favored such transportation. He reached into a pocket and pulled out three credit cards. Yugo assured him that they had never been used and were good for at least a week before the companies noticed.

The parking ramp had been built back when the mall down the street was a thriving business. These days, half the stores were boarded up and the ramp was at twenty percent capacity. Fine with Palmer. He could sleep in the truck. He stuffed a blue sweatshirt in his backpack and kept the green one to wear.

Palmer walked to the bike station. No attendants. All you needed was a credit card. He used a card to unlock the bike. It charged per mile, transmitting the data to the DOT, and they would automatically bill him when he finished. He could leave the bike anywhere. It had a homing device and sooner or later, the DOT would pick it up. Palmer had seen at least a half dozen bikes discarded in ditches, streams, and alleys. Some of them looked like they'd been there a while.

Riding the bike back to the parking garage, he stopped and inflated the tires properly. None of the bikes he'd seen had properly inflated tires. Their users didn't care. Nor did the city. The bikes belonged to no one and everyone. The bike signaled that its rider was an obedient apparatchik.

Palmer found a coffee shop a block down from Waffle House and took up position Tuesday morning, just another aging academic staring at his laptop. He spotted his quarry at eight-thirty walking across the street from the hotel to the restaurant. The Gang of Three. The leader, a no-nonsense former military dude; the tech guy, beard and glasses; and the lady reporter. He admired her courage. Palmer was not inured to the media shit-show. He seldom paid attention to the news. Still, he appreciated that the Weldon-chick had what his dad called moxie. Palmer lingered, checking the NFL draft. Being from Baltimore, he was a Ravens guy.

Forty-five minutes after they entered, the trio emerged and strolled back to the hotel. Palmer paid his bill, went outside, and got on his bike. He waited for a break in traffic and pedaled across the street, pulling into the parking lot of a Discount Tires. They were doing a bang-up business and paid no attention to him as he straddled his bike, staring at his phone. The phone was off. He waited for the Crown Vic to circle around front, watched as the babe and tech support got in, and took off down the bike corridor a hundred yards back. That car was hard to lose.

Palmer was surprised how easy it was to keep up with traffic. The Crown Vic led him to a VFW hall on Verona Road. Palmer watched as the Crown Vic parked in a strip mall across the street. The bearded guy got out, went into a Dazbog, and returned with three cups of coffee. They sat in the car watching the hall. It was a stakeout; he knew one when he saw it.

They're probably waiting for Murray.

But Murray wasn't coming. He'd made that clear. Murray was lying low until Palmer did his job. If this was a regular routine, it simplified things. There was a light industrial strip the Crown Vic passed that had never recovered from the rioting of 2020. Half the stores were still boarded up and covered with graffiti. No one would look twice at a garbage truck. Palmer brought up a map of the area and planned an escape route. He could fit the bike in the back of the truck and use it to get away.

All he had to do was choose his spot. He knew how to strike a vehicle to cause maximum damage. Three for the price of one. Even a Crown Vic with a shielded fuel tank couldn't withstand multiple blows from a twenty-ton vehicle. A road flare, tossed into the crashed vehicle, would ensure any survivors perished.

I just need a few photos of the dead bodies so I can squeeze some more cash out of Murray.

Chapter 43
Thunder Road

Since the death of his wife and daughter, Braxton had turned himself into an avenger. He'd built up his muscles, honed his fighting skills, become a marksman, educated himself on police techniques, and become a security expert. He maintained a bubble of security around himself and his friends and kept his eyes peeled for possible threats.

The Silverado kept reappearing. Sometimes it was in the distance, other times in his rearview mirror. He pulled the Crown Vic into the parking lot of the VFW and waited to see if the Silverado followed. It did, at a discreet distance.

Whoever is driving it is good. He's using other vehicles to mask his approach. We're dealing with a professional.

"What is it?" Faye asked.

"We have a shadow."

"Palmer," Ronin said. "It's got to be him."

"What is he up to?" Faye pressed.

He put himself in the mindset of the man who was stalking them. "If I were him, I'd be looking for a pattern in order to find an opportunity to take us out. One at a time is too risky. He'll want to do it all at once. That means he needs a place where there won't be a lot of witnesses."

"Where is he going to find a place like that?"

Braxton closed his eyes. He didn't know a great deal about the Indianapolis area. There was one place he knew that would fit the assassin's needs. "I have a location. Rural, off the beaten path. He needs to see us go there."

"Where is it?" Faye asked.

"Where they tried to drown me." He started the Crown Vic and pulled out, eyes darting to his rear views, catching occasional glimpses.

He drove to the pond. Seeing the dock and the water in daylight brought a surge of memories, none of which were positive.

"So this is where they tried to sink you?" Faye asked.

"This is also where he brought Walter Fitzsimmons," Ronin said.

Braxton stared at the pond. "We do the same thing tomorrow and the next day. Palmer will see this as the perfect place."

"Um," Faye said. "How do we make sure he doesn't succeed?"

"Keep our eyes peeled. More importantly, we're armed to the teeth. This guy thinks he's the hunter. Flipping the table is going to throw him off, but not for long. We have a narrow window in which to act."

* * *

Murray, according to the tracker in his car, was not moving. *Waiting for his hired gun to take us out.* Percy had not surfaced either. Braxton was growing weary of Indianapolis. For two days, they repeated the pattern. Braxton brought his pistols and rifle. There was something reassuring about having Themis in reach.

On the third day, he drove past the Loaf & Jug on the way to the pond and he noticed a garbage truck in the lot. He caught a glimpse of the driver. He was wearing sunglasses. "That's our guy."

"Where?" Ronin asked.

"That garbage truck back at the store."

The tension in the Crown Vic ratcheted up. Braxton drew a deep breath. "He's planning something." He turned onto the wooded road that led to the pond.

"That's a shitty getaway vehicle," Ronin said.

"I think he intends to plow into us with that thing. Right into the water. Hang around and wait for survivors."

"Well, that sucks," Faye said.

"It makes sense, big vehicle like that," Ronin said.

Braxton drove to the pond, stopped, and handed his ball cap to Ronin. "Ronin, you're behind the wheel. Faye, get out and go over to those trees." He gestured at some pines about fifty feet from the water.

"Where are you going?" Faye asked, as she opened the door.

Braxton got out and moved around to the rear door. He grabbed his rifle case and the army surplus duffle. "I'll be ready."

"What do you want me to do?" Ronin said.

"He's going to come at you. Keep the engine running. Point sideways so you don't drive into the water. Punch it before he makes contact." Braxton took Faye's hat and tossed it up on the dashboard. From the distance, with the slightly tinted windows, it might convince Palmer that it was her head. "Don't let him hit the car. That garbage truck is a monster."

"You're worried about the car?" Ronin said.

"I like the car."

Braxton hotfooted it to a copse of trees with ground cover that had a decent view of the road. He put a shot bag on a log for support and attached a suppressor to the rifle. Braxton's senses were peaking. He could taste the Crown Vic's exhaust, the smell of the pond water, the pines.

The Accuracy International felt good in his hands. Reassuring. He chambered a round and popped out his Kestrel calculator. His phone relayed the light winds and barometric pressure to him, and Braxton made the adjustments to his scope. The range was too short to miss.

He heard the rumble of the diesel engine of the garbage truck before he saw it. The big truck dominated the narrow road. It slowed as it came within sight of the Crown Vic. Braxton didn't have eyes on Palmer, but he imagined he was sizing up the situation.

Fifty yards separated the vehicles. Picking up his shot bag, he repositioned, hoping to get line of sight. The truck's engine roared as Palmer punched the accelerator. It lurched forward as Braxton slid to the ground.

He didn't have a good shot as the garbage truck bore down on the Crown Vic, lining it up for a T-bone. He wondered if the Crown Vic could dodge the rushing vehicle. If it hit Ronin broadside, it would push him into the pond.

Braxton raised the rifle and peered through the sights.

Come on, give me a damn target!

Chapter 44
Rubbish Runners

Palmer felt an icy calm, as he always did when he was about to kill someone. Knox had presented Palmer with the perfect location. He had gone out through the narrow tree-lined road to the pond twice, scouting it out. Knox would be a sitting duck when Palmer came at him with the truck. There was nowhere to hide. Palmer could push Knox into the pond. No one would find his car for days.

His employer, Brownwater, was on the shadier side of the PMC business spectrum. They applied for more legitimate PMCs but failed background checks or simply weren't the right fit. PMCs were often seen as mercenaries, which Palmer thought was a romantic view of what they did. The advantage of working for Brownwater was that they tended to look the other way with side contracts, like the one he was working. If there was trouble, they didn't want their name dragged into it. But they saw such gigs as a way for their people to make ends meet.

This wasn't the kind of life that Palmer had imagined. He envisioned working in Special Forces for life. There had been problems in the Army, though. Allegations of theft. While the evidence was circumstantial, it was enough to get him booted out of the military. Wesley certainly never envisioned himself assassinating civvies with a garbage truck.

If my sergeant could only see me now.

He had purchased a fresh driver's uniform from the company that provided them in the city. Fifty bucks.

At least I don't have to do this reeking of trash.

Stealing the Troll Sanitation truck was easy. While they had good security camera coverage at their garage, their chain-link fence was old, rusted, and easy to cut through. The rear of the facility backed up to a dirt service road. Rather than get his face all over the security camera footage, he simply cut through the fence and rolled out onto the service road.

Palmer knew the police would be looking for the truck, and with the big Troll Sanitation logo and name on the side, his odds of being caught were high. He arranged for a down and dirty wrap company to give him a new name and logo. Rubbish Runners. *Chances are the cops won't bother to run my plates because the name on the sides doesn't match Troll Sanitation.* The wrap was perfect camouflage, allowing him to hide in plain sight.

Palmer knew the Crown Vic was faster and far more maneuverable. On the other hand, it was unusually heavy and would sink without a trace. The key was to make sure that Knox and his people didn't get away. If they weren't stunned or killed in the collision, he had plenty of firepower. Palmer preferred shotguns because they didn't leave bullets that could be linked to his gun. As he learned in his youth, shotguns were indiscriminate and forensically clean.

As he went down the wooded road leading to the pond, he slowed down. He calculated possible reactions. They would see a garbage truck, unaware of his intent. When he gunned the engine and bore down on them, they would be stunned, confused. By the time they realized he was a threat, he'd hit them. He'd get out of the truck. They would be confused, hopefully injured. Palmer would use the shotgun to finish the job. The garbage truck would push the car into the pond. He'd drop the truck near a bike share. He'd spray a bunch of bleach inside, wipe it down for the fingerprints, take off the wraps, get to the Silverado, and head for the airport. No muss, no fuss. The police would never connect the stolen garbage truck to Knox's disappearance, and even if they did, there would be nothing that could tie him to the crimes.

Driving down the narrow road, he came to a small hill. Just over the rise, he'd be visible. He moved the Mossberg so that after the collision, it wouldn't bounce around on the floor.

He came over the rise in first gear, nice and slow. The Crown Vic was parked perpendicular to the roadway, with the pond twenty feet beyond. The driver was one of Knox's associates. He saw a silhouette of another in the passenger seat. Palmer had no idea why they kept coming to the pond.

Maybe they tag team that Weldon-chick.

The engine roared as he aimed for the driver's side door. Hitting second gear, he topped it out as he lined up his ramming attack. A rifle cracked, a boom near the front of the vehicle, and the truck lurched to the right, hard. He tried to compensate when the Crown Vic spun out, heading left.

Another crack and the vehicle dipped to the right. The Crown Vic drove clear. Wesley cranked the steering wheel hard to adjust, but it felt as if the truck was fighting him. As he shifted to third gear, he felt the power drop off, as if something was slowing the truck.

What the hell is happening? Is that my tires?

The realization screamed at him—he was under fire. Old instincts kicked in.

* * *

Braxton's first shot wasn't at the driver; he couldn't see him. He aimed at the front tire. Themis kicked his shoulder as the bullet blew the tire apart. The truck lurched toward him.

Ronin did his part perfectly. The Crown Vic kicked up dirt as its 4.6-liter V8 propelled it out of the path. Braxton chambered another round, aiming for the rear tires. The bullet blew both out with a large *whoomf,* causing the truck to lurch harder towards him.

The truck turned away from him as he reloaded and fired at the last set of rear tires on his side. He blew one up with the shot; the other blew a moment later. Pursuit of the Crown Vic was no longer an option. Ronin turned hard and headed towards Braxton's position.

Chambering another round, Braxton fired at the rear tires on the driver's side, deflating one. The garbage truck ground slowly to a halt as it tried to follow the Crown Vic.

Braxton reloaded as it turned, revealing the driver's side. The truck's brakes squealed as Palmer stopped it with a heave. Ronin passed his position, bringing the Crown Vic to an abrupt halt. Knox's focus was on the garbage truck, waiting for the driver to make a move.

The door flew open and a man leaped down, shotgun in his hands.

Chapter 45
Contract Cancellation

This wasn't the damn plan!

Palmer grabbed the Mossberg and slammed on the brakes. None of this was unfolding the way he had intended, but Wesley was a survivor. He'd been in worse ambushes in the Middle East and always came through.

I need to deal with that sniper first.

I need to move fast. He must be in the tree line. A few blasts from the shotgun should drive him to cover and pin down his location.

Running around the back of the truck, he fired into a clump of low pines and cedars, shredding boughs. No response. He turned to the next cluster. A shot cracked to his left. Palmer's body jerked. He almost lost his grip on the shotgun. Looking down, he saw his uniform wet with dull crimson blood. The moment he saw the gore, he felt the pain in his upper shoulder.

He'd been shot before, overseas. This was different. He was alone here. There was no fire team for support or to extract him to the medics. This time, there was terror.

Aiming for the far left group of trees, he pumped the Mossberg and fired. The kick of the weapon sent a raging fire into his wounded shoulder. Palmer wobbled as pain engulfed his body.

It was then he saw the suppressor aimed at him. Straining, he pumped another round and felt the Mossberg slam into him. The stock shattered, wood splinters flew in the air. A hot, stabbing poker from the bullet rippled through his midsection. Twisting from the impact that had destroyed his gun, he tossed it aside. He still had his

Beretta. With his right hand, he groped for his shoulder holster where the weapon was slung.

Another shot cracked from the woods, hitting his right forearm. Blood sprayed his face, warm and terrifying. The impact staggered him. He fell, losing his grip on his weapon on the way to the ground. Trying to grab the M9, his arm refused to respond. Looking down, he saw his radius bone poking through his skin, snapped like a twig.

Lying on his back, he struggled to get air. The stink of the diesel and the gut-wrenching aroma from the truck invaded his lungs.

It wasn't supposed to be like this!

A shadow fell over him. A hand reached down and pulled his Beretta. Palmer trembled, not from just fear, but the pain. He watched Braxton Knox pocket his M9, then sweep a massive Accuracy International AXSR at him.

* * *

"Hurts like hell, doesn't it?" Braxton said as he aimed Themis at Palmer in the dirt in case he somehow made a move. "Dying always does."

Palmer coughed, wincing from the pain. "You set me up."

"Yup."

"I need to get to a hospital," Palmer choked out.

"You ain't gonna make it. Murray hired you, didn't he?"

"Yeah," he said, coughing three times, each an agonizing convulsion. It was impossible for Braxton to ignore it. He had no intention of acting.

"How much did he pay you?"

"Not enough."

"He wanted us all dead, didn't he?"

Palmer nodded. "Not much choice. It took some digging to figure out who you really were. That Harry Callahan persona—it just didn't feel right. Braxton Knox."

Braxton saw the blood oozing from his wounds.

It won't be long now.

"I didn't want to kill you. You had no part in this. But when you started tailing us, preparing to kill us, it became necessary."

"Why are you doing this?" he coughed. "Long way from Portland for you to come."

"Percy—Murray's nephew. He ruined a man's life. We're here to set that right."

It's what I do now—it's who I am.

"I've got a sister," Palmer managed, fighting the pain. "She needs to know about me."

Braxton eyed him carefully.

He's a mercenary. This guy would have killed all three of us without flinching. Now he's begging that we let his sister know about his death?

In a strange way, Knox admired his arrogance, so close to death. "I'll consider it. But I need to know, does anyone else know who I really am?"

Palmer shook his head. "I never told Murray. I figured I'd do it after you were dead. I've got a guy in the government that helped me ID you, but he's not going to draw attention to himself." The last word he spoke was strained. His eyes stopped focusing on Braxton and looked skyward. "This isn't fair," he sighed.

"Fair? You were going to murder us. I think letting you bleed out here is more than fair."

Palmer's eyes lost all focus. He let out a low gurgle, tensed for a moment, then stopped breathing.

Braxton looked down at the lifeless body. He wanted to feel bad about the guy. A part of him felt he should, but he couldn't.

This guy knew what he was getting into. We're doing what we do because it's right. His actions were driven by cash. He knew what the game was; we just played it better than he did.

Ronin looked down. "We need to dispose of the body."

Braxton slung Themis over his shoulder. "Agreed."

"How did you manage to put a round through the stock of his shotgun? That was a hell of a shot."

"I wasn't aiming at it. I just wanted to take him down. It was a fluke."

Faye joined them. She had been standing behind Braxton. He hadn't even noticed. "That was terrifying and gross."

"It's about to make the jump into morbid," Braxton said. "We need to let Murray know that his hired gun is toast."

"What do you have in mind?" Faye asked.

"Why don't you two get in the car? I can handle it."

Faye left. Ronin lingered in case he needed help. He vomited as Braxton undertook his grizzly task.

* * *

There were two options. One was to drive him and his garbage truck into the pond and let them sink. It was the easiest and cleanest way, but that was problematic. Sunken vehicles leaked oil and fuel, which would rise to the surface and draw attention to their presence. Also, he was unsure how deep the pond was. If they drove in and the vehicle sank ten feet, it would be visible from the shore.

That left fire. That might draw attention from someone nearby, but was the best way to ruin physical evidence. Ronin took Palmer's wallet to make sure nothing survived the inferno. He pocketed the M&P 9 too. There was no point in trying to salvage the Mossberg. Faye and Ronin drove away to get a gas container. Braxton went to work on the body. He used a bayonet to sever Palmer's head, placing it in a heavy duty garbage bag. It was a gruesome and tiring task, much harder than he had expected. He dragged Palmer's body and shotgun into the truck's cab.

When Faye and Ronin returned with a gallon of gas, he soaked the interior and under the fuel tanks. Diesel fuel was tricky to ignite. It needed a higher temperature than just a lighter would generate, which the gasoline would provide.

Braxton packed his rifle in its case. He gathered all the spent brass. He'd have to swap out the barrel and bolt. If the police found bullets in the tire, he didn't want them to have any way of linking them to his weapon. When finished packing the Crown Vic, he returned to the truck and pulled out a pack of matches.

Without teeth or fingerprints, the police would struggle for weeks to identify the body. By then, they'd be long gone.

He struck a match and tossed it in the air. A blast of heat washed over him as the garbage truck became engulfed in flames. A breeze blew in, intensifying the heat. Stepping backwards, he watched as the garbage truck belched black smoke. Flames turned the driver's compartment into a furnace.

He got in the car with Faye and Ronin.

"What was it you put in the trunk?" Faye said.

"You don't want to know."

"Seriously?"

"Let's just say, it's a way to get Murray's attention and leave it at that."

Faye sensed Braxton wasn't happy about what was in the sack. "Murray caused his death, not you. He outsourced killing you."

"When all is said and done," Ronin said, "this all falls on Percy. That dweeb set everything in motion. He brought his uncle and Jack Hawthorne into it. Murray and Jack acted like fourth graders, beating up Faye like they did."

Braxton didn't speak until they passed the Loaf & Jug. Glancing in the rearview mirror, he saw a pillar of oily black smoke curling in the light breeze.

"You know, the root of all of this isn't Percy. It's his mother."

"How do you figure?" Ronin asked.

"She's a shitty parent. One of the worst. Percy shouldn't be living at home on his mother's dime. If she had done her job well, she would have kicked him out years ago. Instead, she enabled that twerp. Her coddling of Percy empowers him to do what he does. People like her think they are doing the right thing, but all she did was create an online bully."

"You're right," Faye said. "I hate admitting it, but you're right. She's like Dr. Frankenstein. She's created a monster and despite the evidence, she protects him."

"She needs a reckoning as well," Braxton said as he turned the Crown Vic onto the road that would take them to the highway and back to Indianapolis.

Chapter 46
Shrinking Circle of Allies

Percy was freaked. The killers were on his tail. Jack Hawthorne was dead. Percy had lost his job because of a nosy reporter. His online friends were ghosting him. To Percy, it was an indication that the bad guys were coming for him. He had been driven from his house at the urging of his uncle. Someone had ripped him off with promises to crack the phone his uncle had recovered. His online world was shrinking, and he was living on the run.

I'm a victim!

He desperately wanted to tell the world his story. In it, Percy was a socially conscious person protecting the world from threats from fascists. Now he was a fugitive with killers on his tail. His friends were being harassed too. Why? Because he stood up and did what was right. It was a story that Percy knew people would buy. It would elevate him in the eyes of others, getting him more clicks and follows than he could dream of. With his spare time, he worked on an outline for the story he would weave about the events and what platforms would get which posts.

People loved victims. Others would rally to him. *Maybe I should set up a GoFundMe so that people can contribute to my expenses.* Rachel Maddow would have him on MSNBC to talk about the hate leveled at him. *I bet I can squeeze a book deal out of this before it's over.* Percy was confident that a lawyer would take up his case against the bookstore for firing him. *I'll get my revenge and get famous for doing it. Hollywood will love this story.* He fantasized about who might play him in the film version. Possibly Mark Ruffalo. Thinking about that made him feel great.

While a part of him wanted the chaos to end, another part wanted it to continue. It was the most exciting thing he had experienced in his life. The power he felt was incredible, and he wanted more.

I was able to upset enough people for a reporter to hound me and get her friends to force me on the run!

It was thrilling. Living in a hotel? While he didn't have all of his computer hardware with him, it was better than staying at home with his mom. It was expensive, but his mother's retirement accounts covered it.

As he lay on the hotel bed, he called his uncle. Within two rings, Uncle Murray picked up. "What do you need, Percy?" his uncle said flatly, almost as if he was annoyed by him.

"I hadn't heard from you in a few days. You said you hired a professional to deal with this shit. I was wondering if anything has changed."

Murray sighed, which Percy found annoying.

He acts like I'm bothering him.

"If anything changes, I'll let you know."

"What exactly is this guy doing?"

"Percy, this isn't the kind of stuff we talk about on the phone. He's a pro. He'll take care of it. That's all you need to know."

"I get that. You've gotta remember, I'm the one living in hiding right now. I mean, I'm still not back home."

"Don't you go back there. Not until this shit is settled. The last thing I want you to do is drag my sister into your ugly-ass fuckfest."

"How long will this take?"

"It takes as long as it takes. Guys like this, they work on their own timetable. This little operation set me back a lot. I had to eat my nest egg. After these fuckers killed Jack, I knew I was going to need some firepower."

"So the guy you got, he's good?"

"I told you, he's a pro. This is going to get resolved and we can both return to our lives. Have you had any luck with that phone?"

Mention of the phone summoned his humiliation at the hands of Blitzerboy who had ripped him off. He knew his uncle wouldn't want to hear about that. When the truth made Percy look bad, he lied.

"We cracked it. The people this Weldon-bitch has working for her are pretty sophisticated. They had a wiper program running. It nuked all of their texts and phone call history the moment we got in on the phone."

"They can do that kind of shit?"

"Oh yeah," he said, flaunting knowledge that he didn't have. "It's real spy-level stuff."

"Fuck me," his uncle groaned…acknowledging that Percy's lie had worked. When he told his story in interviews and online, he needed to include details like this.

"I'm sorry, it's a dead end."

"Well, at least you tried." It was a line that Percy had heard a lot in his life. It was the sound of disappointment.

He dealt with it as he always did, by changing the subject. "Have you talked to Ma? Is she okay with all this stuff going down?"

"I talked to her. I told her you were hanging with me for a few days. I told her you needed some manning up so you could go and get a new job."

Percy winced.

Everyone puts so much emphasis on jobs. It's really just to maintain class status. People think that their jobs define them, like having a good job makes them better than anyone else. It's not about that. Jobs make you slaves to the Man. By not having a job, I'm actually doing society a big favor. I'm taking a stand against a corrupt system.

"Good," he muttered. "I didn't want her to worry."

"Just don't stir the pot. You've already cost me a small fortune with all this crap."

"It isn't my fault," Percy snapped. "Weldon came after me—got me fired."

"I own a business. Nobody fires you because a stranger comes in and says you did something wrong. There's more to your story. Don't try and tell me different."

"Uncle Murray—"

"Don't. I don't want to hear it. You need to get your freaking act together. This isn't normal. I've been cleaning up your mess, and this

237

is the end of it. When my guy does what he has to do, you're going to turn yourself around."

Percy knew that pushing matters with his uncle might backfire on him. He resented the "manning up" comment as much as the shot about him getting a new job. His generation didn't have to rely on toxic masculinity to be manly. He just hadn't found the right woman yet.

"I appreciate everything you've done," he said.

"Yeah, yeah, fine. Look, I've got to go. I have something I need to attend."

"What is it?"

"Jack's funeral. Gotta pay my respects. Keep your head down and don't do anything to make this worse. If we're lucky, this is all going to blow over soon." His uncle hung up before Percy could say goodbye.

Everyone keeps trying to define me in their terms. When this is over and everything is out there, they will see me for the man that I am.

Chapter 47
Cause and Effect

Murray Landreth hated the waiting game almost as much as his nephew. It had already cost him too much money. It wasn't any love he had for Percy, but for his sister. Since hiring Wesley Palmer, he had done what he had to and laid low. It had given him time to do some work around the house, something he had been putting off since his wife died. She had always pricked him with jabs that he owned a business that fixed other people's houses, but never his own.

Murray checked on his crew by phone. He fed them a story that he had COVID and didn't want them to get sick. It wasn't how he liked to run his company, but he also didn't want to be out and about.

It is best to let Palmer do what he needs to do. Then I can put this ugliness in my rearview mirror.

The phone call from Percy only reinforced the need for his nephew to stop doing crap on the internet and get out in the real world. Just thinking about Percy made his eyes roll.

I gave him one to-do for me, cracking that phone, and he managed to botch it. That kid is as fucked up as a football bat.

He went into the bedroom and dug out his only suit. The pants were tight, far more snug than the last time he had worn it for Paula's funeral.

I'm at that age when the only reason you break out a suit is to put someone in the ground.

Today it was going to be his friend, Jack Hawthorne. If it was anyone else, he would have simply put on dress pants and a nice shirt. For his buddy, Murray pulled the pants tight and managed to hook the button as his gut spilled out over the top.

His mind was trapped in a loop, constantly thinking about Jack's death and how it couldn't be an accident. It was consuming. As much as he tried to not think about it, it kept coming back to him, burrowing deep in his conscious thought.

It had to be that bitch's friends. They ran him down; that's the only thing that makes sense. At least I get the satisfaction of knowing they are dead or about to be.

Jack didn't have the cash for a full service. One of his nieces paid for a graveside service at Custer Cemetery in New Palestine, Indiana, outside of Indy. The small cemetery had not been well kept, weeds grew among the grave makers, and the grass needed mowing. A small canopy had been put up, though there wasn't a big crowd. Several members of the VFW were there to provide a military send-off. A few other veterans attended, most of which he knew. Jack's niece and her kin. A Hispanic female.

Murray was thankful that the service was short. Little more than some kind words and a prayer from a minister. The uniformed VFW members gave him his twenty-one gun salute. Most of those gathered twitched during the gunfire, but not Murray. The family didn't have any sort of events planned afterwards. Murray gave nods to the regulars from the VFW as they filtered past.

Rex, the bartender, came alongside and leaned in so his voice wouldn't carry. "That woman over there," he glanced with his eyes at the Hispanic lady. "She's the cop that came in looking for you and Jack."

Murray nodded and headed for his car. He didn't see her come up behind him, but when he opened his car door, she was there. "Mr. Landreth."

Murray had one foot in the car. "What?"

"Do you have a minute?"

"Actually, I'm a little pressed for time."

"I'm Rita Hernandez with the Indianapolis Police," she said.

"Okay."

Hernandez unfolded a piece of paper. "I've been looking into something that took place a while back. A reporter, Faye Weldon, was beaten up. I got a tip you might be the person in this photo."

Holding out the blurry picture, Murray felt his jaw set at the image. It was him and Jack in the bar.

The mention of Weldon made him edgy. "I don't know. That image is pretty blurry," he said, averting his eyes from it.

"You would know if you were involved, wouldn't you?"

"I don't know what you're talking about."

"Were you in Tom's Bistro on the night of the fifth?"

"Nope. I guess you're chasing the wrong guy."

"Doesn't that look like your buddy, Jack Hawthorne?" she asked, pointing at the picture.

He wanted to get in his car and leave, but doing so would only make Hernandez more suspicious. "You're asking if my friend who was just buried is in your picture? Don't you have any decency? For God's sake, this is his funeral!"

"I think you're the guy in that photo. I'm setting up a lineup downtown for Miss Weldon."

"You need to talk to my lawyer," Murray said, sliding into the driver's seat. "I don't think your picture gives you probable cause to haul me in for anything. That image is so grainy, it could be anyone."

"This isn't over," she said in an assuring tone.

"It is as far as I'm concerned," Murray said, slamming the door. He fumbled with his keys, started the car, and pulled out on the gravel road that snaked through the cemetery. In the rearview mirror he saw Hernandez standing, arms crossed.

Great...just fucking great. They got a picture of Jack and me. My best hope now is that Palmer kills Weldon before they haul me in front of a lineup.

As he turned down the main road, another thought hit him. *If Palmer kills Weldon, they may think I had something to do with it. Fuck me! Do I call off the hit? Too late for that. Besides, he'll just keep the money I gave him.* He was trapped, forced to ride out the events that were in motion. *When Weldon is dead, they can suspect my involvement, but there won't be any evidence to link me to her death. Let the cops chew on their theories. I can't go to jail just because they suspect me.*

He stopped at a Pitstop Liquors and got a bottle of Jack Daniels. While he waited, at least he could numb himself. Walking out with the bottle in the paper bag, he was tempted to open it in the parking lot and take a swig, but didn't want to risk any further run-ins with the law. *My luck is already soured today.*

On his way home, he considered an alternative. *What if I kill this Hernandez? If she's dead and I do it right, chances are pretty good that anyone picking the case up will start at a disadvantage.* He hated her smugness. *She confronted me at Jack's funeral. How messed up is that? Doesn't she respect the sanctity of a religious service?* It was as if he were looking for reasons to kill her.

He toyed with adding her to Palmer's list of targets, but that was only going to increase his costs. *No, this is something that I can handle myself. Police get killed every day. Nobody is going to cry over a dead cop. They'll search for me, but if I do this right, I can get away with it. It'll either look random or they'll assume it was one of dozens of cases she has worked on.*

When he got home, he poured a glass of Jack, added some ice and just enough Coke to convince himself he still had some class. After savoring some chest-warming drinks, he went into his bedroom closet, opened his gun safe that dominated the tight space, and pulled out his old Remington Model 7400. He had named the gun Gracie, after his mother. Murray hadn't hunted in a long time. Holding Gracie brought back memories.

All I have to do is find out what days she works and from what division. I'll follow her, find the right location, and put this part of my problem to bed once and for all. Murray had a friend whose brother worked as a cop. He was confident he could get the information with a single phone call.

This time he wasn't going after a buck, he was going after a spic cop. He savored the thought of killing her, and putting his problems behind him.

Chapter 48
The New Oldsmobiles

Braxton changed out the barrel and bolt on Themis as Faye paced the hotel room. "I can't believe you have that thing in the trunk."

"It was necessary, Faye."

"That's pretty gruesome, and my standards are pretty low," Ronin said.

Braxton understood their resistance. Faye had threatened to go out and look. So he told them. Faye didn't take it well.

"It has to be. Murray hired a professional to take us out. Make no mistake, he would have killed us without even flinching...you were there. I need to show Murray that his hired gun failed."

"Why?" Faye asked.

"To force a response."

Faye frowned.

"Murray Landreth is a simple person. He's got a dipshit for a nephew, who got him sucked into this whole thing. He's the kind of guy who can barely run a business. We're talking about someone that hangs out at the VFW because the only thing he did well was in the military. No wife, no real life. Landreth is a very basic person."

Braxton put the rifle back in its case. "His lack of sophistication tells me that he'll be reduced to two courses of action—fight or flight. He'll fight, which means he'll be playing our game."

"What makes you think he won't rabbit?" Ronin asked.

"He's already gotten Percy to go into hiding. His sister is in town. He has anchors. When he sees what's in that bag, it's going to force him into irrational decisions. It will make him afraid and angry. If I were him, I'd want to make sure I didn't end up like Palmer. That means he will bring the fight to us."

"And we want that?" Faye said.

"We do...if it's on our terms."

"So how do we make that happen?" Ronin asked, intrigued.

"The key is to make him believe he's in some degree of control. We create a circumstance so he pursues us to a site we pick for an ambush. Then we take him out."

"Why not just bust into his house and shoot him?" Ronin asked.

"Too many variables. With Percy, we know he isn't used to real-world violence. His uncle is a different matter. The guy's a vet, with combat experience. We know he's prone to violence. He attacked Faye. He brought in Palmer. We go in on his home turf, he might be able to turn the tables on us. I want this bastard dancing to our tune, not his."

Faye sighed, putting her hands on her hips. "Haven't we had enough?"

"I'm learning as I go, Faye. Circumstances have changed me. I'm not the guy that used to teach college classes. I have a mission. I didn't ask for this. People like Percy, they take and take and never give. He arranged to have you beaten. Do you know how messed up that is? People like him deserve what's coming, and I'm more than happy to give it to them. But to deal with him, we need to take out some of the other pieces on the game board. It's not enough to hurt Murray; he needs to die. It really is that simple."

Faye nodded. "I know," was all she could muster.

"This was never supposed to blow up like this. We were going to get to Percy and his friends. Percy changed the rules, bringing in Hawthorne and his uncle. His uncle made matters worse with Palmer. To set this right, we need to respond on our terms."

Ronin nodded. "Alright, so what else do we need?"

"A place to pin him down. Somewhere that has open terrain with some elevation. Some place that we know will be abandoned at night."

"We don't know Indianapolis well," Ronin replied. "Let me do a little digging."

Ronin went to work on his computer. Faye pulled up the local news. "Firefighters in Laurence reported a garbage truck fire. By the time they arrived, the vehicle was a loss. The truck in question had been stolen from Troll Sanitation. A body has been recovered." They all looked at the screen as the Marion County Deputy, a younger version of Wilford Brimley, appeared. "There was no ID on the body we recovered. We have turned the remains over to our medical examiner. Until we get the results from them, we have no further comment." The image shifted to a heavy duty wrecker dragging the burned husk of the vehicle onto its back.

Ronin chuckled. "That medical examiner's report is going to be pretty entertaining,"

Faye shot him an icy gaze. He returned to his computer.

"It looks like Murray took a short drive today," he said, pointing at the screen.

"Where to?" Braxton asked.

"Custer Cemetery in New Palestine."

"Jack Hawthorne's funeral."

"Yup."

"Easy guess."

"Our tracker history shows he stopped at a party store for a few minutes, then went home."

"Keep tabs on him. Now that the police have found what's left of Palmer, there's a chance he might get nervous."

"Based on what you've done, I doubt they will get ID on him for a while."

"True. Still, we have to assume the worst-case scenario."

Ronin nodded. An hour or so later, he spoke up. "I've got two places ID'd for your encounter with Murray."

Braxton stood behind Ronin to see his laptop. "First up, Heidelberg Materials, Aggregates. It's a rock quarry. They have one security guy at night, according to their online org chart. I guess nobody wants to break into a place that big when the only things of value are rock haulers."

The image showed the open-air quarry. With multiple levels, a long sloped driving ramp, deep pools of water at the bottom—there were a number of advantages. *If we can get him chasing our car, get him in there, I could use the high ground to pick him off.*

"Not bad. What else you got?"

Ronin brought up a shopping mall. "Meet the Lafayette Square Mall. Abandoned a while back, except for the Christmas season when a few pop-up stores open up."

"A mall?"

"An *abandoned* mall. It has wide-open areas inside, multiple levels of elevation—everything you want."

"But it's a mall."

"There's no security there."

"But it's a mall."

"Didn't you ever watch *The Blues Brothers?*"

The new Oldsmobiles are in early this year... The chase scene in the mall had been one that he and Suzanna loved. Braxton considered the possibilities and risks of each location. The quarry had a guard. He would have to be subdued before the ambush. The quarry, while providing greater shooting distances, could be blocked off, trapping them.

"So there's no security at the mall?"

"The place is closed up tight. I'm sure the local cops swing by and check it out. I can't even find a contract for an alarm company. No money coming in, no security."

"Can we get a car in there?"

Ronin pulled up another picture. "They pulled out the concrete posts around the doors on the east and north sides for some reason. Probably to bring in dumpsters when gutting some of the old stores. All that stands in your way of getting in there is some old aluminum and a shitload of glass."

Braxton looked at the photo. "Do you have a map for this place?"

"Please..." Ronin replied, opening it up. There wasn't a lot of maneuvering space, but then again, Braxton didn't think he'd need it. He found himself warming to the idea. "Can you get some inside photos?"

"Loan me the car and I'll run a drone through there and scout it out."

246

Braxton tossed him the keys.

"You're not seriously thinking about confronting Murray there, are you?" Faye said.

"Faye, I know you well enough to know you don't ask questions that you already don't know the answers to. Of course I'm considering it. Gunfire in that place won't travel far. Murray may have shopped there at one point, but he's never driven in it. It negates any home field advantage. He'll think he's chased us into a dead end. Then we flip the script on him."

"I knew you'd like it!" Ronin exclaimed.

"This isn't a game," Faye cautioned. "This man is very dangerous."

"I know," Braxton replied coolly. "Just remember, I'm dangerous too."

Chapter 49
Extreme Measures

Murray woke from his stupor at dawn. He had a hangover the size of North America. A sick feeling permeated his gut. That fucking cop was on his case. If she tied him to Palmer, it was lights-out. Murray was not a natural killer. He'd shot at the enemy in Afghanistan, but they were far away, and he was never certain he'd hit anyone. Percy had made him into something new, a man who had to take lives to stay free.

He had the experience. He had a marksman's medal. It was either her or him. The few times he saw Hernandez, she was alone or some distance from her partner. The result of Indianapolis' hiring freeze, and the many who had quit during the pandemic rather than take the jab. Murray would prefer to take her out alone, but if not, he needed to make sure he was able to get away from her partner, if she was riding with one. He wasn't sophisticated enough to booby-trap her car. It had to be a rifle, and it had to be a long shot. But not a real long shot. No mile-long sniper shit. He was confident of his accuracy up to a hundred yards. In the city, that was a chip shot. If he knew her routine, he could take up position atop a building anywhere along the route and wait for her to come by. But how could he know her routine?

It occurred to him to ask Percy. That was a hard no. He'd settled on the realization that Percy could fuck up a one-car funeral. On top of that, involving him would make his nephew an accessory, about which he didn't give a shit, except insofar as Percy wouldn't hesitate to rat him out to save his own hide.

His contact in the police department had told him which precinct Hernandez worked out of. The rest, he'd have to learn it himself. Armed with her precinct, Murray would show up every morning and watch from afar. He'd written down her unit's number. Cruiser number eighty-two. Problem. She knew his car. Solution. The ubiquitous community scooters and electric bikes in which Indianapolis had foolishly invested. You saw them everywhere, usually lying in gutters or in the middle of abandoned lots. Murray knew the drill. The only people who benefited were the politicians who'd authorized them, and the companies, most in China, that made them. Kickbacks for the pols, fat profits for the companies. It had been years since Murray had ridden a bike, but riding a bike was like riding a bike. Once you got the hang of it, it all came back. Besides. The city bikes all had big step-throughs to accommodate women, and transsexuals, he supposed. As for the scooters, no prob.

All he had to do was alternate. Bikes one day, scooters the next. And he could dump them anywhere. They allegedly had homing devices so the city could pick them up, but he'd passed the same abandoned scooters and bikes for weeks before they disappeared. Eight a.m., Monday May 22nd, Murray was waiting down the street wearing blue jeans, a Colts hoodie, and wraparound sunglasses, poking at his phone but really waiting for Hernandez to pull out in her shop so he could follow her. He wasn't worried about keeping up. Police were not in a hurry unless they were chasing down some sucker for a traffic infraction. He did not have long. At 8:35 a.m., her vehicle left the parking lot, heading north, away from him.

Complication. She had a partner. Murray was tempted to abort, but instead decided to see if he could still manage to get a shot at her. Besides, her partner didn't look too intimidating. If he were pressed, he'd put a round in him as well.

That might even throw off investigators, making them think it was a random shooting or someone out gunning for cops in general.

He pressed the power key, waited while it booted up, and then took off in top gear, peddling lightly. It was one of those models you didn't have to pedal to get the power. You could just use the battery. With a top speed of about twenty-five, he easily kept her in sight as she cruised through abandoned strip plazas, boarded-up windows covered with graffiti, past homeless encampments beneath bridges or by gang neighborhoods where young thugs in training whistled harmlessly and stared at the sky as she drove by.

The police cruiser stopped at a homeless camp on South Belmont and Hernanez got out of her car to talk to a particularly rough-looking individual weaving around in a peacoat with a beard like the Ancient Mariner. The derelict was four sheets to the wind. She spoke to him firmly, pointed at his purloined shopping cart stuffed with clothes and canned goods, and shook her finger at him. Good deal. That meant she would probably return the following day to check. Murray had stopped a block down. He liked the location. Ironically, it was only a couple blocks from American Legion Post 64 which he sometimes visited. There were plenty of sniper sites in the run-down neighborhood.

An abandoned four-story apartment building, now festooned with unreadable graffiti, much of it in Spanish. Several abandoned warehouses protected by chain-link fences. It would be a cinch to clip his way in before the sun rose. But he had to be sure. One day wasn't enough to establish a pattern. Murray stayed on her tail until noon when she got on the Sam Jones Expressway and headed toward the airport. He rode the bike back to where he'd rented it, threw it in the gutter, and took the bus home.

Looking at the house, he groaned. The lawn needed mowing. *Fuck it.* He hadn't even fired the mower up this year. Maybe when he got through the current crisis, which was slightly more important. Feeling aggrieved, Murray went into his sagging two-story wood frame house, got the Jack Daniels out of the cupboard, and settled down in front of his television set. Forty-seven streaming channels and nothing to watch. He liked *Cobra Kai*. John Kreese reminded him of some of the guys down at the VFW. Every time one of the kids threw him, her, or itself into the air for a senseless pirouette, he took a drink. He passed out in the Barcalounger. When he woke, it was morning and Tommy Lee Jones was pursuing Harrison Ford. He felt like shit. But the urgency of the situation overrode his desire to stay home and sleep it off. He choked down a microwaved breakfast sandwich that tasted like cardboard; forced himself to drink a quart of water; put on a pair of canvas painter trousers, an old corduroy jacket, and a watch cap; and caught the bus back to the Southwest District. This time, he rented a scooter. It was a cinch to ride once he mastered the nuances of balancing. He waited on the opposite side of the street north of the station this time, and was not surprised when Hernandez's cruiser passed him without a glance, again heading north. Same routine. Strip malls, boarded up windows, homeless encampments. Once again, she pulled into the same homeless encampment where the same bearded vagrant was staggering around, gesticulating wildly, causing others to creep back into their tents or walk in the other direction.

She got out. The bum saw her coming and immediately stopped remonstrating, reverting to forelock tugging humility. Murray could practically hear his tobacco-stained words. "Yes, officer. I understand, officer; it won't happen again, officer." She gave him a look that could freeze water, hands on hips, right hand on the butt of her gun. The homeless man meekly melted, got his shopping cart, and headed south toward where Murray stood, one foot on the scooter, one on the trash-strewn ground. The homeless man passed him without a glance, muttering under his breath.

Well, this is it. Murray had no doubt she'd return the following day to see if that scumbag took her seriously. After that, she was going to arrest him. She did not want to do that. She did not want the reeking bum in the back of her ride. But she would. Murray knew the type. He waited until she pulled out, heading north before zipping around, looking for a good place to set up. And there it was. The roof of that abandoned four-story brick apartment building, its windows boarded up, police warning on the door. Abandoned. Everything about it screamed *stay the fuck out*. Of course, that didn't prevent junkies from prying off the plywood and creeping in so they could shoot up and sleep it off in peace. Murray circled the building. Steel fire escape in back. The lowest rung hung seven feet off the ground, but it would be a cinch to snag with a crowbar.

Feeling pleased with himself, Murray rode the scooter to a strip plaza on life support and caught a bus home. There would be no drinking tonight. Tomorrow was Sniper Day.

Chapter 50
Sniper Day

Murray slept well that night. No booze, just exhaustion. He knew he needed to be crispy for the next day. In the morning, he cleaned his Remington 7400. He hadn't been hunting with Gracie in years. He no longer enjoyed tramping through the forest during deer season festooned like a Christmas tree, so he wouldn't be mistaken for a deer.

Murray's friend in the department had told him about Hernandez's call sign. He had dug out his old-school Bearcat police scanner. It took him a few minutes to get it working, but once he did, he could monitor her communications and where she was.

Murray had a decent scope, a Pinty Rangefinder. He'd bagged deer with it before. He had experience. That was all he needed. He drove his beat-up old Cadillac to South Belmont and parked it on a side street four blocks away. He set up a phony dash cam. He was taking a chance leaving it on the street, but at this hour the junkies and gangbangers were still sleeping off last night's festivities. The dashcam might throw off any would-be thieves.

Dressed in a shabby great coat, watch cap pulled low on his skull, he was indistinguishable from the other homeless as he trudged north pulling a collapsible shopping cart which contained a beat-up golf bag. A nine-iron poked out of the top as well as what appeared to be a wrapped umbrella. He headed down a side street, then up the alley to the abandoned redbrick building overlooking the homeless encampment. He used the nine iron to snag the bottom rung of the fire escape, slung the umbrella over his shoulder, and climbed. It hurt. He wasn't used to climbing. He had to get back to the gym. By the time he reached the roof, he was breathing hard. It was an overcast day and from his perch he could see downtown Indianapolis partially obscured by clouds. The One America Tower. Three Hundred North Meridian. The Marriott.

Once in position, he sat on the worn tar paper roof, slid the rifle out, careful to not knock the scope out of adjustment, and ratcheted a cartridge into the chamber. With any luck, it would be one and done. He eased over to the two-foot abutment and looked. At this hour, there was little activity in the collection of tents, lean-tos, and trash surrounded by shopping cars and a few bicycles. Peering through the scope, he was surprised to find the bearded revenant with whom Herrera had remonstrated. Some people just couldn't take a hint. A low rider cruised the block, passenger window open, hand waving.

"'Ludes, blow, smack, whatcha need, whatcha need…"

A creature swaddled in cloth waddled forward. Could be a man or woman. It spoke softly to the rider who laughed in its face. The car did a humpty-bump and chirped out. Murray reached for a pack of cigarettes, then remembered he'd put on an old coat he'd been meaning to donate and there were no cigs in the pocket.

A half hour passed while he stared at his phone. He played video slot machine for a while, dreaming what he'd do with the money if it were real. The few times he'd ventured to a casino were disasters. He was not a good poker player, and he understood the slots offered the worst odds of any game in the joint. At least while he was playing, the drinks were free.

Every so often, he perked up when the police scanner squelched. Listening intently, he heard Hernandez's voice a few times. Each time, he had a burst of excitement.

At just past ten, cruiser eighty-two appeared around a corner and approached the homeless camp. He had heard the call go to her car… a possible person needing assistance lying on the sidewalk. A possible drug overdose. The object of her attention lay half-twisted on his back, red nose to the sky, snoring so loud Murray could hear it echoing in the distance. It was her beat, her homeless encampment.

I've got her now.

His target wasn't alone. She had the same partner as before. Murray made some quick mental calculations. If he gunned her down, would her partner know where the shot came from? If he did, at this range, was there any risk? His jaw clenched as he realized he was perfectly safe, and that his target wasn't.

He could read disgust in Hernandez's stride. She stood for a minute staring down, then nudged the bum with her foot. He groaned and rolled over. She nudged him again. The homeless guy's arms flew around as if he were warding off wasps and his eyes opened. He started when he saw her.

They were too close to the building for Murray to get off a shot; the angle was all wrong. He would have had to hang over too far from the roof. He would have fallen. Murray waited until she read the bum the riot act. He hoped she wasn't going to arrest him. That would present problems. But no. This was her third and final warning. She shook her finger at him. The bum nodded and shrimped like Uriah Heep. Finally, she turned to go.

She was twenty feet from her car as Murray lined up his shot. Mid thorax. Gently, he squeezed the trigger. The report reverberated up and down the street. Hernandez instinctively whirled, drawing her pistol, lowering her stance. She looked up for the source of the shot. He'd missed.

Damn it all!

His instinct was to run, but he instead went for a second shot. She bolted for her vehicle. It took her five seconds of sprinting to reach her cruiser. Her partner opened his door and was using it for a shield, looking for the source of the rifle crack. Murray lined up his shot, leading her by a fraction of an inch and squeezed. Blood sprayed all over the car from his hit, but she managed to stagger around the back and get in.

He'd injured her. He had one more chance to take her out. Her partner jumped in, trying to help her as she twisted in the driver's seat. Hernandez revved the engine, slammed it into gear, and the car lurched forward. Murray was undeterred. Aiming from the roof, using the parapet to steady his weapon, hoping to hit her behind the wheel, Murray fired his third and final shot. The glass marked the hole, a spiderweb of carnage. The police cruiser swerved erratically, recovered, and roared on down the road, beyond his range within seconds.

I had to have hit her.

The handheld police scanner squealed about an officer shooting, so he knew the clock was ticking.

Time to move!

Cursing, Murray quickly stuffed the rifle back in its bag, humped to the back of the roof, and stepped onto the fire escape. Halfway down, he realized it didn't matter. She was injured. She was off the case. No one else was on his ass like her. They would be obsessed with tracking down the sniper, but they had nothing to go on. There were no cameras in the neighborhood. No one would connect his car, parked three blocks away. Panting, Murray reached the final platform, stepped onto the sprung ladder, and lowered himself to the alley. His fold-up shopping cart was gone, along with his golf clubs. Frantically, he tried to remember if there was any way to ID him.

How could I have been so stupid?

He'd left an identification card in the fucking golf bag!

With any luck, whoever took it had no interest in public service. They would try to sell or trade the clubs, and whatever else was in the cart, to get money for drugs. With the rifle in an umbrella sleeve over his shoulder, he stiff-walked as fast as he could back to his vehicle. Well, there was a stroke of luck. It remained as he had left it, unmolested.

Adrenalin made his skin itchy. Murray made a point to drive like a senior, slowing down at yellow lights, never exceeding the speed limit despite his racing pulse. It took him a half hour to get home. Garbage cans lined the road. It was garbage day. He wondered if he still had time to get his garbage out. He saw the garbage truck approaching from down the block.

Fuck it. The garbage will wait. I need a damn drink.

Parked in the driveway and headed for the door. He stopped. There was something on the stoop. At the foot of the door; something that didn't belong. A dark plastic garbage bag crunched up to the size of a basketball.

What is that?

No one left packages for him, let alone a bag. Murray's chest filled with dread. It was not a package. There was a smear on the plastic, maroon, and what looked like matted hair.

Is that some sort of animal?

He was afraid to look, but knew that he must.

Trembling, Murray picked it up. It was heavy. He walked to the side of the front porch, the side with the driveway, rested the heavy bag on the rail, and opened it. He looked in. Sightless eyes stared up at him, half rolled back, but open. Stumbling, Murray backed away, letting the head of Wesley Palmer fall to the deck as he turned and vomited.

Chapter 51
Fire Away

Sitting in his car, Braxton watched Murray's house discreetly from down the street from the comfort of his Crown Victoria. *I now understand why cops use these cars. If you're in them a lot, they are comfortable as all hell.* He need not have worried that he'd be spotted. Murray was on hands and knees, throwing up, crawling away from the severed head. Braxton picked up his burner phone and called the other burner phone. The one he'd left in the bag, sealed in a baggie, as a courtesy.

Murray looked up, startled. He wiped his mouth on his sleeve. He looked around, panicked and afraid. When he realized where the ringing originated, he rocked back on his heels. He looked up and down the street. His gaze lingered on Braxton's car. Hesitantly, he opened the bag and looked inside. Delicately, he inserted his arm, retrieved the bagged cell phone, and brought it out between thumb and forefinger. His hands were trembling as he pulled it open.

"Who, the fuck, is this?"

"The guy you tried to kill."

There was a pause, no doubt Murray hadn't expected that answer. "Callahan. That's impossible."

"We tried it once your way. Are you game for a rematch?"

"What the fuck do you want?" Murray snarled.

"Did you know I was in the Army?" Braxton said. "Thank you for your service, by the way. I looked at your record. You saw combat. I never really did. I don't know why you didn't just try to take me out yourself. Then you wouldn't be in this position. Win or lose, you'd know you'd faced it like a man instead of attacking a helpless woman. You couldn't even do that by yourself. You had to bring a pal along. Now Hawthorne's dead and you don't know whether to shit or go blind."

"You killed him!"

"Hawthorne got drunk, and I ran him off the road. It was remarkably easy. I'll give you this, he was a tough prick—needed some end-of-life assistance. You should try it sometime."

"I see you, you son of a bitch. You're right. I should have taken care of you myself."

"Your hired gun wasn't good enough to do it. I hope you didn't pay him in advance. Maybe you are good enough to deal with me. Now's your chance. But I'm willing to bet you're not man enough."

Braxton loaded the music he'd chosen for the chase. The radio and speakers in the Crown Vic were probably the least used components, but not today. Pat Benatar's "Hit Me With Your Best Shot" roared out of the speakers. With his windows down, he was sure that Murray could hear it. He flew by Murray on the porch.

"Put up your dukes, let's get down to it. Hit me with your best shot..."

Murray lurched for the umbrella case, dropping the rifle on the deck. Red-faced, Murray checked the magazine and knelt at the end porch railing, sighting in on the Crown Vic. Braxton put it in gear and gunned it, grinning broadly. He fishtailed the car in the center of the street and roared toward the Landreth residence with all the gusto the old car could muster. Braxton lowered the passenger side window and flipped Murray the bird as he passed. Murray didn't squeeze off a shot. Braxton didn't care. All that mattered was the pursuit.

* * *

Murray ran to his car, threw the rifle in the back seat, got in and backed into the street, nearly sideswiping a service vehicle parked at the curb. As he drove, he opened the glove compartment, reached over, and grabbed the Glock that he had taken from Callahan before he had tried, and apparently failed, to drown him.

That son of a bitch is going to pay.

By his own admission, he'd never seen combat.

You've screwed with the wrong vet!

Not like Murray. He'd been in several firefights with Al Qaeda. In battle, he never hesitated. He didn't know if he ever hit anyone. His targets were either too far, or they were involved in a wildly kinetic scene in the streets. The rag heads would drag their dead with them. Well, this time he'd make sure. He'd follow Callahan to the ends of the earth if necessary.

Callahan thought his car was fast? The Cadillac had a V8 too. Murray pressed the pedal all the way and the big car surged ahead. They were doing ninety through a residential area. Seeing some kids skating out into the street, Murray laid on the horn. They barely got out of the way. They flipped each other the bird as he passed.

* * *

Braxton knew the way to the mall. He'd done it five times. The path he and Ronin had picked out avoided streets with stop signs and signals that might cause accidents. They checked police patrol patterns. The last thing Braxton needed was a police car in pursuit.

"Talk to me, Goose," he said over the speaker of his phone.

"I wish you wouldn't call me that," Ronin replied. "Your right turn is coming up. There's a school bus that just moved onto the road." Ronin had two drones up. While movies made car chases seem commonplace and easy, the reality was far different. With Ronin acting as air support, there was a good chance that he could avoid an ugly confrontation.

I want this fight on the ground of my choosing.

The call about a bus made him flinch.

Damn!

A bus meant kids, and the last thing he wanted was to hit a kid.

"Got a route around?"

"Hang on."

Braxton squealed through a tight turn. In the distance he saw yellow flashing bus lights turn to crimson. A check of his rearview told him Murray was close behind.

"Come on, Ro," he muttered as he raced towards the bus.

"You have a left coming up. Take it, then the first right, then right again. That should get you around the bus."

The Crown Vic skidded as he turned left, almost clipping a Kia parked at the corner. Every bit of his concentration was centered on threading the needle and avoiding damage.

As he made the right turn, he heard Murray's Cadillac sideswipe the Kia, crunching metal. "Cherry Bomb" by the Runaways came up on his soundtrack. He angled the Crown Vic around and came back to the street. The school bus was in the middle of the block as he turned again, this time to the left. He saw it in the rearview mirror for a moment, then Murray's Cadillac filled the mirror.

That's right, big boy, keep right on my tail.

* * *

Callahan wheeled hard, turning west on Bainbridge Road. Murray followed, nearly losing control in the middle of the intersection.

How is this bastard getting all of the signals?

Murray had been counting on him wrapping that Ford around a pole or hitting another car, then he could walk up and shoot that bastard. Somehow, he avoided traffic.

A mile on, Callahan turned into the abandoned Lafayette Square Mall. It used to be one of the most popular malls in Indianapolis before online shopping, COVID, and the lockdowns had driven a stake through its heart. It had a Sears at one end and Bloomingdale's at the other. Before that, it was a Gimbels. Gimbels started in Indianapolis. They ended in Minneapolis.

The empty parking lot let them both pile on the speed. At first he was sure that Knox was going to use the weed-filled parking lot to skirt the mall, to try to shake him.

Then he turned right at one of the entrances.

You've got to be kidding me!

Murray watched in disbelief as Knox crashed through the east entrance, sending splintered glass in all directions. If he thought he would lose Murray in the mall, he was insane. Murray had been going to that mall for thirty years before it closed.

"Thanks for making the hole, sucker," Murray muttered. The sound of grinding glass beneath his tires made his skin crawl, but it was over in an instant and now he was inside the main concourse. Where could Callahan have gone? The lights were off but the interior was visible due to skylights.

An engine roared.

There!

On the other side of what was left of the food court, the Crown Vic furiously backed out of a tributary and headed away.

"Must have been a dead end, sucker," Murray snarled, swerving to avoid a table, aiming for his prey. He drove over some garbage left on the terrazzo floor.

Callahan's car reached a dead end and did a skidding turn to face Murray.

Gotcha!

* * *

"The fox is in the hen house," Braxton said as the debris of the mall entrance spilled off of his hood and windshield as he made the tight turn. In front of him, he saw the Cadillac.

"I'm not seeing any signs of police pursuit. He's all yours," Ronin replied.

Chapter 52
White Chocolate

Braxton finished his skidding drift, bringing the Crown Vic around so that he was facing Murray's Cadillac. Gunning the engine, his tires squealed on the polished terrazzo, then caught hold as he headed straight at Murray's car. He knew his target would flinch; it was a question of which direction. Angling his flat black car slightly, he forced Murray's decision.

The music changed, switching to REO Speedwagon's "Riding the Storm Out." The squeal of the guitar echoed over the rumble of the big engine. It set the mood. This was a storm and he was going to weather it.

He'll divert to the left, firing as we pass.

Murray had already lowered his windows to avoid the shrapnel. Held Braxton's own Glock at the ready. While Braxton hoped to hit Murray, the actual intent was to throw off the incoming fire as they passed.

Murray jerked the wheel as the two vehicles passed, both drivers firing. Murray ducked, just as Braxton had hoped. Firing with his left hand as he drove with the right, he knew his shots missed, but had rattled Murray, which was the intent. Murray's bullets hit the side of the Crown Vic behind him. One had come dangerously near his face, going out the open window of the passenger door. He focused on leading Murray deeper into the mall.

As he reached an intersection, Braxton turned sharp and hit the brakes. Murray's Cadillac turned and slid into a bunch of abandoned and broken tables, echoes of the crashing noise music to Knox's ears. He waited, wanting Murray to recover and get on his tail. Ronin's drone had done a good job of mapping out the mall, the layout imprinted in Braxton's memory.

Murray rallied, his tires screeching on the floor as he backed up and aimed for him.

That's right, Murray, come right for me.

He heard the roar of the Caddy as it came right at him, hoping to T-bone his car.

Braxton timed it perfectly, punching the accelerator, just getting out of the way. Murray turned sharply, slamming the driver's side of his vehicle into a kiosk. The kiosk exploded as it crumpled. Murray tried to get behind Braxton.

Just as I planned.

Murray's gun barked, the shots hitting his rear window. The rear window shattered. Braxton's seat lurched.

Shit, he hit my seat!

As he raced down the main aisle, Braxton looked down but saw no sign of blood. The steel plates he had hung on the seat had done their job. A bullet *thunked* the trunk.

Braxton saw the far end of the mall racing at him. Behind him, Murray was tight on his rear. Reaching down, Braxton grabbed the metal ring tied onto the cable hooked to his tire-popping bar mounted under the rear bumper.

Braxton yanked. There was a clunk and clanging behind him, then a series of bangs. These weren't gunshots; they were tires popping. He swerved to the left, then right, swinging his Crown Vic one hundred and eighty degrees.

The Cadillac careened into another kiosk, blasting it apart. Bits of wood and metal littered the Caddy's hood. Murray slammed into one of the pillars supporting the roof, concrete crunching as the bumper groaned. The muffled *whomp* of airbags going off were barely audible in the chaos. Kiosk parts flew off as the radiator hissed.

The engine protested, straining to run, then gave up. Braxton slammed his brakes, stopped, and got out, killing the engine and music. He aimed his Beretta at the Caddy driver's door. Illuminated by the filthy skylight, he saw that his homemade stop stick had blown three of Murray's tires. The sticky sweet smell of old steaming radiator fluid tugged at his nostrils. Braxton moved to the flank, firing at the airbags. The shot cracked through what was left of the front windshield. The bags went limp, a white powdery residue plastering the interior.

"Get out of the car."

Murray fired from the rear seat. One bullet hit the stone floor. Braxton felt a sting. Ricochet! He fired two more shots at the Cadillac, aiming at the rear seat, blasting out the driver's side window. His shin hurt, but he could still move. Braxton darted to the left, seeking cover behind an abandoned coffee stand. He poked his head out the side.

He looked down. His pants leg wet with blood, his pants coated with dust. Pulling up his pants leg, he saw a chip of flooring stuck in his thigh. He yanked it out. It felt better. He peered at the wreck of the car but saw nothing. He heard someone banging on the rear passenger side door. Murray was trapped inside.

"Give it up, Murray!" Two shots.

"Fuck you!" Murray shouted.

Braxton checked his ammo. Despite having three bullets, he loaded a fresh magazine. More bangs from the damaged car door. "You're trapped, Murray. Nobody's coming to help you."

The passenger rear window shattered. Braxton eyed his path, kept low, and moved. He needed the angle for the shot and he was on the driver's side of the vehicle. Moving around the coffee stand, he darted around a pile of old rotting furniture, giving him an angle on the front of the crippled Cadillac.

Murray flopped out of the window, half rolling on the shattered safety glass. He got on all fours, grabbing his gun as Braxton lined up. Exhaling slowly, Knox squeezed the trigger. The Beretta uttered its deadly crack and Murray moaned, wailing as he dragged himself along the floor, moving behind a table that was toppled on its edge, leaving a smear of blood on the floor.

"You can struggle and bleed out, or give up now," Braxton called out.

The gun poked over the top of the table and fired two rounds, then clicked on an empty chamber. Knox shifted, but there was no way to fully flank Murray unless he backtracked and went to the rear of the Cadillac. In the acoustics of the mall, he could hear the familiar sound of another magazine loading into his Glock.

"Why are you doing this?" Murray called out. "Was it that Weldon-bitch? Is that what this is about? She had it coming. She got my nephew fired!" He fired off a rapid burst, randomly spraying where he thought Braxton was.

Braxton switched magazines. "You beat up an innocent woman. She didn't get Percy fired, you dumb-ass. All she did was confront him. His boss found out that Percy had been harassing innocent people while on the job. You beat her up on Percy's word, and that little sack of shit is a liar." Braxton stealthfully made his way back around the coffee stand and his own car, watching where he stepped to avoid giving away his position.

"What about Jack Hawthorne?"

Braxton moved slowly, aiming his voice to the side, hoping the echoes would confuse where he was. "We chased him. It was his own drinking that landed him in the ditch, that and a little nudge from my car. He might have lived, but I couldn't allow that. Beating an innocent woman—that's not something I can tolerate. I put a plastic bag over his head and he died gasping for air."

"I'll kill you!"

"Doubtful. You've been hit. Your life is oozing away. Even if you do kill me, the chances of you getting out of here alive are between slim and none."

Murray's voice was clearly more strained, an indication of the pain he was feeling. "You're a sonofabitch!"

"I prefer to think of myself as the embodiment of justice."

* * *

Murray's leg oozed blood between his fingers. Struggling with his belt, he managed to make a makeshift tourniquet. It wasn't perfect, but it might save him. He had his stolen Glock and his rifle. There were only two rounds in the handgun. He had another magazine, but it was in the car and there was no way that he was going to stand up and get it. With the bullet in his thigh, standing was not in his future. At least the rifle held a few more rounds.

He hoped to taunt Callahan into the open. "When I kill you, I'm going to cut your head off, just like you did to my guy. I'll leave it in a bag outside that bitch's hotel room!"

Braxton laughed. "If you want my head, come and get it."

Knock it off, Murray. Be practical.

He had him where he wanted him, in a deserted mall. He had maybe another fifteen minutes before someone noticed the damage and told the cops. Or maybe not. This neighborhood wasn't exactly filled with responsible citizens. If it were, the mall might still be open.

We came in the side entrance. It might be days before someone spots it.

Behind him was a court area with a fountain in the middle. He edged toward it, using the rifle as a crutch, letting the overturned table block his movement. He saw where Waldenbooks had been and Murray flashed on buying books there when he was a kid.

* * *

Braxton decided to redeploy. The mall had a second story; from there the table would be worthless. He backtracked to the Crown Vic and pulled out Themis. He shifted to an escalator and silently maneuvered up the long dead stairs to the top floor. Someone or something had defecated on the floor at the top of the escalator, and he moved around it, shifting to the left.

All I need is line of sight.

At this range, it was going to be hard to miss with Themis.

* * *

Panting, Murray scanned the court area. The area lay in darkness. No skylights. That's where he would hole up. Fighting back the pain, he made his way there, settling on bits of broken glass. Flopping down next to a planter, he surveyed the area for any sign of Harold

267

Callahan. His gaze wandered up to the second floor where a dark figure peered down at him through a scope. Murray felt the bullet slam him back into the planter, knocking it over. The bullet had gone right through him. Pain rippled up his spine. The report echoed as he fell to the ground. Numbness overwhelmed him from the shoulder down. He couldn't feel his fingers. Looking down, he saw that he'd dropped his pistol. The rifle lay a few feet away, but it might as well have been a mile.

A minute later, Callahan appeared with a bizarre rifle over his shoulder. He recovered his stolen Glock and tucked it in his waistband. Then he picked up the Remington and looked it over.

"I don't appreciate you using my Glock."

"Screw you!"

"Nice rifle," he said, checking the weapon.

"I used it to shoot your cop buddy."

"What cop buddy?"

"Hernandez. I pegged her earlier today."

"She wasn't a buddy. You shot a cop for doing her job."

"Doesn't matter now," Murray muttered, struggling for air. It was getting harder to breathe, forcing him to breathe faster. "Callahan... you motherfucker," Murray said through clenched teeth.

The man smiled broadly. "It's not Callahan, you moron. It's Braxton Knox."

"Who?"

"It doesn't matter. You know, Murray, none of this would have happened if you hadn't decided to intervene for that moron nephew of yours. If you and your buddy Jack hadn't attacked Faye Weldon, you would be sitting at home watching the WWE. How does it feel, tough guy? How does it feel to beat up a woman?"

"We wouldn't have done it if she hadn't gone after my nephew. She started it."

"She wouldn't have done it if your nephew hadn't gone out of his way to attack an ordinary businessman because he refused to make chocolate penises. You know that, right? That's the reason I'm here. Because your nephew decided, out of the blue, to destroy the life of a

Christian candy maker who declined to make chocolate penises shooting jizm. White chocolate, one presumes."

Murray's vision tunneled, and it was getting harder to get air. "Fuck you," he spat as he fought the darkness that was engulfing him.

"All you accomplished was to get your buddy and your hired gun killed. And for what? Penis candy?"

Murray opened his mouth. "I...I did not know that."

Setting down the rifle, Knox pulled his trusty Glock 19 on him, aiming at Murray's head. "Now you do."

Chapter 53
The Sins of the Mother

As they approached Percy's home, Braxton slowed and edged into a spot two doors down. Faye pointed to the house, 1517 Jacobite Street. An older home, not well kept. Shutting off the engine, Braxton pulled out his night vision gear and looked.

"Anything?"

"No. Dead quiet."

"Percy's not there," Ronin said. "His last post on social media was from an IP address different from his house."

"He'll be there after we secure his mother."

"Are you sure you want to do this?" Faye said.

"These SJWs, they are all momma's boys. The products of bad parenting, dependent on their families. I saw that when I taught at Eastern. Parents prop up their fat failures, enable them, coddle them, prolong their adolescence. When they got bad grades, I actually got calls from the parents wanting me to change them."

"How do you want to approach this?" Ronin said.

"You go to the rear door, I'll go in the front. I'll signal you when I enter. You come in about ten seconds later. Faye, you come in with the rifle after we have our target secured."

"Wait a minute. I'm a reporter. I don't carry a rifle."

Braxton looked at her. Her jaw was set. He saw the problem.

"Ronin, you bring the rifle."

"What if she calls nine-one-one?" Faye said.

Ronin pulled out a radio-like device with four black antennas. "Meet the Altron-4. It jams 5G and other mobile signals. You can use it to take out drones if they're close enough. Of course, the

270

federal government has made it illegal to use, but purchasing one is easy enough."

"What if she has a landline?" Faye asked.

"I already checked. She killed the landline four years ago," Ronin said.

Braxton drew a deep breath. A few hours ago, he'd dueled Murray. He'd cleaned his wound and bandaged his shin. He'd been caught off guard when Murray said he'd shot Officer Hernandez. Ronin found the news article. She was still alive, but had been hit twice by an unknown assailant. While no friend, Braxton still saw them as kindred spirits.

She was the only person in the police department to go looking for Faye's assailants.

Hopefully she'd recover.

Pulling on Nitrile gloves, he checked his Glock to make sure he had a round chambered. "Alright, let's go."

Braxton got out and approached the front door slowly. One of the porch floorboards groaned, enough to make him pause, listening for sounds inside. He heard a television.

Good, that will cover our moves.

Waited a few moments to give Ronin time to get into position.

He checked the door. The knob wasn't locked, but the deadbolt felt like it was in place. *Probably a grade-three lock.* That would complicate matters but not by much. Deadbolt locks created the illusion of security. Braxton had studied locks for months. Now was time to put it to the test. Holstering his gun, he pulled out a hammer and a screwdriver.

Pulling out his radio, he toggled it on. "Ronin, I'm going to breach the door. You'll probably hear a bang or two."

"Gotcha."

Braxton brought the hammer and down on the lock hard. *Bang.* It drove the housing down.

Inside, a female voice called out, "Who is that?"

Braxton stuck the screwdriver into the gap at the top of the lock. He latched onto the inner mechanism and twisted the deadbolt free.

The door sprang outward as he dropped his tools, grabbed it, pulled it open, and entered.

The house looked like a grandmother's. It smelled of cat. He found an old woman standing in front of a La-Z-Boy, her mouth open. "Help!" she cried as he cleared the distance, putting a hand over her mouth.

She struggled, but not much.

"Don't say a thing," he said.

Terror flashed in her eyes as he guided her out of the living room and towards the kitchen in the back. It was hard to tell if she was resisting, or just slow.

Ronin entered from the back porch, carrying Murray's rifle. Knox shoved Percy's mother into a chair. "Where's your phone?"

"I—on the stand next to my chair in the living room," she stammered. Ronin went and returned with Faye.

"What do you want?" Thelma asked, her head whipping around at the three of them.

"Where's Percy?" Braxton said.

"He's not here. He left days ago."

"Call him. Get him to come home."

"I won't!" she snapped. "I don't know who you are, but if you think I'll put my boy in danger, you're wrong!"

Braxton pressed his Glock to her forehead. "Lady, if you don't call him, you're of no use to us."

"Wh—why do you want him?"

"Your son has ruined a lot of people's lives. He needs to own up to that. He needs to pay the price."

"My Percy is an angel! He would never hurt anyone!"

Braxton withdrew the weapon and glared at her. "I don't know what's worse, him or you."

"What do you mean?"

"Your coddling of him allows his brand of bullshit to happen. What kind of parent are you? You have no idea what is going on in your own house. Your kid is ruining people's lives. He's broken up families, gotten people fired. Bankrupted them—he's a monster."

"My boy is gifted."

"No. He's not. He's the byproduct of two generations of parents who never did their jobs."

"He loves me and I love him."

"You're confusing love with enabling stupidity. Percy doesn't have morals because you never instilled them in him. As a result, he believes likes and clicks on social media are validation for what he does. You, though, you're worse. You made him what he is."

Tears ran down her cheeks. "You just don't understand him."

Braxton shook his head hard. "The thing is, I *do* understand him. The problem is you don't." He held out his hand. Ronin handed him her phone. "Here's how this is going to go down. You're going to call him. You'll tell him he needs to come home, that you are hurt. I'll be holding a gun to your head. If you try anything stupid, he'll hear the gunshot and the bullet blowing your brains out. Capisce?"

Tears flowed onto her floral night smock. She nodded. "What are you going to do to him?"

"We're going to hold a little court," Braxton said.

Chapter 54
Home Is Where the Heart Is

Percy was now staying at Brad's Motel, a relic from the fifties out on Highway 135 on the far west side. Fifty-five dollars a night, cash. He was worrying that his regular withdrawals from his mother's retirement account might raise suspicion. He glared at the clerk. *Stupid sand nigger sitting there so smug with his face buried in a titty book.* Percy held him in contempt. People from the Middle East didn't have the respect for gays and women that he felt they should have. The man barely looked up as he took the cash and handed Percy a key, an actual physical door key. Percy opened the door to his room and was assailed with the scent of dust and Pine-Sol. At least they cleaned. Looking around the shabby room with its threadbare carpet and faded quilt, he got the sense he was the first visitor in a while. A painting of a golden palomino, mane snapping in the wind, hung over the bed. It looked like it came from a thrift store.

Percy slumped on the bed and reached for the remote. The TV didn't work. He sighed. What did he expect for fifty-five bucks? He brought out his laptop. At least he got Netflix, if this dump had internet. Two bars. Better than he'd hoped. He brought up WXIN Fox59, the local news station. *"Breaking breaking breaking,"* screamed the banner. There'd been a break-in at the deserted Lafayette Mall. Police suspected gang activity. There was one fatality; police were investigating. Had nothing to do with him.

Percy was at his wit's end. He didn't know what else to do. The thugs working for Faye Weldon were still out there like the fucking Alien, waiting to pounce, unstoppable. Not even her people could trace him to this shithole of a motel, which he'd chosen at random while driving by. His mother didn't need the car. She could barely walk. He could always phone the Kroger and arrange for a delivery to her house, so she wouldn't starve. Ramen noodles and chicken soup. Maybe some bananas. He'd call her later. He put his laptop on his belly and brought up Netflix. He was halfway through the new first season of *The Rings of Power*. This was what Tolkien should have written! A strong female lead, lots of ethnicity. It was a digital monument to DEI and Percy loved it. This was the kind of entertainment that would draw people to the woke ideology.

The people that like this understand people like me.

As he watched the fight scenes, he frowned. Martial arts was for fools. Percy patted the pistol lying at his side.

Let someone mess with me. Let them try.

He could have taken his dad's .38 police special. Instead, he had brought his KelTec PF9. When he had purchased it, the gun shop owner told him it wasn't very good; he tried to upsell him to a Sig Sauer. Percy knew better. Besides, he loved the look of him holding the KelTec.

The other reason he hadn't brought the .38 was that it reminded him of his father. His dad was a failure as far as he was concerned. A night watchman, a glorified rent-a-cop. How pathetic was that? His dad hadn't been around much when Percy was growing up. He was pretty much left to his own devices. His mother was a much bigger figure in his life, alternately loving and scolding. It seemed like for years their conversations were all the same.

"Percy! Don't you want to be someone when you grow up? Don't you want a nice house, nice things, a nice car, to get married and have a family?"

"Not now, Ma! I'm busy."

She would bring him things to eat while he was online, tracking down some white supremacist. No wonder he weighed what he did. As he watched the episodes of *The Rings of Power*, he started to really appreciate the forces of darkness. Orc lives mattered! While a number of online critics slammed the series, he felt he understood it at levels they never could.

This isn't a fantasy; it's a commentary on current social values.

His phone rang. It was his mother!

How in hell…is she psychic?

She always phoned at the most inopportune times. He picked it up.

"Yeah, Ma."

"Percy," his mother said, voice trembling. "I need you to come back here right now."

"What's wrong? Dishwasher on the fritz?"

"No. I feel faint. I fell down. I need help."

"Do you want me to call 911 for you?"

"No, Percy! I want you to come back here and lift me up off the floor yourself. I'm not paying a thousand dollars for a ride to the hospital when you can come help me."

Percy sighed. Wasn't this just like his mother to insert herself back into his life just when he was feeling a trace of independence? "Okay. I'll be there in a half hour."

She hung up. A soupcon of worry penetrated his perfervid imagination. Maybe she really was in trouble. He did a quick calculation. If she died while waiting, how much would he inherit? He was her only heir, other than Uncle Murray. He already had access to her retirement account. It wasn't a lot—chump change. Five figures at best. She was, after all, his mother. He supposed he owed her some sort of allegiance. He closed his laptop, putting it in his backpack, and slinging it over his shoulder.

If I'm going home, I can download a few more movies off my desktop.

Percy heaved himself off the bed and trudged wearily out into the cool night air where his mother's five-year-old Chevy Volt rested. He got in the car, pushed the button, backed up, and headed for the highway. As usual, the Volt was silent. Percy had urged his mother to get the Volt to save the environment. It took nine hours to charge. It went two hundred miles on a full charge. But Percy drove with pride because he was saving the environment.

Twenty-five minutes later, he pulled onto the two concrete strips separated by weeds that constituted the driveway, leading to a one-car detached garage. The one-story wood frame house was lit from within, a slight TV glow showing. Percy trudged up the steps and tried the door. Unlocked. The house was dark, which struck him as strange. He hit the light switch and nothing came on.

That's weird.

"Ma!" he called out. There was no response, but he thought he heard shuffling in the kitchen.

This doesn't feel right.

She always locked the door. Reaching into his backpack, he pulled out the KelTec and pulled the hammer back. The gun was a dead weight in his hands, far too heavy, but he held it trembling in front of him. He'd played enough *Grand Theft Auto* to know how to fight if he had to.

He approached the kitchen door slowly, beads of sweat trickling into his shirt collar. "Ma?" he called out. Again, no response. He licked his lips.

* * *

Thelma Kornbluth was tied to the chair using strips of a cut dishcloth; not the kind of thing that would leave a mark. A strip of duct tape covered her mouth. Braxton had warned her not to make any sounds or he'd kill Percy. Braxton wore night vision goggles.

Braxton was on one side of the door, Ronin the other. Faye sat on a kitchen table at one side. In the light blue glow of the night vision gear, he saw a gun poke through the swinging door to the kitchen.

Percy wants to play!

Braxton brought his Glock up slowly as Percy inched in.

Ronin grabbed Percy's extended arm. Ronin wasn't wearing night vision gear; he had made out the arm in the ambient light from the back door and windows. It meant that Braxton couldn't fire as Ronin and Percy struggled. Percy fired, the flash momentarily lighting up his night gear, then he fired again as Ronin struggled with him. Another shot rang out, popping Braxton's left ear as he holstered his weapon and threw a punch at Percy's head, hitting him in the throat, just below the ear. The pistol went off again, this time aimed at the floor as Ronin wrenched it free from Percy's hand.

Braxton grabbed Percy and threw him to the floor. The portly man was heavier than he thought. He hit the floor and he cried out. Braxton kicked him in the ribs. Percy moaned.

"Faye, lights," Braxton said, switching off his night vision gear. The lights came on. Percy squirmed. Braxton pulled his Glock and aimed it at the bridge of Percy's nose. "Hold it right there, pork rind!"

"Oh shit!" Faye called out. Even Ronin gasped. Glancing off to his side for an instant, he saw the source of their horror. Thelma Kornbluth had been shot in the head. Her gore was splattered all over the kitchen. Drips of blood fell from the small curtains over the sink.

Percy saw it too and tensed up even more. "What have you done?" His voice was a mix of horror, terror, shock, and righteous indignation.

"Us? This was you. We were going to do it, but it looks like you saved us the effort," Braxton grabbed Percy's XXXL hoodie at the throat, lifting him with every bit of his strength and a rush of adrenaline. Percy's eyes were fixed on his mother and the blood splatter on her 1970s chipped white kitchen cabinets.

"Welcome home, Percy. Time to pay the piper."

"Why are you doing this?" he stammered, then he saw Faye Weldon.

"None of this would have happened if you hadn't gone out of your way to put a man out of business, ruin his life, because he refused to make chocolate penises spurting white chocolate jizm. Am I right?" Braxton snapped.

"They weren't giant penises! They were tiny, decorative penises. He's a vile homophobe and deserved what he got!"

"Tell me, Percy. If he had made them, and you got some, would you suck that cock? Is that why you decided to harass Mr. Higby, because you were really a closet homosexual?"

"I'm not queer! I mean, there's nothing wrong with that. I like girls! Ask anybody!"

"Have you ever had a girlfriend? I'm not counting the poor women you've probably stalked. You're a virgin, aren't you? None of this would have happened if you'd got laid. You watch online porn and fantasize that it's you, because in real life, you couldn't land a sober girl under three hundred pounds. Isn't that right?"

Percy looked like a red balloon about to explode. Braxton backhanded him as Ronin moved to hold his hands behind him, cutting his backpack off. "You're pathetic. A waste of DNA. People like you only know how to destroy. You ruin everything you touch. Now you've killed your mother." He paused, listening for police sirens. There were none. No surprise in such a run-down neighborhood.

"I didn't do that!"

"Yes, you did. It was your gun that did it. And that rifle over there," Braxton nodded where the rifle was propped up against the cupboard, "that was the gun your uncle used to shoot a cop today."

Percy was confused, Braxton could read it in his face. "Your uncle is dead. You roped him into doing your dirty work for him, along with Jack Hawthorne. They are both dead, along with the hitman your uncle hired. Your friends on the net, they're through. You have no friends, and you just shot your own mother. There's no cavalry coming for you, Percy."

Ronin rummaged through the backpack, pulling out Kornbluth's notebook computer. "What's your passcode?" Ronin asked.

"Why?"

"Just answer him," Braxton said, shoving the Glock into his Adam's apple.

"Six, nine, six, nine," he said as a dribble of snot oozed from his right nostril. Tears flowed. "Why do you need my code? What are you going to do?"

"You're going to post a manifesto, one where you admit that you shot your uncle and mother. You're overwhelmed by guilt and will denounce woke ideology. The manifesto will talk about your reasons for committing suicide. Too much guilt for you to deal with. You will be an object lesson for others who think your woke bullshit is just fun and games."

The color drained from Percy's face as realization choked him. "Please, I'll do anything! You don't have to kill me. I have access to my mom's money. Take it, it's yours, just let me live. I'll never tell anyone about this, I promise."

Sweet music to Braxton's ears.

"Give us your passwords and we'll talk about it."

Let him think there's a chance.

Percy rattled them off as Ronin wrote them down. When he was finished, he looked at Braxton, thinking he had bought salvation. He looked relieved. "Please, I'll keep quiet. You have my word. You don't have to kill me."

Braxton picked up the KelTec that lay at Percy's mother's feet. He held the gun at Percy's temple, angling up, as it would if Percy were holding the weapon. Ronin moved out of the way. "I know you'll be quiet. Tell your uncle hello from Braxton Knox."

Percy's mouth opened. The words never came. Braxton squeezed the trigger.

Chapter 55
"Deja Vu All Over Again"

Faye, Ronin, and Braxton sat in his room at La Quinta watching the evening news. An earnest newsreader with perfect hair, undeniably female, spoke urgently in front of video of fire trucks outside the Lafayette Mall.

"It began as a fire in an abandoned Indianapolis landmark and ended with a bizarre horrific murder suicide. Firefighters responded to an alarm this afternoon from the now-shuttered Lafayette Mall and found the remains of a car fire. Authorities have tentatively identified the driver as Murray Landreth, a longtime Indianapolis resident. The body was burned beyond recognition, but police determined his identity from the license plate and a wallet on the body.

"Police went to the residence of Landreth's sister, Thelma Kornbluth, and found her shot to death along with her son, Percy. Percy Kornbluth recently lost his job at the University of Illinois Bookstore and was believed to be despondent. He posted to his Blue Sky and X account last night confessing to the murder of his mother and his uncle before he killed himself. Thelma Kornbluth, his mother, had a long history of depression. According to experts, depression is often a genetic condition which can affect entire families. Police took down his online manifesto pending further investigation, though unnamed sources claim that this entire ugly affair is likely to be closed soon.

"Percy Kornbluth admitted that he stalked and harassed numerous people online with no real justification. When approached about an article about his role, he enlisted his uncle, Landreth, to, and I quote here, 'deal with that reporter.' When police became involved

281

in the case, Percy allegedly learned that his uncle had shot an investigating officer, so he killed him. Police recovered a rifle at the scene and are running ballistics to compare against bullets recovered from the police shooting of Officer Rita Hernandez yesterday.

"In other news, a group of parents are suing the District Four School Board for having them arrested when they appeared at a public meeting demanding answers on why Sojourner Truth Middle School was advising children about gender-changing surgery without notifying the families—"

Braxton muted the sound. Smiling, he handed out plastic cups filled with an inch of Buffalo Trace purchased at Dave's Liquors.

"I think our work here is done." They all raised their glasses and touched plastic.

"That manifesto you posted did the trick," Faye said to Ronin.

"It should. You wrote the original draft. We just added the most recent events, like Murray's death and Hernandez's shooting."

Braxton took a burning sip. "It was good work. It tied a nice bow on everything, laying it at Percy's feet, where it belonged."

Ronin pulled out Percy's laptop and brought it up. "To whom it may concern," he read. "I have devoted much of my life to social justice. I was a committed warrior in the struggle to expose white supremacists, homophobes, haters, and closet Nazis. When a reporter threatened to dox me, I thought I could get out of it with violence. I asked my uncle to deal with that reporter. He and a buddy beat some sense into her. At the time, I thought that was smart. Now I see it for what it is. He made me an accessory to his criminal acts.

"My uncle told me that the police were onto him, so he shot the cop that was investigating him. He even hired a hit man to go after the reporter. When I found out what he was doing, I confronted him, and killed him. I had no choice. Things had gotten out of hand.

"I have come to realize that my following of the woke hivemind was all a tragic mistake. I ruined people's lives and as a result of my actions, people got hurt and financially ruined. I know I could never make it right. So I decided to end my life.

"I couldn't leave my mom alone. I killed her brother and with her medical problems, I couldn't bear to leave her alone in this world. So I put her out of her misery.

"To people online who called me a friend and admired me: I was wrong. You were wrong. There is no such thing as social justice. Ruining people's businesses, families, and everything else we did was horribly wrong. I see that now. We weren't making the world a better place. All we were doing was making others miserable. We did it for likes and clicks. Looking back, I was more of a Nazi than anyone I ever called that. I wish there was a way to fix what I did. I can't leave the world a better place, but I can leave it.

"Yours most sincerely, Percy Kornbluth."

Ronin wiped a crocodile tear from his eye and sniffed. "Touching."

"I prefer nonfiction," Faye said. "Once I get home, I'm calling Higby for a follow-up."

Braxton turned to Ronin. "Speaking of Higby, what about Percy's mother's retirement account?"

"Percy's last act was to set up Mister Jason Higby as the sole beneficiary," Ronin replied. "At least, that's how it looks online. There may be some contesting, but Percy doesn't have any other relatives. Mr. Higby is going to get something when all the dust settles." Ronin tossed back his drink. "Urp," he belched.

Money couldn't fill the gap of a lost life. Braxton understood that better than most. It did help take the edge off, though.

Maybe he will be able to restart his business. Who knows? If nothing else, it gives him the opportunity to start over.

"I have a nine a.m. flight tomorrow to Portland," Faye said. "I can't wait to shake Indianapolis off my boots."

"Good. We could all use a little break," Braxton said. "I'll see you all back in Portland in about a week. I'm going to visit Mt. Rushmore and Yellowstone National Park. I always wanted to see the Little Big Horn Battlefield…maybe I'll swing that way. Ronin, you want to come?"

"Nah, I gotta get back."

Faye seemed to study his face; he could feel her eyes. "You look a little depressed, Braxton."

"Naa. Not depressed. I only have one regret."

"What was that?"

"I didn't use one *Dirty Harry* line during this entire affair. I had Murray on the ground at my feet. I should have said, 'I know what you're thinking. *Did he fire six shots or only five?*'" His response generated a chuckle from his friends.

"A blown opportunity. Maybe next time?" Ronin replied.

Braxton set his cup down. "I'm going to visit Officer Hernandez. Who wants to come?"

Faye raised her hand. "I'll go."

"Ronin?"

"Nah, Imma stay here and make sure our digital trail is wiped clean."

Hernandez was at Kindred Hospital. Braxton parked on a ramp down the block. A police officer stood in the lobby holding a cup of coffee. The front desk directed them to room 426. Braxton bought a bouquet of flowers in a vase. Hernandez was sitting up in bed with a tube in her arm and her shoulder heavily bandaged.

"Well, well, well," she said. "If it isn't Harry Callahan and Faye Weldon."

Faye set the bouquet on a table. "How are you? I'm so sorry this happened to you."

Hernandez shrugged, winced. "Goes with the job. Now I get to ride a desk for three months. Could be worse."

"We saw on TV that they ID'd your shooter," Braxton said.

"Yes. They believe Landreth to be my shooter. They recovered a rifle at his nephew's place and they're running ballistics tests now. With a confession posted online, it's really just a formality. The case is pretty much wrapped up."

"He must have felt you were onto him," Faye said. "He felt the walls closing in."

Hernandez stared at Braxton. "Maybe. They are wrapping the investigation up and tying a bow on it. Percy Kornbluth was a horrible person. Him shooting himself was probably best for everyone."

A black officer entered, waved at Braxton and Faye. "How y'all doin'?" He went to the bed and carefully hugged Hernandez. "How you doin', baby?"

"Hanging in there."

"Well, we won't take any more of your time," Faye said. "Speedy recovery."

The cop looked at them. "Who are these fine folks?"

"That's Harry Callahan, boyfriend," Hernandez said.

The black cop grinned, clearly getting the joke. "Ahuh."

"Nice to meet you," Braxton said.

The cop shook his hand, then Faye's. "Duane Albright."

Hernandez winced as she shifted in her bed. "You know, Mister Callahan, you never told me where you got the names of Murray Landreth and Jack Hawthorne. It kinda feels like you were ahead of the curve with all of this." Even with painkillers, there was suspicion in her voice.

"That's right, Officer Hernandez," Braxton replied. "I never did tell you." He cracked a wry grin.

They left.

They had the elevator to themselves. "I'm surprised they don't know your real name."

"Maybe they do, but see no percentage in getting all huffy about it. We gave them everything investigators wanted, a case all wrapped up with no loose ends. If they did dig deep, they'd figure out that the guns that killed Murray won't match the ballistics from Percy's pistol. But why look into that? Everyone implicated is dead."

"Almost as if you planned it that way. Maybe they just don't have enough time."

"All the more reason for us to hit the road."

They returned to LaQuinta. Ronin was gone. Faye hugged Braxton hard. "Call me when you get back."

"Will do."

Braxton checked out before noon and hit the road. First stop, Rocco's Garage. Rocco was on a chassis trolley beneath an old Ford

150 when Braxton arrived. Seeing legs, he rolled out, got up, wiped his hands on his coveralls and shook.

"You've been a busy boy. How's the car holding up?"

"That car will outlive us both."

"Glad to hear it."

"Just wanted to stop by, see how you're doing, do a little Bondo work, and thank you for your help."

"Leaving town?"

"Yes. I'm driving back to Portland."

"Beats flying."

Braxton laughed. "I doubt I'll ever fly again. My work requires driving."

"I don't blame you. I remember when it used to be fun. What do you need to patch up?"

Braxton gestured to two bullet holes in the car, courtesy of Murray.

"Someone take a shot at you?"

Braxton feigned a surprised look. "Wow, you know, those *do* look like bullet holes."

It took an hour for Rocco to patch up the damage, including the holes punched in the trunk. When he was done, Braxton paid his tab.

"If you're ever out this way again, I'll find a spot for you in the garage."

"Thanks, Rocco."

"If you ever want to sell me that car, I'll make you a good offer."

Braxton grinned. "No chance."

Chapter 56
Half Past Midnight

It took him two days to reach Sidney, Nebraska, arriving by four in the afternoon. Pulling into the Sleep Cheap parking lot, he went to the office. Memories of helping the girl came back. He half expected to see her at the desk, but instead there was an older woman, one whose age could be counted by the wrinkles on her face.

He checked in, paying cash, filling out the index card with his information, registering as Harold Callahan. "The last time I was here there was a young girl working here. Cheryl, I think her name was."

The woman shook her head. "She's my granddaughter. Poor kid. She just got out of the hospital."

"What happened?"

"Two local boys beat her up. She was in the hospital for a week. Broke her cheekbone and nose, and cracked a rib. She's scared half to death after this. Her parents are going to homeschool her. Those boys messed her up good, not just her face, but her head."

Braxton felt anger rising like hot lava.

Please don't let this be my fault.

"Why would they do that?"

"They had been harassing her and a guest cut one of them up. The kid lost his finger knife fighting with someone who was better than him right here, according to Cheryl."

"I take it the police arrested them."

The old woman grimaced. "You'd be wrong. One of the boys is the son of a sheriff's deputy. They denied doing it, she got scared and decided to not file charges."

It was my fault. My intervention is why they beat her up.

He didn't know what to say as guilt squeezed his chest.

Cheryl's grandmother handed him his key. "Cryin' shame. You can't get justice in this county, I swear."

"Where do these kids hang out?" he asked casually.

"Cedar Lanes. It's a bowling alley. Why?"

"Just curious," he replied, walking to the door.

* * *

Cedar Lanes wasn't big. The brick building was on 11th Avenue with a parking lot out front. A block south was a wooded lot, where he set up his position. Themis was nestled on a shooting bag, with a fresh barrel. His Kestrel ballistics computer was doing its job as he adjusted the thermal sights. He had parked almost a mile away, sneaking into position perpendicular to the road.

The thought of two men beating Cheryl made his stomach knot. Memories of his own little girl, Angela, surged in his veins and pulled at his heart. The fact that the legal system would not do anything only made matters worse. Small-town thinking; that and an incestuous relationship with law enforcement. If his daughter committed a crime, he would have held her accountable. Otherwise, how would she ever learn?

At ten after ten, a ten-year-old Camaro with hand-painted flames extending from the front wheels pulled in. He recognized it instantly. "What are the odds?" he said, checking his readings, adjusting the scope. At this range, he'd have to work hard to miss.

Doing a solo job without Ronin and Faye came with risks. If he were caught by the police, his days of administering justice would be over. That didn't matter. This was about goons beating up an innocent girl.

His mind churned over the options as the two men got out of the Camaro. Shoot them going in or coming out? There was little doubt he could take them right then. They had parked their Camaro at the edge of the parking lot. He had a good line of sight, perfect weather.

Logic took hold. It was far better to get them on the way out. Fewer people, fewer potential witnesses. They would be hopefully drunker, would make for garbled eyewitness accounts. Braxton summoned his restraint and waited.

Hours passed. Finally, at half-past midnight, the remaining bowlers and drinkers filtered out. His two targets were laughing. One of them had a young girl under his arm. That was a complication he hadn't anticipated.

I need to make sure my shot is dead-on.

His first target would be his best shot; he knew that from experience. He opted for the one with the girl. The young man moved to the car, opening the driver's side door as Braxton brought him into his crosshairs.

Themis barked, muffled slightly by the suppressor. It snugged hard into his shoulder as the bullet hit the youth at the base of his throat. He was knocked back a half-step, his female companion not fully understanding what was happening. It was seductive to watch him suffer, but Braxton reloaded and aimed at his second target. Once more, he squeezed the trigger.

The girl screamed. His second round slammed into the chest of the second man, dropping him like a bag of potatoes. The girl's screams filled the night air as he picked up his spent brass and slung Themis over his back. It took twelve minutes to reach his Crown Vic. As he put his rifle in the back, he heard the wail of police sirens in the distance.

It's a thankless job, but someone has to do it.

The next morning he showered, packed, and went to drop off the key. The older woman was still on duty, part of the burden of a family business. He put the key on the small counter.

"You know what? Those two boys we were talking about—they got shot last night. Dead as doornails!" she said.

"You don't say."

"Whoever did it was good. They haven't been able to figure out even where the shooter was. He got them in the dark. That was some serious shooting."

"Sounds like karma to me," he said, straight-faced.

"Some coincidence. You come in asking about Cheryl, and then the two punks that attacked her end up dead."

Braxton shrugged. "Sorry to disappoint you, but I was asleep."

"There's not a lot to do working the night shift here. I saw your car leave and come back."

She knows.

Braxton didn't reply. He let the unspoken accusation hang in the air between them.

She pulled out his registration card and tore it up, tossing the shreds into a wastebasket. "Then again, my eyesight isn't what it used to be."

Braxton nodded. "Tell Cheryl I hope she feels better soon." Before the old woman could respond, he went out the door.

Epilogue: Sheffield the Fox

Ronin was just outside Portland when his special phone rang. He knew enough to pull over when that phone rang. Only one person knew that number. In fact, it was the only reason he owned that phone to begin with.

"Hello, Seymour," the voice said the moment he connected. There was only one person that called him that, his quasi-former employer.

"Hello."

"I've been tracking how things went in Indianapolis."

"It got messy," he tried to explain. "But in the end, things came together."

"The reparations to the victim was an excellent touch. Dare I say, classy?"

"That was Knox's idea."

"It's good. I will be contributing to that effort. I particularly liked the manifesto. That has been trending on my platform as well as those of my competition. It's put a lot of people who support the woke mindset under the magnifying glass, which I love."

"Faye and Braxton came up with that."

"I'm pleased you didn't kill Percy's accomplices."

"It wasn't necessary. It's hard to explain, but there's some compassion with Braxton at times. There's an edge to it, but he's not a heartless man."

"I'm glad to hear that. I'm going to be sending you some additional resources. Some of which is sitting in your mail room right now."

"Thank you." His mind danced with thoughts of what it might be.

"You might need help. That PMC, Brownwater, they are starting to poke around Palmer's death. People like them are unaccustomed to being challenged the way you did. I have another asset planting misleading clues for them to waste their time with. I thought you should be aware of their activities."

How does he know about Palmer? Ronin caught himself. *Of course he knows. He's got almost unlimited resources.*

"Thanks for the heads-up."

"Of course. So what is Knox planning next?"

"In fairness, I don't know."

"When you find out, keep me posted. Until then, good job."

With that, the call and the conversation came to an abrupt end.

* * *

On the fifth day since leaving Indianapolis, Braxton pulled into the pine-strewn yard of his cabin up a dirt trail off Highway 26. It had been his grandfather's, and sometimes his father visited with a couple of his buddies, to hunt deer. His dad and Monsieur were on the porch when he pulled up. The bulldog raced up to him, and Braxton kneeled down and rubbed him down good.

His dad wasn't a hugger, but did shake his hand when he reached the porch. "I take it you took care of the business."

"Yup."

"Good. Not much going on here. Your dog missed you."

Braxton glanced down at him. "He looks like he's put on a few pounds."

Grayson Knox shrugged. "What can I say, he's my grand-dog and it's hard to say no."

His dad didn't ask for details, nor did Braxton offer any. They chatted, mostly about day-to-day happenings. Portland was boring, and after his trip to Indianapolis, boring looked good.

His father seemed hesitant to leave after dinner. Braxton understood that. Grayson had been out of the assisted living home for a few weeks and enjoyed his freedom. As the sun set, Grayson finally said goodbye, leaving Braxton with Monsieur. He texted Faye and Ronin to let them know he was back, did his laundry, and anticipated a night in his own bed.

He stoked a fire in the stone fireplace. He checked the solar batteries. They were at twenty-five percent. It was not a great site for solar power and his dad had told him that there had been clouds for four days in a row. Grayson had used the generator and the refrigerator was cold.

It was good to be home, to relax with the knowledge that he was on his own and would be left alone. Most people just wanted to be left alone. That was something his enemies just couldn't understand. With their zeal to change the world, their zeal to punish all who didn't believe as they did. It had always been so. It would always be so.

Braxton had picked up apples, bananas, clementines, and milk. There was no mail delivery at the cabin. Tomorrow was Friday and he'd pick up his mail at his post office box. He kicked back in the ancient recliner and turned on the television. Five minutes in, he heard a scratching at the front door. He got up, went into the kitchen, and picked up the bag of dried dog food and a sack of freshly purchased cut carrots. He opened the front door and there was a raccoon standing on its hind legs, front paws clasped, looking up like a parishioner or an asylum seeker. Returning inside, Braxton filled a bowl with kibble and sliced carrot, then put it on the porch.

As if on cue, ten more raccoons appeared in the yard, including a mama with four kits, and scurried up the wooden steps. Braxton watched them go at it. "Hang on," he said. He went back in the house and got another bowl. This was the biggest gang of freeloaders yet. Braxton got a kick out of them. Monsieur growled at them. Braxton held him at bay. "Save it for the real bad guys," he said. "We can use all of the friends we can get." Once the food was gone, so were the raccoons.

Braxton made a mental note to have his RAV4 transported back to Oregon. The Crown Vic was a great car, and he had some ideas about additional modifications he wanted to do to it. The Bondo-patched bullet holes needed sanding and the whole car needed a fresh coat of paint. The car wasn't registered, but he was sure it had been picked up by more than a few traffic cameras. For the time being, he'd cover it with a tarp, until he needed it again. His RAV4 was more nostalgic, a relic of life with his family. It would remain his regular driver.

He went back in, collapsed in the recliner, and turned on the news. The pillow guy came on...on and on. Fabulous savings. Sale extended. He switched to another news channel. The middle class was fleeing California and the governor had no clue. A popular cosmetic was being recalled due to the danger of cancer. Jaguar declared bankruptcy. A bear at Central Park Zoo had become an internet sensation by dancing the Macarena. Someone had brought a boom box and that bear got up and boogied. Now it had an OnlyFans account and was worth three million dollars.

Changing the channel got him more commercials. A new drug with lots of X's and Z's was guaranteed to cure psoriasis or your money back, with the world's fastest talker bringing up the caboose warning about side effects which included, but were not limited to, impotence, anal seepage, whatever that was, unibrows, arthritis, and the possibility of growing a tail. The last ones he made up in his mind for self-amusement, though he didn't doubt they could be actual side effects.

What the hell is anal seepage?

The next commercial was for an electric Cadillac. Braxton switched back to the first news channel. A perfectly coiffed newsreader addressed the camera in front of a video of a man being marched out of his house in shackles by seven SWAT-type enforcers.

"...all began when a Samaritan alerted New York authorities that William Garfinkle had adopted a baby fox, also known as a kit, and raised it at his home in upstate Pottersville. Four years ago, he created an Instagram account for Sheffield the Fox, which now has over a half million followers. Garfinkle had rescued the baby kit when the mother had been hit by a car. Garfinkle had a weekly show in which he showed Sheffield playing, grinning, and enjoying belly rubs. It should be noted that state law prohibits the owning of foxes, wolves, coyotes, hyenas, and other undomesticated animals. The reason for this is foxes can spread diseases like rabies, leptospirosis, mange, and roundworm.

"Garfinkle sought a shelter for Sheffield but was unsuccessful. He bottle-fed the fox for several months before returning Sheffield to the wild. Garfinkle released the animal into his backyard, but a day later, he found Sheffield on his porch with half of its tail missing. Garfinkle said he opened the door, Sheffield ran inside, and that was the last of Sheffield's wildlife career.   "In other news, Oberlin College has announced that they are eliminating their DEI department."

Braxton whipped out his laptop, connected to the satellite antenna, and looked up Sheffield the Fox. What he found spiked his blood pressure through the roof.

The Police Benevolent Association of New York State (PBANYS), which represents the state's Environmental Conservation officers, stated that they had received a complaint regarding Garfinkle and his abuse of Sheffield. Mr. Garfinkle was contacted by an Environmental Conservation Officer and warned that his ownership of Sheffield was illegal. They claimed that Mr. Garfinkle informed them that his intent was to comply by releasing the animal to the wild. Garfinkle later denied this in an interview with *The New York Times*, stating that he had no intention of setting Sheffield free. The NYSDEC initiated its investigation after further complaints were received, leading an investigator to review Garfinkle's social media accounts and discover that Sheffield was still in his care, along with a pet raccoon named Fritz. The Pottersville Health Department (PHD) Environmental Health Services received additional complaints regarding Mr. Garfinkle's unlicensed animals. They coordinated with NYSDEC, who confirmed that they were aware of at least one fox and four raccoons being kept on the property illegally.

Garfinkle claimed that the NYSDEC used excessive force during the armed raid, which lasted five hours. In an interview with *TMZ*, Garfinkle stated, "They treated me like I was a terrorist. They treated this raid as if I was a drug dealer. They wore body armor and were fully armed." The PBANYS said in its press release that of the twelve personnel who executed the search warrant, only three were uniformed Environmental Conservation officers. These officers were focused on securing the couple's eighty-acre property and not seizing the animals. Other involved personnel including plainclothes officers. The union said that it was the CCHD's decision to test Sheffield and the four raccoons, not the NYSDEC's.

Both Sheffield and Fritz tested negative for rabies, and were euthanized the next day per state policy.

Braxton closed the laptop. For long minutes, he just sat there staring into the darkness. He reached for his phone. Memories of the FBI raid on his house that had cost Angela her life came back, summoning a deep anger within him. Government overreach and innocent pets killed.

People should be up in arms over this.

Reaching down, he rubbed Monsieur behind his ears. His bulldog cocked his head and licked his fingers, as if he could read his thoughts. Braxton grabbed his phone and called Ronin.

"What's up?" Ronin answered.

"Have you heard about Sheffield the Fox?"

Printed in Great Britain
by Amazon

61797574R00171